BADD
MEDICINE

A BADD BROTHERS NOVEL

Jasinda Wilder

BADD
MEDICINE

ONE

✦

Ramsey

HERE I AM STUCK WASHING FUCKING DISHES. AGAIN. Of all the shitty jobs in the damn place, why do I always get stuck washing the dishes? I'm part owner of Badd Kitty Saloon—I should be tending bar or placing orders, but no, I'm in the back corner of the goddamn kitchen, clouded in steam, spraying dirty dishes, and operating the dishwasher.

Fuck this.

I cursed under my breath, grumbling and complaining in an unending monologue, but fifteen minutes later I was finally caught up. The bar had been busy all day and I was hoping things were letting up.

"Fuckin' finally," I growled as I slammed the

door shut on the last load in the dishwasher.

And then, of course, Matty, our busser, arrived with another tub full of dishes in from the dining room.

"Are you motherfuckin' kidding me right now, Matty?" I snarled as I threw him a dirty look.

He looked at me, and the color drained out of his face. Matty was barely sixteen and this was his first job. He weighed about a buck twenty soaking wet, didn't need to shave, and his voice still cracked on occasion.

"S-sorry, Ram. I—the dinner rush is just about over, and—"

I sighed, stuffing my temper down, stacking the plates as Matty scraped the food off and placed them on the washing station. "Ahhh, don't worry about it," I told him. "You're doin' a great job, Matty. I'm just cranky 'cause I hate getting stuck washing fuckin' dishes."

"Sorry, Ram," Matty said. By way of explanation he added, "Tony was feeling sick yesterday, so I wasn't really all that surprised when he called in today. We're just about caught up out there, so I should able to take over once the last few tables are turned over."

"Quit apologizing so much," I muttered. "Ain't your fault Tony got sick, and it's not your fault I'm stuck washing the goddamn dishes."

"Sorry."

I arched an eyebrow at him. "Are you apologizing for apologizin' too much?"

He stammered. "I—I…"

"Repeat after me: Quit being a pussy and deal with it, Ram."

He paled further, looking as if he was going to pass out. "I—I can't say that to you!"

I stared at him. "Fuckin' say it, Matty. Grow a pair of balls, would ya?"

He blinked at me, fiddling with something in the big black bus tub. "I, um…quit being a…uh—quit being a pussy and deal with it, Ram." He grinned shyly as he stammered out the phrase, his braces showing.

I nodded, holding out my fist. "There ya go. And look, I didn't even eat you."

He bumped his fist against mine. "I'm gonna go bus the last few tables."

"You do that. And Matty?" I called out. He stopped in his tracks. "Just fair warning, I'm probably gonna bitch when you bring that tub back in here, so just, you know…don't take it personally."

"Okay," he mumbled and with that he left.

I went back to work spraying, scrubbing, and sorting dishes. By the time I had everything spick-and-span, Matty arrived with another full bus tub.

"This is pretty much the last of it, Ram," he said,

scraping and stacking. "There's only a couple tables left out there."

"Thank fuck," I mumbled. "So, after this load, I can quit doing this bullshit?"

"I think so, yeah." He hesitated and I glanced at him.

"What?" I asked. "Spit it out."

"For such a tough guy, you sure do whine a lot."

I blinked at him; he held his ground, but I could tell he was shaking in his boots after making that comment. Took some balls, that did—I outweighed the kid by about a hundred and twenty pounds. I let him stew for a second, and then I couldn't hold back my laughter anymore. I guffawed, laughing until I was breathless.

When I was done, I held out my fist to him. "Good one, Matty! You're learning."

He tapped my fist again. "Learning what?"

"How to talk shit like a man," I said. "I'm bein' a whiny little bitch and you called me out on it. Proud'a ya, kid."

He grinned broadly. "I was scared you'd knock my head off."

"Nah. I got a sense of humor. You try that shit with Rome, he may just clobber you." I cackled again. "Of course, if you talk shit and he clobbers you and you take it like a man, he'll respect you forever."

Matty frowned. "Yeah, but if Rome clobbers me, I'm not sure I'd survive it."

I laughed again. "Eh, Rome wouldn't hit you hard enough to break much except your nose."

"I've never been in a fight," Matty mumbled. "Getting my nose broken sounds painful."

I frowned at him. "What do you mean, you've never been in a fight? No playground scuffles? Nobody ever socked you and you socked him back?"

He shook his head. "Nope. I usually get along with people."

I scratched my jaw. "Really? Weird. I'd been in so many fights by the time I was sixteen that I couldn't have counted 'em all." I eyed him. "So you mean to tell me you've never been punched?"

"Nope. Never."

I huffed in irritation. "I'm tempted to sock you just to get you over that." I hesitated. "And you've never hit anyone either, I'm guessing?"

"Nope."

I shook my head. "Yeah, I'm gonna have to take you out back and beat the shit out of you just on principle."

He trembled. "Um, maybe that's not such a great idea."

I laughed. "Don't piss yourself, kid. I'm fuckin' with you." I smirked. "Mostly."

"Mostly?" he said, his voice cracking.

"One'a these days, I'm gonna bring you to my cousin Baxter's gym and teach you how to throw a punch and how to take a punch."

Matty shrugged. "That I might be okay with if there's, like, gloves and headgear and stuff."

I snorted in derision. "Yeah, but honestly, there's no replacement for the experience of having someone's fist knock your nose sideways. Dude, that hurts so fuckin' bad the first time, but the pain pisses you off and you swing, and you feel his jaw crunch…and let me tell you, that shit is *satisfying*."

Matty backs away. "Look, I'm…gonna go, now."

I turned back to my work and laughed again. "Yeah, yeah. Sissy."

Rome swaggered into the kitchen a few minutes later, a towel thrown over his shoulder. "I hear you're terrorizing our busser, Ram."

I kept spraying dishes and sorting them into the rack. "I wouldn't say terrorizing. More like…indoctrinating him into the wonders of a good fistfight."

"He says you threatened to take him out back and beat the shit out of him on principle," Rome says, leaning against the wall behind me.

"It was a fuckin' joke. Jesus," I muttered. "The kid's never been in a fight. Never hit anyone, never been hit. It's a fuckin' crime."

Rome snorted. "So he grew up a bit more sheltered than we did. Good for him. That doesn't mean you can go around threatening to smash his face in."

"That's not what happened." I muttered under my breath about whiny kids and then, without warning, I turned and sprayed Rome in the face with the hose. "And also, fuck you for sticking me back here again. This is the third time this fuckin' week I've gotten stuck washing fuckin' dishes."

Rome danced out of the way, drying his face with the bar rag, and then snapped me in the chest with it. "You're such a whiny fucking bitch, Ram. Seriously. It's not that bad."

I snatched the towel from him as he tried to snap me again. "Says the guy who never gets stuck washing dishes."

"'Cause you suck at bartending! You either under-pour or over-pour, and you can't figure out the computer to save your fucking life." He reached out and snatched the towel back from me. "And you're such a potty mouth, I can't let you wait tables or you'll offend all our customers."

I rolled my eyes and went back to the dishes. "Yeah, well not all of us are built for working at a goddamn restaurant."

Rome hesitated, glancing out of the kitchen to make sure he wasn't leaving any customers waiting at the bar, and then turned back to me. "Ram, look—"

I shook my head, not turning around to face him. "Don't."

"Don't what?" he snapped. "You've been a miserable pain in the ass for fuckin' months, bro. If I didn't know you literally never spent time anywhere except here or out in the woods hugging trees or whatever the fuck, I'd think you were tripping over a chick."

"I'm not tripping over a chick," I said. "No chicks in my life to trip over."

"No?" Rome said, and I heard the grin in his voice. "No one?"

"I'll hose you down again if you go there, Roman." I turned and aimed the sprayer at him. "I swear to fuck I will, and then I'll beat you senseless."

He raised his hands. "Are you even hooking up with anyone?"

"How is that any of your business?" I asked, shoving the rack into the washer, snagging a new dry towel and wiping down and stacking the washed plates and bowls.

"Just wondering. You're being so fucking dumb, I'm wondering if you've got blue balls or something. Not like you couldn't haul down some ass if you wanted. I'm just sayin'…you're acting like a miserable son of a bitch."

"I don't have blue balls," I mumbled.

"Yeah? When was the last time you hooked up?

I shrugged. "Couple weeks ago."

Roman grabbed a stack of dried dishes and helped me put them away. "Yeah? Who with?"

"Just some chick. Met her hiking. She was from Michigan, on a backpacking trip with her girlfriends."

"And?"

I frowned at him. "What, you want details?"

Rome just grinned. "Sure. I'm a one-woman man, now, so I gotta live vicariously through you."

I snorted. "And who's fault is that?" I grabbed another stack of plates. "Fine, whatever. So I met her up on Deer Mountain. Her friends had fallen way behind, so she hit the peak ahead of them. We were up at the top together, just the two of us. We sat and talked for a while, and then hiked the rest of the way down together. They had a tent set up in the campground, and since her friends were still finishing the hike, we ducked into their tent and smashed."

Rome smirked. "And? How was it? Was she any good? What'd she look like?"

I shrugged. "She was pretty hot—kind of a short stack, brown hair, blue eyes, nice juicy ass but not a whole lot up top. She was a talker though, let me tell ya. The whole time we were fucking, she was talking, like it was just a conversation—it was kinda weird, to be honest." I sorted the clean silverware

into the tray, ready to be rolled into cloth napkins
later. "It was fun. Not the best sex, but fun. I made it
a game to get her to shut the fuck up."

"Did you?"

I grinned. "Had to put somethin' in her mouth
to make her shut up, but yeah."

"Dude, you're such a dog."

I laughed. "You know it, bro." I eyed him. "Is
it true what they say about getting into serious
relationships?"

Rome cocked an eyebrow at me. "Depends on
what you mean."

"You stop getting BJs."

Rome snickered. "I don't know, man. I hav-
en't found that to be *totally* true. But then, when
you get into a real relationship that stops being..."
He shrugged, hunting for the words. "I dunno how
to put it without sounding pussy-whipped, which
I ain't. I guess once you experience what it's like to
have sex that *means* something, getting sucked off
stops being as rewarding as it is when you're single.
When you're just out for a hookup, and you don't
care what happens, that shit is awesome. When you
start craving the—shit, I don't know...the closeness
or whatever, it stops being about just getting your
rocks off."

"Sounds horrible," I said.

Rome, once upon a time, would have agreed with me. Now he just rolled a shoulder. "I dunno. It's better, I think." He smirked again. "Now, don't go takin' that to mean my shit is vanilla, cause it ain't. My girl is down to get plenty dirty."

I rolled my eyes at him as I untied the rubber apron I'd put on to keep my clothes dry. "Sure, sure." I eyed him with a grin. "When was the last time you and her fucked anything except missionary?"

"This morning," Rome said, arms crossed, a satisfied grin on his face. "Up against the shower door."

I had to cover my surprise, because I'd honestly expected him to not have an answer. "Right. We all know shower sex is overrated."

His grin widened. "I didn't say it was shower sex. I said it was up against the shower door. Not the same thing." He turned away. "And that's all the details you get, bro."

I frowned, trying to figure out what the difference was. I eventually gave up. "Whatever the fuck."

"Don't be jealous," he said, and then paused for effect, tapping his chin. "Or, *do* be jealous—of the fact that I get fucked like a champ on the regular, and you're still chasing random ass like a fuckin' college bro."

I tossed the apron at him. "Again—what the fuck ever, dude. I'm outta here."

He wrinkled his brow at me. "Where are you going?"

I shrugged. "I dunno. Dinner? A movie? Chase down random ass like a college bro? Hiking? Whatever the fuck I want."

Rome hung up the rubber apron and followed me out the back door. "I got shit covered tomorrow, by the way, so you can take the day off. Maybe see if you can find a chick who wants to bone you more than once."

"You mean a chick *I* want to bone more than once? Not fuckin' likely, bro. I got no attention span for that shit." I waved as I shrugged into my hoodie. "Fuck taking the day off—I'm taking the rest of the week. I need to get some air, man. I can't breathe in this fuckin' city."

"The rest of the week?" Rome leaned in the doorway between the restaurant and the alley. "Where are you gonna go? You know?"

I paused, turning to face him. "Nah, I dunno. I'll probably just pack a bag and hit one of the trails, see where I end up."

"Well, take care of yourself, and make sure you log in with the ranger station if you're going into the backcountry."

"Yeah, yeah. What, do you think I'm green or something?" I waved again, and headed out on foot for the apartment. It was after ten at night by this time, and I was hungry, but I'd also been at the saloon all day and just wanted to go home and change into clothes that didn't smell like old food. I also knew there wasn't shit to eat at our place or, if there was, it would require cooking, and god knows that was NOT in my skillset. I could do a few basics in the kitchen, but I had to be motivated, and right now I didn't feel like wrangling up something to eat. I was in a foul mood for reasons other than kitchen duty, and I didn't care to look at them too closely. I just said fuck it and went home. I'd probably end up eating leftovers or a bowl of cereal.

I reached our apartment building ten minutes later, fishing my keys out of my jeans as I jogged up the stairs to our unit on the third floor. As I got closer to our door, though, I heard noise coming from inside--music thumping and whumping, auto-tuned pop bullshit, along with cackling female voices.

Fuck. The girls were over.

That was the problem living with brothers whose girlfriends were best friends and roommates—they'd made our apartment their secondary home. Two of the three were in steady relationships with my brothers Roman and Remington, and they and their friend and roommate Izzy were at our place as much as they were at their own. I often found myself at their place too, dragged along with my brothers as a fifth wheel. Although, Izzy was as much of a fifth wheel as I was. We were both fifth wheels together—not together, though just…shit. I wasn't sure what I meant.

I steeled myself, as I went into the apartment, which was filled with deafening horseshit music with a stupid trippy beat and a happy, poppy chorus repeated *ad nauseam*. GAH. All three of the girls, Juneau, Kitty, and Izzy were in the kitchen, wineglasses in hand, two empty bottles and a third half-finished on the counter…and they were baking. Flour was literally everywhere, on the counters, on the floor, in the air, on them…it looked like they'd had a flour fight, and the apartment was the loser. Baking soda, chocolate chips, butter, eggs, vanilla, bags of sweetener, all sorts of shit I didn't know we had—or maybe they'd brought it with them—cluttered the counters. There were baking sheets on the stove with cookies cooling on them, a tray of brownies, another tray of something that looked like croissants but with chocolate chips…

"I'm hungry," I said, startling all three girls so badly they all jumped and shrieked.

Izzy, the closest, spun in place, spilling wine on the floor. She slapped my chest, leaving a white flour handprint on my black hoodie. "You scared me, you asshole!"

"Yeah, well the music is so loud I could hear it out on the street!" I said, shouting to be heard over the deafening music.

She shrugged and turned away. "You gotta have music when you bake."

I honestly did my best not to ogle her, but I lost that battle after about ten seconds. She was dressed more casually than I'd ever seen her: skintight black leggings with bright purple leg warmers straight out of an 80s jazzercise video, and a bright yellow tank top that was intentionally way too big, knotted under her breasts to show her entire midriff, the whole thing hanging off of one shoulder, showing a violently orange sports bra. Her hair was pulled into a loose ponytail low on her neck and draped over her right shoulder. She had a white handprint on each ass cheek, flour on her cheekbones and dusted across her nose.

The woman was stupid fucking sexy. Those leggings were basically just black nylons; so tight they were like a second skin, showing off the strong curves of her legs and highlighting the thick, juicy, upside-down heart-shaped perfection of her ass. And the top? Even a sports bra and baggy tank top couldn't hide the bulging, heavy roundness of her enormous tits, and the way she had the tank top knotted up right under them to show off her torso from diaphragm to hipbones. She had fit, toned flat abs and a narrow waistline—she had an honest-to-god hourglass figure, and I had to fight a fucking hard-on every moment she was around.

Mostly because every time I looked at her, I remembered meeting her for the first time at the hospital all those months ago. We'd all been there visiting my dad, but she had not hesitated ducking into an empty room with me. My intention had been to slip on a condom and just fuck her on the bed, or even up against the wall, but she'd had other ideas. Such as pushing me down into the cheap, uncomfortable hospital recliner beside the door, yanking my jeans down around my ankles, and wrapping those plump lips around my cock. She'd had on lipstick that was a bright, vivid scarlet—I remember that very clearly because when I went home and took a shower, I'd had that red lipstick smeared in messy rings on my cock.

Shit. I'd been home for less than two minutes and I already had a semi. I was forced to think about forest fires, and bald, angry principals and sad puppies to get it to go away.

Of course, Izzy sauntering away from me didn't help, because those handprints on her butt shook and jiggled and swayed with every step, hypnotizing me, begging me to put my hands on those handprints.

I had to suppress a snarl as I followed her around

the island to the stove, where the goodies were. "Can I grab a couple cookies?" I asked, reaching for them.

I got whacked across the hand with a spatula. "Ah-ah-ah!" Kitty said, giggling. "Not yet. They're not cool yet."

I had to stop myself from snatching the spatula from her. "I don't care. I haven't eaten since lunch and I'm fuckin' starved, and I need those cookies." I reached again for a cookie.

And got my hand smacked, this time by Izzy. "No! They're for a fundraiser at Ink tomorrow morning. You can't have any!"

I did snatch the spatula from her. "Just gimme one, goddammit."

She lunged for the spatula, and I held it out of reach, not bothering to hide the fact that my eyes were following the bounce of her boobs.

"Give that back!" she snapped, jumping and grabbing it from me, whacking me not just once more, but twice with it. "And quit leering at me, you bloody caveman!"

I grabbed a cookie off the tray and danced out of reach before I could get my hand smacked again. "I'm taking one whether you like it or not. And if you wear clothes like that, it's because you want to be leered at."

She stopped, one hand on her hip, the other

clutching her wine glass, eyes blazing. "That is the most disgusting, chauvinistic, sexist bullshit I've ever heard in my life, Ramsey Badd. Surely you can't be *that* much of an unevolved Neanderthal, can you?"

I lifted my chin in defiance. "You like being admired, and you know it."

"I dress to look nice. I dress to be comfortable, to feel good, and to look good—for *myself*. Not for asshole men like you to stare at me."

"You wear pants so tight I can see every dimple on your ass, so I'm gonna look."

Izzy narrowed her eyes at me. "I do *not* have dimples on my ass, fuck you very much. My ass is smooth as silk, and you're just pissy because you can't have it."

I was tempted to throw our little hospital rendezvous in her face, but with Kitty and Juneau around I didn't dare—and I think she was gambling on that. We had an unspoken agreement that, as far as anyone else knew, it had never happened, and that we wouldn't acknowledge it to one another.

Not really sure why we've both insisted on holding to that arrangement, but we have for the past year. People may suspect something happened, but I know I haven't breathed a word to my brothers, or cousins, or anyone else about what happened. In fact, the only reason I know it happened at all is my memory of it, and even that could be chalked up to a fever dream, or some kind of warped fantasy.

However, standing here facing off against Izzy, a still-warm and gooey chocolate chip cookie in my hand, I knew exactly what she looked like under those leggings. I knew what her creamy pale thighs looked like—and I knew she was probably commando under those leggings. I also knew she kept her pussy waxed totally bare, and I knew she liked to scream...*loud*. I knew she came more easily and more readily than any woman I've ever laid eyes, hands, or mouth on—and *fuck*, if I could get her naked and alone for, say, two hours, I could probably make her come so hard she'd pass out.

Fuck it. Seriously, fuck it.

I took two long steps toward her, stopping to stand directly in front of her, mere inches separating us. I sank my teeth into the cookie, staring at her the whole while. I ate the whole thing in two bites, licked chocolate off my thumb and forefinger and then smirked at her.

"Trust me, babe, I know *exactly* how silky smooth your ass is," I whispered. I felt a rush of guilty be-musement at the sharp gasp she gave me, and the way her hazel eyes flared wide. "That's not something I'll forget."

"You *bastard*," she hissed.

"Don't tell me you're embarrassed?" I went on,

definitely pushing my luck. "I'm not. You tasted sweeter than that fucking cookie."

"I knew it!" Kitty crowed. "You guys *did* screw!"

Izzy whirled on her friend. "We did *not.*"

I leaned against the island. "She ain't lying. We didn't fuck."

Izzy glared at me. "You can just shut up," she snapped. "*You've* helped enough. Now get the fuck out of here."

I smirked. "Sorry, babe, but this does happen to be my apartment."

"Don't call me babe!" she snarled, stepping up into my space. "And fine—we'll leave. Come on, girls. We're taking this baking party somewhere else." She whirled away.

Kitty and Juneau exchanged glances.

"Ummm, Izz?" Juneau said, making an apologetic face. "We kind of...can't. We have a batch of cookies in the oven, three batches cooling, and two more ready to go in. We're kind of committed."

Izzy groaned, tilting her head back. "Dammit." She glared daggers at me. "You had to show up and ruin everything, didn't you?"

I shrugged. "I don't see how I ruined anything. The cookies are fantastic." I snagged another one and sauntered away. "Seriously, babe, these are fuckin' delicious."

"QUIT CALLING ME BABE!" she shouted.

I paused in the hallway. "Gonna make me?"

She growled, and I felt a rush of arousal at the fierce look in her eyes, the wild, angry way she stomped down the hallway toward me, every curve bouncing and jouncing. "You, Ramsey Badd, are a fucking asshole."

I smirked. "Yup, 'fraid so."

Her hand flashed up and smacked me across the face—and fuck, it stung, but I forced myself to not react.

"Oooh," I taunted. "You slapped me. I'm *so* upset!"

She howled in rage and went to slap me again, but this time I caught her wrist. "Let me go!"

I stared her down. "You get one for free, because I'm being a dick. But that's all you get for free." I held her wrist and dragged her closer to me, until our bodies met—her breasts and my chest, our hips, our thighs, everything but our noses. "I'm sick of the game, Izz. I'm sick of pretending nothing fuckin' happened between us. It did, and I enjoyed the shit out of it. Hell, I'll be the first to admit I wouldn't mind revisiting what happened."

I paused, and let the silence draw out, let her shake and tremble in anger and arousal.

When I continued, it was in a whisper only she

could hear. "I'd like to get you totally naked next time, though. If I can make you scream the way I did with just my tongue…? Ohhh, honey. I got ten fingers and a big fat cock—I could make you scream so loud the neighbors would call the cops."

"You big, stupid, arrogant son of a bitch," she snarled, yanking at my grip.

"Got most of that right—I'm big, I'm arrogant, and I'm a son of a bitch, literally and figuratively. I ain't stupid, though." I slowly, gradually released the pressure on her wrist, letting her go. "And Izzy?"

She yanked her wrist away. "What?" she huffed.

I moved in, telegraphing my intentions so there would be no doubt, no mistake, no confusion. Just so it was clear—I didn't slam my mouth against hers; it wasn't a kiss so sudden she couldn't have pulled away.

But she chose not to.

She watched me close in, her eyes on mine, still angry, but now the anger was laced with conflict: it was in the subtle way she parted her lips speaking of arousal, the way she sucked in a breath speaking of readiness.

I slanted my lips against hers, slid my tongue along her lower lip, nuzzling, shifting my mouth, brushing my nose against hers, and not quite firmly latching our mouths together.

She actually, literally, growled like a trapped wildcat and pushed up against me to finish the kiss, and she was the one to turn it hot, to make it aroused and erotic, her tongue slashing against mine and my tongue being sucked into her mouth. Her fists knotted into my hoodie, hauling me down and refusing to relent from the kiss, refusing to back away or give up. Classic Izzy.

For my part, I growled into her mouth and tasted her tongue and bit down on her lip as she hauled me down. I couldn't help a huff of amused, aroused laughter from rumbling through my chest, which quickly turned into a groan of frustrated need as she pushed against me, flattening those big soft melons of hers against my chest, pressing her hips into mine, a moan of her own escaping as she felt the evidence of how this kiss was affecting me.

I wrapped an arm around her waist, placed a hand on the back of her head; my right arm was tight around her waist, cupping her right hip, and when she moaned into my mouth, my hand slid, entirely of its own accord, around to grip her ass cheek.

She pushed her hips against mine, and then huffed into my mouth as she pulled her lips away from mine, briefly touching her forehead to mine.

And then she backed away, lips firming into a thin hard line, eyes narrowing. "Now you know what you'll never have," she said, her voice sharp and snippy.

I just laughed, a harsh, sarcastic chuckle. "Who you think you're teasin', sweetheart?" I smirked at her, licking my upper lip suggestively. "Yourself, as much as me, that's who."

She growled, sounding more than ever like a pissed off wildcat. "Fuck you."

"Is that a promise?" I reached up and brushed a dusting of flour off the bridge of her nose with the pad of my thumb. "You know what sucks for you? You can't even do a dramatic exit right now, 'cause you're in my house. I'll tell you what—I'll save you the effort and go into my room, and I'll stay there till you girls are done baking. I'll even offer to clean up after you, if you leave me some cookies and brownies."

She had nothing to say to that so she whirled around, stomping—or rather, flouncing—back toward the kitchen.

I waited until she was at the end of the hallway, and then called her name. "Izz?"

She turned with a haughty look in her eye. "*What*, Ramsey?"

"I'll be thinking about you."

She narrowed her eyes. "Don't waste your time. I know I won't be thinking about you."

I just laughed, opening my bedroom door.

"Anyone ever tell you you're a shitty liar?"

My reward was another of those maddened wildcat snarls, which only prompted me to laugh all the more as I went into my room and closed the door behind me.

I found myself licking my lips as I flopped onto my bed. The question was...

Which was sweeter—her lips, or that cookie?

TWO

Izzy

I KNEW I WAS BEING RIDICULOUS AS I STOMPED ANGRILY back into the kitchen, but my blood was boiling. I honestly couldn't remember the last time anyone had ever made me so mad—well, short of Tracey, the Evil Stepmother From Hell, but she was a special kind of vile. Average, non-Satanic people simply didn't have the ability to affect me emotionally the way Ramsey was currently affecting me.

Kitty and Juneau were rolling dough into balls and pretending to not have heard any of the preceding events as I stormed into the kitchen. They both slowly, warily, lowered their spoons and dough balls to the counter.

"Ummmm…what just happened, Izzy?" Kitty asked.

"I don't wanna talk about it," I mumbled, doing my damnedest not to take my ire out on my best friends.

Juneau peered at me through narrowed eyes. "Izzy…" She slid closer to me, a ghost of a smirk dancing across her features. "Did you and Ramsey…?"

"No." I kept my eyes on the cookie dough, but wasn't really paying attention to what I was doing.

Juneau burst out laughing, and then immediately stifled it. "You did!"

Kitty looked at me more closely, then—specifically, at my mouth. "HOLY SHIT! You *kissed* him!"

"Did not." Again, I knew I was being patently ridiculous—my lipstick was certainly smeared, and my lips were probably swollen. It *had* been a hell of a kiss.

Kitty stood in front of me and grabbed me by my arms. "Isadora Styles. It's *us*. Don't lie to us." She wiped at the lower edge of my lower lip with her thumb. "Your lipstick is messed up, and your lips are swollen, and I've never seen you this flustered."

My eyes snapped up to hers. "I'm *not* fucking flustered!"

She just arched her eyebrows. "Oh no? When was the last time you yelled at me like that?"

"I'm not yelling!" I yelled.

I looked down at my hands and realized I'd rolled enough dough into a ball to make a cookie nearly a foot across. In an annoyed sigh, I tore the ball in half and then in quarters, and then rolled the pieces into balls, and set them on the baking sheet. And then, out of sheer desperation to keep from screaming, I shoved the fourth quarter of raw cookie dough into my mouth.

"Sorry," I said, around the mouthful of dough. "I'm being a bitch." Although, it sounded more like: *Saw-hee. I'm be-uh a bih.*

Kitty covered a grin with her hand. "Izzy. Just… just talk to us."

I finished chewing and swallowing, my head ducked down, trying to breathe slowly and calm my pulse. "He makes me furious. I become unreasonably angry for little or no reason at all." I toss my ponytail behind my back. "I don't even get it. All he has to do is—is *look* at me and my blood boils. He strings two words together and I go insane. It's embarrassing."

Juneau laughed as she resumed rolling cookie dough into balls. "Oh boy, do I understand that. Remington has the same effect on me. I've been dating him for a year, and he can still make me crazy like that."

Kitty laughed too, taking the trays out of the

oven as the timer beeped. "I think it's a Badd thing: all Badd males have an innate capacity to make you unreasonably angry with a single look." She set the hot trays on the counter and slid the prepared trays of cookies into the oven and reset the timer. "Bast, Bax, Brock, the twins, all of them can do that. Xavier not as much, or at least not in the same way. He has a bunch of odd little quirks that can be infuriating sometimes, though. And god knows Rome has the ability to make my head explode."

"I hate it, though," I said. "I've always prided myself on staying pretty even-keeled most of the time."

Kitty and Juneau exchanged long, meaningful glances, and then both burst out in hysterical laughter. Kitty, gasping, bent over double, stumbled over to me, and wrapped me in a slow, tender hug that somehow managed to be gallingly condescending.

"Ohhhh honey," she murmured. Yep, her voice was dripping with condescension. "You are the least even-keeled person I've ever met."

I frowned at her, pushing her away. "I resent that, Katerina Maureen Quinn," I snap.

She arched an eyebrow at me. "Ooh, the full name," she said, faking a shiver of fear. She cupped my face and kissed my forehead. "Isadora, sweetheart, darling, my best friend. You are not even-keeled *at all*. You're excitable, spastic, impulsive, and unpredictable. And that's part of why we love you so much."

"I—" I cut myself off, mouth flapping. "Okay, fine. But how often do I get truly angry at anyone?"

She rolled a shoulder. "You're right—you don't get actually, truly angry all that often."

"That's all I meant—I'm even-keeled in that I don't get angry, and Ram just makes me *so—fucking—angry*. And I don't like that."

"It's because you like him," Juneau said.

"I do not. I hate him."

"At this point?" Juneau grinned at me. "It's basically the same thing."

"That's stupid," I said. "Hating someone and liking them aren't even remotely the same thing."

She snorted. "Do you even remember eighth-grade crushes?"

I rolled my eyes. "Well, sure, but we're not in eighth grade anymore. I'm thirty years old."

"Doesn't mean you've matured past that emotionally, though."

I looked up from cookie prep and frowned. "You're calling me an emotional eighth grader?"

She nodded. "Yep."

I glared. "Well, screw you too."

She laughed and gave me a side-hug as she

scraped the last of the dough onto a spoon and rolled it, plopping it on the tray in a single huge cookie. "You know I love you, Izzy."

I shoved her away, but it was *mostly* good-natured. "I love you too, but I'm *not* the emotional equivalent of an eighth grader. I'm fully emotionally mature, thank you very much."

Juneau patted me on the head. "You're also not very self-aware, it seems."

I took the empty bowl and put it in the sink, washing it for something to do with my hands, and to calm my irritation. "You two are pissing me off."

"Because you're still mad at Ramsey for being so likable *and* so annoying."

Kitty was using a spatula to scoop cooled cookies from the trays onto the platter. "Izz, I'm sorry, but she's kind of right."

"How am I lacking in self-awareness, then, if you're both so fucking smart?"

Kitty set her spatula aside and leaned against the counter, munching on a cookie. "Hey, these *are* good!" she said, staring at the cookie in her hand with admiration. "Okay, for example—do you realize that you have never, ever dated a guy for more than a month since I've known you?"

I snorted. "Duh."

"Furthermore, do you realize none of the guys

I've ever seen you hookup with have ever been older than twenty-five, and that none of them have ever been successful at anything other than being pickup artists?"

"That's not true!" I protested, but then I had to stop to think. "That's not true…is it?"

Kitty shrugged. "I mean, there may have been the isolated one-night stand here and there, where the guy was like, twenty-eight or even thirty, but that would be the exception rather than the rule."

"Hector was successful," I said.

Juneau's eye roll was venomously, searingly sarcastic. "Yeah…maybe at dealing dime bags of low-grade pot, and nearly getting you arrested for vagrancy and possession."

"He also had a great cock and a really nice car." I frowned again. "And you've both noticed this?"

Juneau nodded, taking a cookie herself. "I've noticed it. You tend to pick up hot, young sleazeballs."

"Sleazeballs?" I demanded. "Really?"

Juneau nodded. "Yup. The douchier they are, the better."

"You ever see *Don Jon*?" Kitty asked. "Joseph Gordon Levitt? That's the kind of guy you specialize in."

I glared at her. "Not true. Patently untrue."

Kitty laughed, tucking her hands under her

arms. "God, these are almost too good. I'm about to eat them all." She pointed at me, then. "Your denial of this just proves my point about you not being self-aware."

Juneau eyed me sidelong as she ate a second cookie. "What Ram said about the way you dress and why?" She held up a hand to forestall my protest. "While it was absolutely sexist and awful, it's also kind of true."

"You cannot be serious!" I snapped. "Please, *please* tell me you're joking."

Juneau sighed. "See?" She brushed crumbs off her hands. "You dress for attention. You like being admired. You're built like a goddess and you know it, and you like flaunting it a little bit."

"So now I'm an attention whore on top of being emotionally immature?" I was near tears, and tried desperately to hold it in. "Wow. Awesome. Thanks a lot for the support."

I pushed away from the counter and headed for the door, snagging my purse off the floor where it sat near the front door.

"I'm out. I'll see you later."

Kitty and Juneau both followed me to the door, grabbing me and pulling me back inside before I could escape.

"Izzy, wait, wait—please wait," Juneau said,

wrapping me in a hug. "We love you. You have quirks and foibles just like the rest of us. You claimed you weren't un-self-aware, and we were just pointing out that maybe that's not entirely true."

"We're not calling you immature or an attention whore, Izzy," Kitty said, hugging me from the other side. "You're our best friend and we love you more than anything. We're just trying to…help you be a little more self-aware, babe."

"Don't call me babe," I murmured. "I hate it."

"You do? Since when?" Juneau asked.

"Since Ramsey Badd started calling me that."

Kitty laughed. "You like him."

"I DO NOT LIKE RAMSEY BADD!" I shouted.

"YES YOU DO!" we heard Ram call from his bedroom.

I glared at my friends. "You guys suck." Kitty and Juneau stifled their laughter, and that sent me over the edge—again. I knew I was being ridiculous and unfair, but I couldn't help it. "I'm so fucking glad you guys find this so fucking hysterical. Fuck you both."

And with that, I stormed out of the apartment, stomped down the stairs and out into the late evening of a Ketchikan summer. I was on foot, steaming with irrational anger, and upset with myself for being that way in the first place. That led to a pathetic cycle with me being even more mad at Ramsey, which fed into

me being mad at myself for being mad at Ramsey...
and so on, and so on.

GAH.

I was a hot mess and I didn't really even know
where I was going, just that I needed to move, needed
to get away from Ramsey, and that apartment, and
my friends who seemed to find the whole situation so
bloody funny.

Somehow, I ended up standing outside of Badd
Bar & Grill. I stared through the open doors at the
late evening crowd milling inside, Sebastian and Zane
both behind the bar mixing drinks and pouring shots
and beers, chatting and grinning and teasing each
other. Bax was leaning against the propped-open door,
nose in his phone, the screen lighting up his face.

He glanced up and saw me. "Oh, hey, Izzy." His
smile was quick and friendly. "What brings you here?"

"I...don't know, to be honest."

He nodded, shoving his phone in his pocket. "A
few of the girls are at the family booth," he said, jerk-
ing a thumb over his shoulder at the interior. "Go on
in, get a drink, and relax. They'll sort you out."

"They'll...sort me out?"

He chuckled. "Yep. You look...complicated, and
trust me, no one is as good at uncomplicating shit as
those ladies in there."

I sighed. "I look complicated? Awesome."

He held up his hands. "I'm just—"

I cut him off. "It's not you, it's me. I'm just in a really shitty, *complicated* mood."

He arched an eyebrow. "Got anything to do with my cousin?"

The glare I gave him could have melted an iceberg. "No."

He widened his eyes and he nodded warily. "*Ohhhh*-kay. Not related to Ramsey. Got it."

Once more, I had to force myself to react rationally when I felt anything but. "I'm sorry, Bax. Like I said, it's not you. Ignore me. I'm gonna go get a drink."

He just smirked. "Lucky for you, I'm immune to being offended. See ya 'round, Izzy."

I entered the bar and wove my way through the crowd to the Badd Family Booth, which was the booth closest to the service bar and kitchen entrance. At some point recently, some enterprising member of this absurdly large extended family made an actual plaque and hung it on the wall over the booth, permanently reserving it exclusively for them and their friends or guests. Sitting in the booth were six women: Claire, Dru, Mara, Eva, Aerie, and Tate.

I honestly wasn't sure which couples were married, which were engaged, and which were significant others. I didn't know them all that well, but I did know that they had to be pretty amazing women to have captured the attention of Ketchikan's legendary Badd brothers. Each of them was a true individual, and each had her own style, including the identical twins Aerie and Tate.

Each woman was so beautiful it was honestly annoying, and a little intimidating; what was even more intimidating to me was how close they all were. There were two more women in the family: Harlow Grace, international A-list movie star extraordinaire, whom I'd met a couple times at family get-togethers, and Joss, a quiet, serious, and somewhat mysterious young woman with long black dreadlocks and dark, exotic skin.

Harlow—whom the rest of the family simply referred to as Low—was with, in whatever capacity, Xavier, the hyper-intelligent youngest brother, and they balanced their time either in Harlow's condo in LA, on her yacht cruising between LA and Ketchikan, or here in Ketchikan in their sprawling converted warehouse-slash-robotics laboratory.

The Badd brothers, along with their cousins and business partners, were an eclectic bunch, and each of them was talented in special ways. They were all generous to a fault, and they all had a wicked sense of humor. A conversation with one, or all of them was sure to be interesting.

Joss was with—again, in what capacity I wasn't sure—Lucian, the quietest and most enigmatic of the Badd brothers clan…or, rather, the original Ketchikan Badd brothers clan, as opposed to the newcomer Badd brothers, the triplets. Joss and Lucian ran a bookstore/coffee shop two doors down, on the other side of the office and recording studio owned by the twins —both sets, because, confusingly, Aerie and Tate, identical twins, had married Canaan and Corin, also identical twins, and they had worked together to open a record label which was next door to the bar.

The eight women were all super close—not just friends and sisters-in-law, but best friends…they were actual sisters regardless of blood or legal connection. They had inside jokes and nicknames, and they borrowed each other's clothing, and hung out with each other pretty much all the time.

I mean, I was close with Kitty and Juneau, but this group of women took closeness to a whole different level.

They saw me coming and Tate jumped up, snagged a chair from a nearby table, and set it at the head of their table. I sat down, and the women all greeted me.

Tate grinned at me. "Hi, Izzy. Welcome to the club."

I laughed. "The club, huh?"

"When four or more of us are gathered in the name of Badd, it becomes the Badd Lovers Club." Tate eyed me mischievously. "So, when I say welcome to the club, I hope I mean that literally."

I groan, tilting my head back. "I've only had three glasses of wine, which is nowhere near enough to deal with an inquisition on that subject."

Aerie reached out and patted my hand. "Well, I'm not sure I can stop the inquisition, but…" She uncorked a bottle of red wine that was sitting on the table and poured a healthy measure into a clean glass that was pushed down to me at the end of the table. "I can help with the sobriety situation."

Eva, who was one of the most effortlessly elegant, kind, and soft-spoken women I'd ever met in my life, smiled at me. "We won't inquisition you, Izzy."

Claire snickered. "Speak for yourself, Evie. I'm totally going to inquisition the shit out of her." She turned to me. "You have to know we're like sharks smelling blood. You've only ever shown up here when you're with Kitty, so if you're here this late at night on your own there's something going on. Izzy, there's gossip, and I want it."

The table interrupted into laughter and then they quieted when I said, "I honestly don't know why I ended up here."

"There's only one way to figure that out," Claire

said. "Tell us what's going on."

I sighed. "It's stupid."

"That means it must be Badd related," Dru said. "You have the look of a woman just beginning to learn how infuriating, confusing, and arousing it is to deal with a man who has Badd blood in his veins."

I didn't want to admit that she was right, but I couldn't lie, either. They'd see right through that.

"You hit the nail right on the head," I said, finally. "Infuriating, confusing, and arousing. Mostly infuriating, though."

"If the focus isn't on 'arousing,'" Claire said, with a leering smirk on her elfin features, "then that means you haven't fucked him yet."

"Not…not exactly," I mumbled.

Mara, quiet so far, pounced on my response. "Not exactly, huh?" She arched an eyebrow, toying with the end of her long blonde braid. "Meaning, you've done *something* with him, up to but not including sexual intercourse?"

"Pretty much," I said.

"…And?" Claire prompted.

I stared at her. "And what?"

"And start talking, bitch! Details! We need all the salacious, dirty, inappropriate details." Claire wiggled her butt on the bench. "Come on, girl! Spill!"

I sighed. Normally, I'd be all for spilling the

details, in filthy, graphic detail. For some reason, I just wasn't feeling it, this time. "Okay, look—it was over a year ago, and it was just a quick…thing. One time only, and a mistake."

All six women just stared at me.

Tate, sitting closest to me, had her cell phone out, and was watching her own twins sleep on a monitor app; her babies were two and a half, identical twin boys named Liam and Richard. She glanced up at me from the monitor, a knowing smirk on her face.

"One time only and a mistake," she echoed, and patted my hand. "Keep telling yourself that, Izzy."

Her sister, Aerie, gave me an eerily identical smirk. "I know I don't know you very well, Izzy, but you don't seem like the type to think a random hookup, or whatever it was, was a mistake, nor do you seem like the type to be reticent to share details."

I toyed with my hair. "You're right—I'm not usually like this." Might as well go for broke—if anyone has experience dealing with the maddening bullshit of a Badd, it was these six women. "The truth is, Ramsey just…" I trailed off, shaking my head.

"Can make you spitting mad so fast it's silly?" Dru suggested.

"Flips between being an asshole and absurdly charming so fast you get dizzy?" Mara added.

"Turns you on so fast you're worried your ovaries

might explode?" Claire said.

"Confuses you more than any human being alive?" Eva said.

"Makes you want to stab either him or yourself in the eyeball?" Tate added.

"Makes you want to either fuck him, shoot him, or get thee to a nunnery?" Aerie asked.

I couldn't help a laugh. "Yes to all of the above." I rubbed my face with both hands. "It's like you *know*."

The six of them exchanged a barrage of glances, and then spoke in unison: "Oh, we know." And then they all burst out laughing.

"Honeybuns," Claire said, "the truth is that having one of those men in your life is kind of like bungee jumping. It's terrifying, kind of stupid, exhilarating, and absolutely incredible all at the same time."

"Ooh, I have a great analogy," Mara said. "Being with a Badd is like riding a rollercoaster blindfolded. You never know what's going to happen, but you know it's going to be equal parts crazy and amazing."

"But I don't *want* him in my life!" I whined. "He's obnoxious, arrogant, maddening, and stupid, and I hate him."

"Ahhhh," Tate said knowingly. "You're still at that phase."

"Which phase would that be?" I asked.

"The phase where you're in denial about how

you feel," Aerie answered.

"It's like the stages of grief," Mara said. "Denial, anger, bargaining, depression, and acceptance."

Dru cackled while laughing. "Oh my god, Mara! That's it exactly!"

"Except on a daily basis." Eva said, joining the laughter.

"Or on an hourly basis, depending on his mood," Claire said.

I shook my head. "If you're trying to sell me on being with a Badd, you're not doing a very good job. It sounds exhausting."

"It is," all six said at once.

"But *so* worth it," Dru said, a tender smile on her face as she watched Sebastian work behind the bar.

"It's a lot of things," Eva said, her own eyes on Bax. "But it's never, ever boring."

"I'm just…I'm not there. He makes me too crazy, and I've had enough of crazy in my life," I said.

Claire, whom I felt was a kindred spirit, poured me more wine—I hadn't even realized I'd finished my glass. "Izzy, you want to know the truth?"

I nodded. "Always."

"You and Ramsey?" Her pause and her smile were sympathetic. "It's inevitable. He's got his hooks in you. You can fight it all you want, but you're gonna end up in his bed and in his arms, and your stupid, brittle, callous little heart is gonna be his."

I was tempted to throw the wine in her face just to make her shut up. I didn't, because I refused to waste perfectly good wine, but the temptation was there.

"Shut up," I whispered. "You don't know that."

She just laughed. "Honeybuns, I *do*. You and I?" She gestured to me, and then at herself with a well-manicured index finger. "We're basically the same person. I could probably guess the basic history of your life story."

I arched an eyebrow. "Oh, this I *have* to hear."

She put her index and middle fingers to her temples, furrowing her brow in faux concentration as if focusing her third eye on me. "I see…an only child, or one sibling at the most. You probably grew up either wealthy or upper middle class. Life was great, tra-la-la-la-la—BAM, shit happens, trauma ensues. What, I don't know—could be anything. Just trauma of some kind that totally wrecked your life and closed you off, heart, mind, and soul, to the whole world. You trust no one, not really. Even your best friends probably don't ever to get to see the real, secret, deep-down, ooey-gooey-rich-and-chewy center of who you really are." She peeked at me, and then kept going. "You use men, you enjoy them for their bodies, you have fun, but that's it. If you've ever had anything like a real relationship, it was short-lived, and you sabotaged it yourself. The thought of letting anyone—let alone a man—into your life in any kind of meaningful way makes you break out in hives, and you've probably never actually met a man who could tempt you with that prospect. But Ramsey does, which is why he can put a bug up your ass so easily."

I had to remind myself to breathe. "You're just describing yourself," I muttered, hoping I sounded nonchalant.

Claire smirked at me. "Yep. But you can't honestly tell me I'm not at least close to the mark on most of it." She held up a finger. "Also, I described myself as I was when I met Brock, not as I am now."

"And let me guess, you're all better now, magically healed by the redemptive power of Brock's mighty cock."

Claire snickered. "I knew we were kindred spirits!" She smiled at me. "No, but his cock can work wonders. To be honest, it's who he is and how he loves me that did the real healing."

I tried not to roll my eyes. "Oh Jesus, please spare me the sappy Hallmark holiday movie bullshit."

"I am the least sappy person you'll ever meet, Izzy. I speak the truth." Claire stabbed a finger at me. "You just don't want to hear it."

I blew out a breath. "No, I really don't."

"Exactly," Mara said. "Stage one—denial."

"I have to go," I muttered. "I think I've had too much wine."

"BAX!" Claire shouted, startling all of us.

A few seconds later, Bax ambled up to the booth. "You bellowed, milady?"

"Our dear miss Isadora Styles is a little toasted and requires a walk home," Claire said.

"I'm not toasted, and I don't need a walk home."

"Yes, you are—" Aerie started.

"And, yes you do," Tate finished.

I sighed. "God, you're all so annoying." I looked up at Bax, who was six-feet-plus and so heavily muscled he looked like he could bend I-beams with his bare hands. "Fine. But only if you promise not to so much as mention Ramsey to me."

Bax gave a blank stare. "Who?"

"Exactly." I stood up, and realized I was bit woozier than I'd thought. "Whoa." I stared down at my empty glass. "How many of those did I drink?"

Claire shrugged. "I was wondering if you realized how fast you were drinking."

I frowned. "I remember the first glass, and the second…"

"After that, I'm not sure your glass was ever empty," Eva said, holding up an empty bottle. "That was mostly full when you got you here."

"Holy shit. No wonder I'm so tipsy." I glanced over at Bax, who was watching with amusement. "I guess I'll be glad of the escort after all."

"Sure you're good to walk?" Bax asked. "I could run you over in the pickup."

I shook my head, but carefully. "No, I think the walk will do me good."

I waved at the table. "Bye, everyone. Thank you...I think."

They all waved, and there was a chorus of good-byes as Bax paused to kiss Eva—very, *very* thoroughly.

"Remember the five stages," Mara called out, when he finally let go of Eva and led the way toward the exit. "You're combining stages one and two, so bargaining is next."

I laughed and waved over my shoulder as I walked away. We passed the bar, and Bax paused.

"Yo, Bast—toss me a bottle of sober juice," he said.

Sebastian chuckled, ducking to grab a bottle of water from a cooler under the bar, and tossed it to Bax. "Walking her home?"

Bax nodded. "Yep. Back in a few."

Sebastian nodded, shaking a mixed drink. "Sounds good. We'll be fine."

Once out of the white-noise din of the bar and into the silence and cool of the night, I felt much

better, even as I realized that I was far more intoxi-
cated than I had thought. I gestured in the correct direction, and headed that way, Bax walking beside me.

I only made it a few steps before I stumbled into
Bax, who caught me and set me upright.

"Whoa there, darlin'," Bax said, laughing.
"Hitting you pretty hard, huh?"

"Don't call me darling," I snapped, steadying
myself.

He just laughed again. "Aww, don't take it personally. I call everyone that."

"Well, I don't like it."

He shrugged a massive shoulder. "All right, all
right. Don't get your—"

I whirled on him, intending to give him the
evil eye, but the effect was ruined when I stumbled
again. When I was steady on my feet once more, I
resolved to walk carefully and slowly, with no sudden
movements.

"Do not patronize me, Baxter Badd," I said,
eventually.

He was unfazed. "I'm not. Just how I am."

"Telling me not to get my panties in a bunch is
patronizing."

"Actually, I was gonna say don't get your knickers
in a twist. It's funnier."

I huffed. "You're not British—you're not allowed

to say 'knickers'.'"

"I can say whatever the fuck I bloody well like," Bax said, in a decent—and funny—arch English accent.

"You're hysterical."

We walked in silenced for about five minutes, and then I felt him working up to asking me a question. I shot him a look.

"Out with it," I said.

"Did my girls get you sorted out?"

"They got me drunk, is what they got me." I eyed him. "And…they're all your girls?"

He nodded. "Yep. I mean, Eva is *my* girl, as in, like, my lady love or whatever the fuck you wanna call it, but the others are my girls too, in the sense that I feel a familial and protective sort of affection and love for them."

I snorted a laugh. "Your lady love?"

He nodded unselfconsciously. "Yep. I mean, we're not married or engaged, but we're together for life so she's a hell of a lot more than my girlfriend. Is there a word for that? Partner makes it sound like we're gay together or something, so that's out."

I hummed in thought. "No, you're right. I don't think there's a common colloquial term for long-term, unmarried, romantic life partners."

"So…did they…get you sorted out?"

I groaned. "Bax, come on. Is this gonna turn into some kind of Dr. Phil moment for you, too? Why is everyone so interested in my life all of a sudden?"

"No reason," Baxter said, a little too easily and quickly.

"Well, now there's *definitely* a reason."

He shrugged. "You won't want to hear it."

"Try me."

"No, remember? You forbade me from talking about a certain someone as your condition for me walking you home."

"Oh." I sighed. "Ramsey."

He nodded. "Yep."

"Why is everyone so interested in him and me getting together?"

Bax rolled his eyes at me. "Isn't it kind of obvious?"

"No."

"You're single, he's single, and something clearly happened with you and him a while back—at least, according to the family grapevine. But more than that, if you and Ram get together, it would, like, complete the family." He watched me carefully as he said this. "And remember, you asked."

"Wait, the family grapevine?" I asked.

"Well...yeah."

"What's that?"

"Kitty is the general manager of Badd Kitty Saloon, owned by Rome, Rem, and Ram, our cousins, and partially owned and managed by Bast, our oldest brother. Kitty is romantically engaged with Roman, the owner and manager of Badd Kitty—and Kitty is your best friend. Kitty is also good friends with pretty much all the ladies on my side of things—everyone you met today plus Low and Joss. She's at Badd's pretty much all the time, and the ladies are at Badd's whenever they're not at home or working, so they're always chatting. Basically, whatever happens to anyone is circulated among the ladies, right? You're a chick; you've got to know how that works. And then of course, the ladies will share the juiciest gossip with their respective dude, and then when us guys get together to drink, or get tats, or work out, or whatever, we talk about it."

"Guys gossip?"

Bax laughed, nodding. "Ohhh, yeah, we do. Just as bad as chicks. We just do it while pushing plates, and we act like we don't really care when you ladies talk about it."

"Pushing plates?"

"Pumping iron," Bax clarified. "Lifting. Working out."

"Oh." We reached my apartment building, and I fished my keys out of my purse, found the right key for the front door with only a minor amount of difficulty, and then paused as I entered the building, holding the door open with my foot. "I'm good now, thanks."

Bax shook his head. "Job's not done until you're actually in your apartment," he said. "A significant percentage of assaults happen in stairwells and elevators in your own building, or a building you're familiar with."

I blinked at him. "Oh. I hadn't thought about that." I thought about how many times I'd trotted up the stairs to our unit, alone, late at night, sometimes half in the bag. I thought about the sort of creepy older guy who lived alone two floors up, whom I sometimes passed on those same stairs. "Yeah, that's a good point."

He accompanied me into the building and pushed past me to head up the stairs first, and I didn't miss the fact that he went up the stairs sort of twisted, so he could see ahead up the next flight. I did feel infinitely safer going up these stairs with a man like Baxter accompanying me. We reached my apartment, and I unlocked the door.

"You want to come in for a second?" I asked, out of habitual politeness.

He shook his head. "Nah. I gotta get back." He jutted his chin at the apartment behind me. "Why don't I take a look through your unit real quick, though?"

I hid a smile of amusement and amazement. "Ummm, not necessary, but thanks."

He brushed past me anyway, striding into the hallway, poking his head into the bedrooms and bathroom, and then exited into the hallway again. "You're clear."

This time I didn't hide my smile. "Thank you for the escort home, Baxter."

He nods. "You're in the circle, Izz. Means you get the Badd protection treatment."

"Even if I don't end up with your cousin?"

"Even if you don't end up with my cousin." He smirked at me. "The Dr. Phil in me says you will, though. You just don't realize it yet."

I sighed. "God, not you too."

He shrugged. "Ram is a good dude, Izz. He hides it behind acting like a total douchebag most of the time, but deep down, he's a good dude."

I only just barely suppressed a snarl of irritation. "Good for him. I'm not interested in whether he's a good dude or not. I'm not in the market for *any* dude, good or otherwise."

"Not being in the market for a dude is usually when the dude finds you," Bax said.

I did snarl, then, and it wasn't a pleasant or

ladylike sound. *"Baxter."* I glared at him. "Enough."

He held his hands out to placate me. "Yeah, yeah. I won't say anything else."

I rolled my eyes as he turned away. "Everyone has an opinion," I grumbled.

"Yeah, well, opinions are like assholes..." he started.

"Everyone has one," I finish. "I know. Thanks again."

"You got it," he said, pausing to shoot me a wink and a finger gun.

I grinned at his cheesiness. "And Bax?"

He paused again. "Yo."

"You're a good dude, too. I wasn't sure I'd feel comfortable walking home with another woman's boyfriend."

"Well, I'm a thousand percent committed to Eva, and I look at all ya'll as sisters, basically. So, as fine as you are, Izz, you can't pull my attention away from my lady."

I laughed. "Your lady. You're so old-fashioned."

"You know it!" He ambled for the stairwell, then, tossed a wave over his shoulder. "See ya 'round, Izz! And lock the door!"

I did as he said, locking the door as he walked away. I contemplated whether I wanted food, a bath, or Netflix, but in the end, I was just too tired and drunk for any of it.

I collapsed fully clothed in my bed, only barely managing to wiggle out of my bra and toe off my shoes.

I fell asleep wondering why everyone was so sure I'd end up with Ramsey, why they all thought it was *so* fucking inevitable. I didn't even *like* the man. He was obnoxious, arrogant, and totally ridiculous, and just because I was crazily physically attracted to his stupid ass didn't mean I was going to, like, suddenly fall head over heels in love with him.

You had to spend time with someone for that to happen, for one thing, and I had zero plans of letting that happen.

THREE

Ramsey

MY GEAR WAS SPREAD OUT ALL OVER MY FLOOR, MY bed, my desk, and my dresser. With my checklist in my hand, I ticked off each item as I counted it;

"...extra socks, check—I've got...let's see, one, two, three, four, six pair. That's good." I had a habit of talking to myself out loud as I went over my gear list for a trip like this. "What's next? Hatchet—check. Bowie knife? Check, plus a spare. Pistol? Check. Ammo? Check. Could use more, but it'll be enough. Clothes?"

I went through my clothes again, making sure I had clean underwear, thermal underwear in case it got unexpectedly cold, plenty of T-shirts, a thick sweater, a pair of jeans, plus a fleece shell jacket, a wool beanie, and thin but warm gloves. It was summer, but you never knew what could happen out there, and I believed in being prepared. I could carry the extra weight easily, and the warm gear only took up a tiny corner of my backpack.

"Check," I said, when I was sure I had enough clothing. "Food?" I very carefully went through my food supply, making sure I had enough food for the three days I planned to be gone, plus two day's extra rations in case of emergency. "Check. Canteens? Check. Flares and flare gun? Check. Portable cooktop and fuel? Check. Toilet paper? Check. Matches, lighter, and flint and steel? Check. Fishing line? Check. Hooks? Check. Fishing pole? Check. GPS unit? Check. Paper map? Check. Compass? Check, plus a spare. Tent?" I examined the tent, making sure it was intact and that I had the rain shell and all the stakes and poles, and then checked it off my list.

Item by item, I made sure I had everything I'd need to survive on my own in the wilderness. And then, once I had double and triple-checked that I had everything, I began packing it all into my backpack, which was a long, laborious process, and one I took as seriously as the checklist itself, if not more so— the even distribution of weight was essential to being comfortable on long hikes.

Finally, I was ready. I had my lighter, flint and steel, Bowie knife, pistol, ammo, compass, and hatchet all on my person, either in pockets or on my belt. The rest of the supplies I might need while on the move, such as canteens, GPS, and maps were within easy reach without taking off the backpack. I'd made sure every item was secured in such a way that nothing would jangle, shift, flop, or sway, and I made sure the items I would need at a moment's notice were easily accessible and easy to put back, and that the items secured to my person wouldn't rub or jostle against the backpack.

All that was left now was to actually head out. I shouldered the backpack, adjusted my well-worn, sweat-stained, frayed-brim California Department of Fish and Game ball cap on my head, settled my Oakleys on my face, and headed out of the apartment to my battered old pickup truck.

When the three of us brothers first moved to Ketchikan, we'd all shared the one ancient, rattling, deathtrap pickup we'd driven up here from Oklahoma but, in time, each of us had acquired a used truck for personal use. Mine was a blue Silverado, only eight years younger than I was, with over a hundred and fifty thousand miles on it; the owner had replaced pretty much all the major parts over the years, though, so it ran like a top, and I'd gotten a great deal on it. It had a three-inch lift on the suspension and thirty-inch Toyo off-road tires, an exhaust kit to pump up the horsepower output a bit, and a fairly new A/V head unit receiver. Basically, my truck had everything I'd want in a customized truck, but I didn't have to do any of the work myself, which was why I'd paid the guy his asking price.

I tossed my backpack in the bed and strapped it down, and then drove over to the saloon to give my brothers the heads-up that I was leaving.

I arrived to find Juneau, Remington, Kitty, and Roman all having breakfast together, and Izzy was fifth-wheeling it.

Roman and Remington eyed me as I approached the table, taking in my high-end hiking boots, the military surplus web belt kitted out with a pistol, knife, bear spray, and compass.

"Taking off?" Rome asked.

I nodded. "Yeah. Thought I'd just swing by and let you know."

Rome dipped a sweet potato French fry in ranch dressing. "How long you gonna be gone?"

I shrugged. "Planning on three days or so."

Izzy was eyeing me curiously. "Road trip?" she asked.

I laughed. "Not exactly."

Roman chuckled. "Ram doesn't do road trips, Izz. He just about went batshit on the drive up here from Oklahoma."

"Being trapped in a car is the only hell worse than getting trapped in a city," I said.

She frowned in confusion, eyeing the gear I was strapped down with. "But you said you're going to be gone three days."

I nodded. "Yeah...on foot."

She blinked at me as if my words weren't registering as intelligible English. "Three days? On foot?" She shook her head. "Why?"

I frowned, tilting my head. "It's called *hiking*, Isadora."

She shot me a glare. "You don't have to be a dick about it, Ramsey." She shook her head again. "I just...I guess I can't fathom why anyone would want to walk anywhere for three days."

I spun a chair around to straddle it, reached out, and stole one of her sweet potato fries. "Backpacking is the only time I'm ever really...I dunno. Free, I guess. Getting out there, alone, just me and my gear and the trail? That's fuckin' heaven, to me."

She was still staring at me as if trying to understand. "And you just...start walking? Just like that?"

I shrugged. "Pretty much, yeah. I've got my backpack in the truck that has all my gear in it. Once I get to the trailhead, I'll park my truck and get going."

"Ohhh. So you don't just walk out there like that?" She gestured at me with a finger.

I laughed, hard. "You really are a clueless city girl, ain'tcha? Yes, Izzy, I have gear. Tent, food, clothes…" I leaned toward her as if telling her a secret. "I even have a Kindle so I can read at night, because yes, I *can* and *do* actually read."

She narrowed her eyes at me. "I do realize you're not the uneducated country bumpkin you pretend to be, Ramsey."

"I don't pretend to be an uneducated country bumpkin," I snapped.

She widened her eyes. "Oh?"

Rome was cackling uproariously. "Oh man, oh man, oh man. You two are too fuckin' much." He wiped tears from his eyes, and then elbowed Izzy. "Sweetheart, he's not *pretending* to be an uneducated country bumpkin…he *is* one."

"Fuck you, Rome," I snarled.

"Hey, all three of us are," Rome said, holding up his hands. "We grew up in Buttfuck, Oklahoma, and we barely graduated high school. That makes us uneducated country bumpkins."

Izzy seemed embarrassed. "I just…I only meant that I know you're not stupid. I know you can read," she said, her voice quiet.

I grinned at her. "Aww, babe. I didn't know you cared."

She glared, then, and if looks could kill, I'd be dead. "Don't push your luck, asshole." She tossed her hair to the other shoulder with an annoyed huff. "And don't call me babe."

"I live to push my luck...*babe*." I winked at her. "That's how you know you're alive." I rose, then, and headed for the door without a backward glance. "I'll see ya'll in a few days."

I paused at the bed of my truck to check that my backpack was still strapped down nice and tight. As I did so, I heard the door of the saloon creak open and slam closed, and I assumed it was Rome coming to give me more shit for leaving him and Rem to run the bar without me.

Without turning around I said, "I told you months ago, Rome—don't expect my help around there much longer. I'm done, bro. I need air."

"Are you really going to go hike in the wilderness alone for three days?" I heard her soft, musical voice.

Something about that voice, man; it got my cock hard just hearing it.

I turned slowly, eyeing Izzy as she stood on the sidewalk, purse on her shoulder. She was dressed to kill, as usual: skintight knee-length white skirt, a sleeveless green top that plunged daringly between her breasts, three-inch white heels, silver bangles on her wrists, and a string of pearls tight around her neck...and fuck me running, the look was killer.

I didn't realize someone as young and fashion conscious as Izzy would wear something as old-fashioned as pearls, but it just worked for her somehow.

"Jesus, Izzy," I murmured. "Why are you always dressed like that?"

She frowned, glancing down. "Like what?"

I indicated her with a finger sweeping from head to toe and back up. "Like that." I bit my lip and shook my head. "Like a billion fuckin' dollars. Like you're about to go meet the fuckin' president or some shit."

She shrugged. "It's just how I dress, Ramsey. I like to look nice, and I feel best when I'm dressed well. I'm not trying to impress anyone, and it's certainly not to get *your* attention, or anyone else's."

I rubbed the back of my neck, remembering the comment I'd made that she was referring to. "Shit... Izzy, listen—that was a dumb thing for me to say. I was just trying to push your buttons."

Her eyes narrowed, staring daggers at me. "Well, it worked."

"I'm sorry," I said. "I don't generally make a habit of apologizing to anyone about anything, but...I do apologize. You're a classy dresser."

"Classy?" she asked, arching an eyebrow.

I shrugged. "Yeah. Classy. Sexy, but…sophisticated, I suppose. I dunno."

"Not slutty?"

I sensed the trap, but plunged ahead with honesty anyway. "I think sometimes some of your outfits could be seen by some as slutty. Not by me, though."

She huffed. "Nice."

"Hey, you asked. You want me to lie to you? If you want someone who'll blow smoke up your ass, go find someone else. I call shit like it is. Dress however you like—you said it yourself, you dress for you and not anyone else, so who cares what I or anyone else thinks?"

She waved a hand dismissively. "This is a stupid conversation. I don't know why I asked." But then she moved up to the side of my truck and leaned in to look at my backpack. "Wow—that's a lot of gear."

I gently nudged her away from the truck. "Watch yourself, Izz. This truck is dirty and that skirt is awfully white." I patted the backpack. "Yeah, it's a lot of gear, but then it takes a lot to survive in the wilderness."

"What do you mean, *survive* in the wilderness?"

I shifted to lean back against my truck, so I was between her and the vehicle—leaving only a scant few inches between her and me. "Not sure what you're not understanding, Izzy. Here's how hiking works in my world: I pack everything I need in that backpack, and I *go...away*. I walk out into the countryside, where there are no restaurants, no grocery stores, no malls, no department stores, no Wi-Fi, no cell service, no hotels, no bathrooms...out there, there's nothing but trees, lakes, rivers, animals, and me."

She shuddered. "No bathrooms is where you lose me." She eyed me. "How do you stay clean?"

I snickered. "A little-known secret: it's called soap and water. You see, there's these things out there called *lakes* and *rivers* and *waterfalls*. And you take off all your clothes and you get in the water, and you scrub off with this stuff called soap. And then you lay out in the sun all naked and happy until you're dry, and then you get dressed, and bingo, you're clean. It's kinda like taking a shower, only better."

She managed to narrow her eyes, glare at me, and roll her eyes at me all at the same time. "You're such a fucking dick, Ramsey."

I just laughed. "Well, shit, Izzy, how else do you think I get clean? You think I just spend three days stinking?"

She nodded. "Absolutely."

"I do happen to care about personal hygiene, you know. I brush my teeth and wipe my ass and wash my hands and everything."

She tilted her head back in a gesture of long-suffering annoyance. "Wow. You are the most sarcastic person I've ever met in my life. How did I not realize this until now?"

"Because you've been avoiding me for the past year?"

She steps closer to me, eyes sparking. *"I've* been avoiding *you*?"

"Yep."

Her body language and facial expressions were screaming warning signs at me to stop this line of attack, but it was too much fun to piss her off. She was hot as fuck when she was pissy. Granted, she was hot as fuck all the time, but when angry she was just that little bit extra that turned me on like flipping a light switch.

"Newsflash, toolbag—*you* avoided *me*."

I guffawed. "Toolbag?"

"Yeah—you're not just *a* tool, you're a whole bag full of them. In fact, you're such a tool, I might just start calling you Ace, like Ace Hardware."

"Fine by me, diva."

"If that's supposed to be an insult, you need to rethink your insults. I consider 'diva' a compliment."

"You would." I pointed at her. "You did avoid me, though. Like the plague."

"*You* are the plague."

"You didn't seem to think so when I was eating your pussy. You screamed so loud they sent security to see who was being murdered."

She flushed, and I was amused to see that she was even capable of blushing. "And that's why I avoided you. You're an immature, arrogant bastard."

"Hey, just telling the truth. I heard security talking over the radio about someone screaming bloody murder."

"Need I remind you that you couldn't stand up after I was done with you?"

My eyes blazed, and I moved deeper into her personal space. "No, Izzy. You don't need to remind me—I remember that very, *very* well." I let a slow smile slide across my face. "In fact, I'd be down for a repeat."

"Not happening."

"No?" I tsked. "Too bad. I think I could make you come at least three times, each time just as hard."

"You could not. That was a fluke." She wasn't backing away from me, letting me stay in her personal space, staring up at me with a defiant glare.

"Oh yeah? You think so? Hop in my truck and let's find out."

"No, thanks." She jutted her chin at my truck. "You're going hiking, remember?"

"Yeah, but I could take a few minutes to *hike* that skirt up around your waist and make you scream again." I licked my lips. "Be a nice little snack before I leave."

She blinked a few times, and then backed away. "I have another question."

I was left slightly off-balance by the sudden shift in topic. "Ummm, okay."

"Where do you shit?"

I couldn't help a laugh. "Dig a hole, shit in it, and bury it. No mess." I reached back and patted the back-pack. "I even have toilet paper."

"Sounds messy."

"Not really. Squatting is actually a better poop-ing posture anyway." I rolled my eyes at her. "You wouldn't last two hours out there, would you?"

"I could, I just choose not to."

"You choose not to because you know you wouldn't make it a single mile."

I saw the moment I'd fired up her ire. Her eyes blazed, snapped, sparked, her chin lifted, and her ex-pression hardened. "You think I'm weak?"

"I think you're a spoiled, rich, city girl who's never spent a single night away from air conditioning and Wi-Fi." I wasn't faking the dismissive tone in my voice. "You've probably never done a day's labor that involved the possibility of breaking a fucking nail."

And I may have gone a little too far, judging by the raw fury in her eyes—her anger was so palpable and venomous, I reared back.

"You don't know the first thing about me, Ramsey, so *fuck...you.*" She lifted her chin. "I could last three days out there with you."

I snorted. "Yeah, okay. *You*—miss prim and proper and always in a miniskirt and pearls—*you* are going to go on a three-day hike into the Alaskan bush? You're going to shit in holes, get eaten by mosquitoes, eat out of cans, and carry a fifty-pound backpack?"

She paled, but didn't relent. "Just because I've never done it doesn't mean I can't."

I eyed her steadily. "I know you're not weak, Izzy. That's not what I was saying. You're clearly in shape, you work out, and you're obviously a strong girl. But surviving in the wilderness is a whole different ball game, sweetheart. It's not just about being physically able to carry the pack, or make it up the trails."

"No? Then what *is* it about, almighty nature god?"

"It's mental. It's being away from the comforts you're used to. This isn't glamping in an RV with a TV and a microwave and a bed. It's sleeping in a sleeping bag in a tent on the ground. It's fucking *hard*, literally and metaphorically."

"I'll say it again—you know *nothing* about me, or what I've endured in my life." She stabbed a finger in my chest. "I'm going with you."

"The hell you are. The whole point of this trip is to get away from people—all people. You'll just slow me down and annoy the shit out of me."

"You don't think I can keep up."

"No, I don't."

"I'm going. I'll show you I can keep up."

I let out a slow breath. "Izzy, honey—you have nothing to prove to me."

"You think I'm weak. You think I'm spoiled."

"Yes. Well, no, but yes. I think you're a city chick who knows nothing about the wilderness or camping or hiking. Do you even own a pair of jeans or hiking boots? Do you have the first clue about what to pack or how much?"

Her chin lifted again. "No, but I'll figure it out."

I laughed. "Yeah, okay."

"You are seriously such an—"

"Such an asshole. I know." I sighed. "You're not really serious about this, are you?"

"Serious as a heart attack."

"You really want to come on this hike with me, just to…what? Prove something to me? Spare us both, babe."

"Don't call me babe." She glared up at me. "Give me a few hours to get ready."

"A few hours? Sweet cheeks, you have to buy everything—clothes, gear, and backpack. And you have no clue where to even start."

"Sweet cheeks?" She hissed. "Asshole." She jabbed a finger into my chest again. *"Watch* me."

I glanced at my watch. "It's eight o'clock right now—I'll give you three hours. I'm leaving at eleven with or without you." I leaned in through the open window of my pickup and snatched the crumpled piece of paper that had my packing checklist on it. "I'll even help you out. This is my list. Obviously you don't need everything on this list—like, you don't need a pistol or flares or a tent or a survival knife or any of that shit. Just the backpack, lots of extra socks, durable clothes, and boots—don't skimp on the boots or you'll be miserable. And food—you're carrying your own because I've got mine rationed for one person. Ask one of the people at the outfitter store—they'll help you."

"Why can't you help me?"

I sighed. "Fuck. Fine." I flung open the passenger door of my truck. "Jump in. I'll show you what to get."

She eyed me as she climbed in and buckled up. "You're really going to let me come?"

I snorted. "I didn't think I had an option. Plus, I think I know you well enough to know you're stubborn enough to try it on your own, and if you did that, you're liable to get yourself killed." I grinned.

"Plus, this oughta be entertaining, if nothing else."

"Asshole," she muttered.

"You ever get tired of saying that?"

"You ever get tired of acting like one?"

"Nope," I said, popping my lips on the *P* sound.

"Figures."

Our first stop was a secondhand clothing store. I parked and hopped out; Izzy was slower to emerge from the truck.

"What are we doing here?" she asked, staring at the sign like she'd never seen a secondhand store before.

I led the way in without answering, and she had to trot to keep up; I headed right for the women's section, angling for the jeans. I indicated the rack of denim. "Pick a few pairs. Don't look for style, look for fit—not too tight, not too baggy. Roomy enough to move around freely, long enough to hang over boots without dragging on the ground."

She started sorting through the hangars looking for her size. "I don't wear secondhand blue jeans. I manage a fashion boutique, Ramsey."

"You gonna wear these after this?" I asked.

She made a face as if disgusted. "Hell no."

"Then buy them secondhand. Save money. You really want to spend fifty or a hundred bucks or whatever on brand new jeans? Plus, these'll be worn in—not as stiff or uncomfortable."

She selected four pairs of jeans and headed to the changing room to try them on. A few minutes later, she came out with three pairs, leaving one pair in the changing room.

"Okay, now what?" she asked.

"Shirts. Cheap T-shirts you don't mind ruining. Flannel shirts, too, or something like that. A thick hoodie or two."

She perused the shirts section, taking half a dozen different T-shirts and, to her credit, she picked for fit rather than style, although I noticed even the shirts she chose were cool in a retro sort of way. She didn't find any flannels or hoodies she liked, so she went to the men's section and found a few of both that were small enough to fit her; although, she didn't try either the flannels or the hoodies on, and I wondered if they were going to fit her across the chest. Not that I would mind if they didn't.

She lifted her selections. "Next?"

I indicated the register. "Check out. The rest we get new from an outfitter."

I stood back and let her get rung up, noticing she paid cash for everything. As we headed for the truck, I opened mouth and put my foot in it.

"I'd have taken you for a credit card sort of chick," I said.

She got into the truck, tossing her bags of clothes into the backseat. "Shows what you know about me. I don't have a credit card."

"At all?"

She shook her head. "Nope. I learned that lesson the hard way."

I headed toward my favorite local outdoors outfitter. "Oh?"

She wrinkled her nose, sniffing the air in the cab. "I didn't know you smoked."

I tugged on the three pine-scented air fresheners hanging from my rearview mirror. "I don't—the guy I bought this truck from was a smoker. I'd rather choke on pine tree scent than smell old cigarette smoke." I glanced at her. "So. What was the lesson about credit cards?"

She sighed. "It's embarrassing."

"I once opened up a credit card, spent fifteen hundred dollars on booze, porn, strippers, and rifle ammo, and then closed the account and moved." I chuckled.

Izzy spluttered. "You did *not*."

"Sure did. Thought I'd gotten away with it, too."

"Did you?"

"Hell no! Next time I registered an address, I got a bill for almost three grand."

She snorted. "How do you spend fifteen hundred

dollars on porn and strippers?"

I shrugged. "Honestly, the porn and strippers was only about three hundred bucks, and most of that was for a private lap dance. The rest was booze and ammo."

She rolled her eyes. "Men and strippers. I swear. So stupid."

I chuckled. "I agree, as a matter of fact. The lap dance was for a buddy."

"You don't like strippers?"

"Well, I don't know any strippers, but I'm sure they're lovely people. I just don't get the point of strip bars. What's the fun of a bunch of naked chicks shaking their tits and ass at me if I can't touch 'em?"

Izzy laughed, throwing back her head—and goddammit, her laugh just *had* to be so fucking musical and beautiful. "Exactly! I went to a strip bar once, and I couldn't see the point."

"Male or female strip bar?" I asked.

She rolled her eyes. "Female, meaning naked women."

I frowned in confusion. "Really? Why not a Chippendales sort of place?"

She arched an eyebrow at me. "Because cocks are good for one thing, and it's not looking at. Objectively speaking, penises are ugly and weird. They're only fun in a...um...hands-on way, if you know what I mean."

I burst out laughing. "Yeah, I think I do." I frowned, my laugh halting abruptly. "Not about dicks, though, obviously."

She snickered. "No? So, you're not a hands-on dick sort of guy?"

"Nope. Not so much," I answered. "More of a hands-on tits sort of guy."

She rolled her eyes again. "Nice."

"So, you, a heterosexual female, didn't see the point of a strip club full of naked women? Who'd'a thunk it?"

She laughed. "Yeah, well, I was with a group of girls who wanted to go to one, mainly because the drink specials were really killer, but I was just like... why? Why get all worked up and whatever about these strippers—who honestly weren't all that hot anyway— and you can't even touch them? What are you sup-posed to do, go in the bathroom and whack off? Yuck. I just didn't see the point." She shrugged. "The drink specials were good, though, and the men were all too mesmerized by the strippers to bother us."

"I feel the same way. I mean, don't get me wrong, I like tits and naked chicks as much as the next guy, but like you said, getting all hot and bothered and then having to keep my hands to myself is not my idea of fun." I winked at her. "I'm a hands-on kinda guy."

Her gaze cut to the window. "Yeah, I noticed," she muttered.

"What was that?" I asked. "Didn't quite catch that."

"Nothing."

I laughed. "That's what I thought." We arrived at the outfitters and headed in. "You never told me what the credit card lesson was."

Izzy sighed, pinching the bridge of her nose. "I ended up on my own pretty young, and got a job nannying for this family. Well, they moved up here to Ketchikan, and I came with them thinking I'd keep living with them. I was a live-in nanny, so I had room and board and all that covered as part of the job. But then once they got settled in up here, they kind of abruptly decided they didn't want a nanny anymore. So I was here in Ketchikan, where I knew no one, alone, eighteen, with no job, no home, and a few grand in savings." She was examining the backpacks and canteens and rope, just sort of looking at the all the various equipment as she spoke. "So I found a cheap apartment with some random chicks who needed a roommate—"

"Kitty and Juneau?"

She shook her head. "No, this was before them. These roommates are why, when I finally met Kitty and Juneau, I sort of latched on to them. These bitches, the first two girls I lived with? They were toxic." She waved a hand. "But the point is, I found a place, and found a shitty job folding clothes in a department store. I wasn't making it. The job didn't pay enough to make ends meet, so just to survive, I opened up not one, not two, but *three* credit cards. The assholes were giving them away like candy, and I was so young and naive I didn't really understand how they worked. So I was racking up debt and only making minimum payments, if that, most of the time."

I winced. "Ouch. That never goes well. *Three* cards?"

She nodded. "Yeah. Three, with fifteen hundred on each, and I maxed them all out in less than a year. And I really was trying to keep them for emergencies only."

"Except, when you have a credit card, everything feels like an emergency."

"Yeah, exactly."

"How'd you get out of that one?"

She laughed. "Oh man, I didn't. Not for a long time. I maxed them out and couldn't pay them off, and the job still wasn't paying shit, and the rent wasn't getting any cheaper, and I was already barely eating, because that was the only place I could find to cut expenses." She shrugged. "I walked by this storefront right as a lady was putting out a now-hiring sign. I asked if I could apply, and she interviewed me right then and there, and gave me the job—and she paid me double what I was making. So, I kept living like I had been, cutting corners and scrimping every penny, only I put every dollar I had into paying those cards off. And then, once they were at zero, I cut them up and never opened another one. I have a debit card for my one checking account, and that's it. I pay cash for pretty much everything as much as possible, because if I don't have cash for what I want, then I can't afford it."

I took down the backpack I thought she should get. "Yet you're about to spend at least five hundred bucks on gear for a last-minute backpacking trip to prove a point to a guy you don't even like?"

She gave me a nasty look, taking the pack from me and examining it. "I'm not trying to prove anything to you."

I just arched an eyebrow at her.

"Okay, fine then. I am, a little." She toyed with zippers and compartments and straps and buckles. "But I'm also proving something to myself, via you." She hefted the bag. "Why this one?"

"For the price, it has the features that are most important. It's comfortable, wears the weight well, it's durable, and it's got great back ventilation."

She frowned at me. "Back ventilation?"

I helped her put it on and clip everything into place, adjusting the straps to fit her properly.

"Yeah. You wear a backpack all day, the place you sweat the most is your back where the bag lays against you, and that shit gets miserable real fast—hello chafe city. So yeah, back ventilation is a big deal."

"I never would've considered that."

I sighed. "I know." I tapped the list in her hand. "For most of this, you don't really need to worry too much about brand or price, especially this being last minute, and probably a one-time deal. You don't want to spend a fortune on gear."

I helped her pick out the rest of what she needed until the list was completed and she had a sizable pile on the counter by the cash register. The young man checking her out was thin and whipcord lean, with blond dreadlocks under a slouchy beanie, and a wispy chin beard.

"First backpacking trip, huh?" he asked, grinning at her. "Where you goin'?"

Izzy shrugged. "I dunno. Ask him." She jerked a thumb at me.

"I was thinking the Johnson Pass Trail," I said.

He nodded knowingly. "Good one. Nice and easy. A strong hiker can do it in one day easily, but if you want to just go slow, you can make a couple nice fun days out of it." He indicated Izzy. "Good choice for a first-timer."

"Good to know."

"Lots of bugs this time of year," he said. "And I mean a shit-ton. You want to really protect against bugs."

I went back and grabbed extra sprays and a few other sundries. When she was rung up, I watched Izzy gulp a little at the total, but she took out her debit card.

"Izzy, you don't have to—"

"Shut up. I'm going."

I held up both hands. "All right."

She took a deep breath, glanced at the pile of gear, then at the total on the screen—and then at me, with a long, lingering stare. The stare hardened, and her jaw set, and she swiped her debit card with a determined lift of her chin.

Damn—she was really going through with it.

We piled the gear into the backpack and carried the rest that wouldn't fit and piled it onto the backseat. Our next stop was a grocery store for food supplies—canned beans and fruit, beef jerky, things like that. Once her food was paid for, bagged, and added to the pile on the backseat of my truck, we sat in the parking lot for a moment.

"Now what?" Izzy asked, glancing at me.

"Now we go to your apartment, take your stuff

out of the packaging, go through the checklist to make sure you have everything, and then pack it."

"Okay."

We drove in silence to her apartment, and I helped her carry the stuff up to her room. We spread it all out, took it out of the packaging and ripped off the tags, and Izzy sorted it all piece by piece, going through the checklist.

"Okay, I think I've got everything," she said, glancing at me as she handed me the list back.

I smirked. "I think you're forgetting a couple things."

She frowned. "I am?"

I nodded. "See, some of these items on the list have their own sub-lists. Like clothing." I indicated the pile of shirts, jeans, hoodies, and thick socks. "You don't have any bras or underwear."

"Oh."

I couldn't stop a smirk. "I mean, I know you like to go commando under those sexy little skirts you wear, but that ain't practical on a hike."

"You don't know that." She went to her dresser and opened the top drawer. "Wait—regular bras, or sports bras?" she asked, holding up one of each.

I shrugged, leaning against her bedroom door-jamb. "Well I don't fuckin' know, I ain't got tits." I flicked a finger at the sports bra. "I guess since we're hiking, a sports bra would make more sense, though."

She grabbed a handful of sports bras and tossed them on the pile, and then rummaged in a different drawer, rifling through a dizzying rainbow of colors and styles of underwear.

She shot me a look, catching me watching her. "Quit being creepy."

"I'm not being a creep, I'm just surprised."

"At what?" she asked, sounding like she was gearing up to be pissy.

"At the fact that you have so many pairs of underwear," I said, ignoring the warning signs of an about-to-be-pissed-off female.

She narrowed her eyes at me. "What, you think I just traipse around commando all the time?"

I stifled a laugh, sidling over to her dresser to peer into her underwear drawer. "Yeah, kind of."

"And you're basing this on what?"

Her underwear drawer held a dizzying array of thongs, boy shorts, briefs, high-waisted French cut briefs, barely there lingerie bits—scraps of lace and silk in a profusion of bright colors. "I'm basing it on the fact that when I pushed your skirt up in the hospital, you were naked as a jaybird underneath. And also, I fully admit I've spent quite a lot of time staring at your ass, and I rarely ever see panty lines."

She whacked my hand away. "Get your dirty paws

away from my underwear!" She shoved me backward, and then snatched a thong out of her drawer. "Have you ever heard of thongs?"

I eyed her up and down pointedly. "You're wearing underwear right now?" I smirked, trying not to picture what that'd look like, because I *did* want to go hiking, and if I pictured Izzy in a thong, we'd never leave. "You're telling me you're wearing a thong?"

She narrowed her eyes at me. "It's none of your damn business what I'm wearing."

"What color?" I asked, moving to tower over her, invading her space. "Black? Pink?"

She backed up…into the dresser. "None of your business."

I smirked, trailing a fingertip over the hem of her skirt. "If I tugged this up I have a feeling I'd find your pretty little pussy bare. Wouldn't I?"

"Shut up. You don't know that."

"No, I don't know. But your response tells me I'm right. You'd tell me if you were wearing a thong right now." I slid my finger upward, past her knee, taking the hem of her skirt up with it. "What color is your underwear, Izzy?"

She knocked my hand away and squeezed past me, taking a handful of underwear with her. "Stop that." She set the underwear with the pile of clothing and perched on the edge of the bed, crossing one leg over her knee. "Anything I'm forgetting?"

"Yeah."

She frowned at me. "What?"

"That I know you're attracted to me. You can't pretend you're not."

She shot to her feet, tugging the skirt down. "I'm not pretending. I'm just ignoring it, because it doesn't matter." She pushed me toward the door. "Now leave. I need to change."

"We still have to pack."

"After I change."

I grinned, glancing down at her legs. "Why the rush?"

"Because you keep staring at my legs like you're hoping I'm going to accidentally flash you or something."

"I was kinda hoping for a *Basic Instinct* sort of thing, I admit."

"Dream on, Bullwinkle," she said. And with that, she closed the bedroom door in my face.

FOUR

Izzy

I LOCKED MY BEDROOM DOOR AND SLUMPED BACK AGAINST it.

What the hell had I gotten myself into? A *three-day* backpacking trip...alone...with Ramsey Badd? What the fuck was I thinking? God. My stupid ego, my stupid mouth, my stupid temper.

Three days in the middle of the fucking woods, eating beans out of a can, shitting in a hole in the ground I'd dug myself, getting devoured by mosquitoes, and sleeping in a tent.

Alone.

With Ramsey.

Stupid, stupid, stupid.

There was no backing out now, though. Ego and pride had gotten me into this, and ego and pride wouldn't let me back out. Ego and pride would also be what kept me going when I wanted to give up.

I shucked my blouse and fancy lace pushup bra, and then my skirt. Yes, damn the man: I was commando under the skirt.

And aching from the threat of his touch. All but dripping with arousal at his presence, his heat, his mammoth muscles and the shaggy beard with its woodsy scent, and those bright virulent blue eyes. Could he smell me? Is that how he knew I was commando under the skirt?

I sometimes thought he was part animal, so it wouldn't surprise me if he had the scenting ability of a bear or wolf.

I slid on a pair of baby-blue cotton boy short underwear, wriggled into a sports bra, and then stepped into a pair of jeans. God, they felt weird. I hadn't worn jeans in years—not since I got the job with Angelique Leveaux, owner of Couture Ketchikan. Once she hired me, she gave me a hefty discount on her clothes so I could afford to look the part. And, after that, I just got addicted to the feel of silk and lace and cashmere, the knowledge that I looked expensive and successful. I enjoyed dressing nicely—yes, for myself…and, I had to admit at least to myself, because I did enjoy the way it felt to be admired, desired.

I buttoned the jeans, wiggling my hips and tugging them up higher. Ugh. Who wears these things? Stiff, rough, and so…so…*casual*. I shoved my hands in the various pockets to smooth out the lines, and then checked myself out in my mirror, twisting this way and that. Okay, well…fine—I looked pretty hot. The jeans fit me great, cupping my butt and giving it a lift, making it look nice and round and taut and firm. My thighs were strong, my calves slender. Flat across the front, a nice bell-shape to the hips. Okay, okay…I could get into this.

A soft, swift knock on my door was followed by Juneau and Kitty both entering—and they opened the door wide enough that Ram, standing in the hallway, got a nice little glimpse of me in jeans and a sports bra. His eyes widened, his brows raised, and his chest swelled—he looked me over head to toe twice before Kitty closed the door behind her.

"Um, hi?" I said, grabbing a retro Sonic the Hedgehog T-shirt from the pile.

Kitty and Juneau stood against the door, staring in confusion at the array of supplies.

"What's going on, Izzy?" Kitty asked, her voice hesitant and wary. "What is all this?"

I shrugged into the shirt and frowned at myself in the mirror; the ensemble needed something. But what? Ah! I grabbed a thick brown leather belt from the floor of my closet and threaded it through the belt loops, loosely buckling it and then tucking just the front edge of my T-shirt in behind the buckle. There…much better. Still something missing, though. Hmmmm. I cast a glance around my room, ignoring Kitty's question.

I spied the solution to my fashion conundrum on the top shelf of my closet. Sitting long forgotten, half buried under a pile of old purses was an old, faded Tennessee Titans ball cap of my father's. I'd brought it with me when I'd run away all those years ago, and had long since forgotten it. When I was a little girl, he'd worn that hat every Saturday. He'd wake up, make Mom and me breakfast—scrambled eggs, bacon, and toast—and then put on that hat and mow the lawn. And then, when he was done with the lawn, he and I would ride bikes to a local ice cream stand.

I went to the closet and took the hat down, and I couldn't resist sniffing it—it still smelled like him: grass clippings and gasoline and old sweat. The room was silent as I gently adjusted the snapback tighter, threaded my ponytail through the opening, and settled the hat on my head.

I don't think I'd ever worn a ball cap in my life; it felt strange.

And strangely right.

I let out a long, slow, sad sigh.

Juneau looked truly, genuinely worried. "Izzy, talk to us. What's going on?"

I rarely showed emotion like that, rarely gave away any clues as to the past I'd left behind; I had to cover my slipup.

I gestured at the gear on my floor and bed. "What's it look like? I'm going hiking." I kept my voice brusque and breezy.

Kitty and Juneau traded glances.

"Um…say what?" Kitty asked. "Hiking?"

"Yes, hiking." I sat on the edge of my bed and put on a pair of thick socks with padded heels and soles designed specifically for hiking, and then began lacing up my new boots. "Surely you've heard of it. Apparently you just sort of…go walking in the woods or something."

Another long glance between Kitty and Juneau.

"Izzy—you've never once gone hiking in the years we've known you." Juneau eyed my outfit. "I don't think I've even seen you wear jeans and a T-shirt, much less a *hat*."

"Because I haven't…not for a long time, at least." I eyed them. "Don't make a big deal out of this, please."

Kitty just blinked at me. "Izzy. Izz. Isadora. Honey." She put her hands on my shoulders. "You don't hike."

"First time for everything," I said.

Juneau moved to my other side. "How long is this hike?"

"Three days," I mumbled.

"THREE DAYS?" they both asked in very loud unison.

"Yes," I hissed. "Now stop being weird."

They exchanged yet another meaningful look.

"And…you're going with Ramsey?" Kitty asked.

I nodded.

"Alone?"

I nodded again.

"Just you and him? Alone, for three days? Hiking together?"

I nodded a third time.

Kitty bit her lip. "Um, honey?"

I groaned, tipping my head back. "What?"

"There's no tent here," she said, gesturing at the pile of gear.

"Nope."

Kitty's eyes lifted. "So…you're sharing a tent with him?"

"It'll be totally platonic." I knew I was lying to her and myself, but hell, I had to keep up appearances at this point. "It's fine."

Juneau was snickering, now. "Izz, honey, have you ever *been* in a tent?"

"Nope."

"A sleeping bag?"

"Nope."

She was restraining her laughter. "You realize the tent he has is probably barely big enough for two people? As in, it'll be a tight fit for *him* because he's a Badd and he's fucking enormous." She bit her lip to hold back another burst of laughter. "There will be absolutely nothing platonic about the sleeping arrangements in that tent, trust me."

I rolled my eyes. "When was the last time *you* went hiking or camping, Juneau?"

She stared. "Izz—I'm Native Alaskan, sweetheart. I grew up in the bush. I didn't have running water or electricity for the first ten years of my life. I slept in a tent in the summer and in a camper in the winter and, more often than not, I didn't even sleep in the tent, I just wrapped up in a blanket on the ground."

"Really? I didn't know that," I said.

She shrugged. "We all have our secrets, I guess."

Kitty was fiddling with different pieces of equipment. "One question, Izzy."

I had my boots on and laced, and I stood up. "Okay?"

"How?"

"How what?"

"How did you manage to get yourself into this?"

I sighed. "Because I'm a big fat idiot, that's how. Because I have a huge ego and a temper, and that GUY OUT THERE—" I shouted this so Ram would hear, "makes me mad...crazy even. He doesn't think I can do this." I eyed them. "*You* two don't think I can do this. And that, my dear disbelieving best friends, is why I *am* doing this. To prove him, and you, and everyone, wrong. I am not a spoiled city girl."

"I—" Kitty started, and then bit her lip. "Okay. But Izzy, it's not that I don't think you can't, I'm just surprised...you've never shown the least bit of interest in nature, or being outdoors, or anything of the sort. And this just seems a little..."

"Rash?" Juneau said.

I shrugged. "It's totally rash, reckless, and idiotic. But I'm not backing out now. I just spent over five hundred dollars on this gear, and I'm going to use it." I stomp a foot in irritation. "That was my Longchamp purse fund, goddammit."

"He's getting to you," Kitty said.

I nodded. "Yes, he is."

Juneau and Kitty pulled me in for a group hug, and then let me go.

"Well, if nothing else, at least we know Ram won't let anything happen to you," Juneau said.

"Why do we know that?" I asked.

"Because Ramsey Badd strikes me as the most

capable outdoorsman in the entire extended Badd clan," she said. "From what Remington says about him, Ramsey would live in a hut in the woods like a mountain man hermit if he didn't have his brothers to keep him close."

Kitty nodded. "You're in the best possible hands."

I stared at her, wondering if she meant that as a double entendre. And, judging by the delayed snorts and guffaws, she didn't mean it and was only catching on from my glare.

"Not like that," she protested. "I didn't mean it like that."

"But that's also true," Juneau said, snickering.

"Shut up," I snarled. "Nothing's going to happen."

Juneau patted me on the head. "Ohhhh sweetheart. Keep telling yourself that." She went to my bedside table, opened the top drawer, and pulled out my small pink silk drawstring bag full of...umm, personal supplies—my clitoral stimulator, lube, and condoms. She wrapped the bag inside a T-shirt, which then blended in with the rest of my supplies. "Just in case."

Kitty examined my stock of condoms. "Um, problem, Izz."

I arched an eyebrow. "And that would be...what?"

"These condoms are going to be too small."

Juneau took a look, and winced. "Oooh, yeah.

Way too small."

I frowned. "Oh, knock it off."

She held up a square foil packet. "Izz—these are *not* going to fit Ramsey Badd."

I huffed. "So? It doesn't matter. He's not going need it. Nothing is going to happen."

Kitty held me by the shoulders again. "Isadora Styles, quit lying to yourself." She tossed the condom back in my drawer. "I know you messed around with him, so I know you know regular condoms aren't going to fit. He's a magnum and you damn well know it."

I wiped my face with both hands; if I let myself go back and remember, he *was* rather incredibly well-endowed. As in, *huge*.

"I don't need condoms," I snapped. "We're not going to fuck."

Juneau wrapped her arms around me and rested her head on my shoulder. "Sure, I believe you. But just please, *please*...bring some just in case?"

I groaned, rubbing my face with both hands again, and then went to my bedside table. I tugged open the bottom drawer, rifled through to the bottom, and pulled out the string of magnums I'd stuffed down in there after the last guy, well-endowed enough to use them, had been here. I unrolled the T-shirt, loosened the opening of my bag of goodies, stuffed the string of magnum condoms into the bag, re-cinched it, and rerolled it in the T-shirt.

"There. Just in case." I rolled my eyes at them. "But nothing is going to happen. I don't even like him. He's arrogant and annoying and disgusting."

"Yep," Kitty said. "And sexy, and charming, and funny, and weirdly addicting."

"Shut up. He is none of those things."

"Which is why you're going on a three-day hike with him," Juneau said, a sly grin on her face.

A knock on the door startled us all. "Izzy—time to go. You ready to pack yet?"

I shooed Kitty and Izzy. "Enough of the intervention. I'll be fine."

"There's no quitting once you're out there," Juneau said, "so just...be really, really sure you're ready for this. There's no shame in not going."

"Yes, there is," I grumped. "I'm not quitting. I don't quit. Now go away—I have to pack."

Kitty and Juneau exited my room, leaving my door open.

"All yours, champ," Juneau said, patting Ram on the chest. "Be nice, okay?"

Ramsey eyed her curiously. "Okay...sure. The nicest." He entered my room, glancing at me as Kitty and Juneau vanished into the living room. "What was that about?"

I shrugged. "Just them being weird."

His gaze went to my open bedside table drawers—the top drawer being open is an issue, because the number of dildos and vibrators is, frankly, embarrassing.

He blinked, and covered a grin with a hand. "Looking for something in particular in there?"

I turned away, refusing to let him see me blush. "Yeah. Phone charger."

"In your dildo drawer?"

I reached into the open drawer and lifted out the three extension outlets built into the drawer, one of which did indeed have a cell phone charger plugged into it. "Yep. See?"

I unplugged the charger and tossed it on my bed, and slammed the drawers shut, hoping that was the end of it.

Alas, it wasn't.

"Nice try, but, uh…you know there's nowhere to plug that in out in the forest, right?" He grinned. "And also, there's no signal even if you did have a fully charged phone."

I sighed. "Whatever."

He held out a hand. "Phone."

I blinked. "What?"

"Give me your phone."

Warily, I took my phone from my purse and

handed it to him. He powered it off, stuffed it back into my purse, and then reached into my purse and withdrew my wallet.

"ID in here?"

I nodded. "Yeah…why?"

He opened my wallet, found my ID, slid it out, withdrew my debit card and a wad of cash and tossed the wallet back into my purse. Then, he moved to stand in front of me and shoved the ID, debit card, and cash into my hip pocket, his fingers barely making contact with any part of me except the outer edge of the pocket.

"There," he said. "That's all you need to bring. Leave the purse, leave the phone, leave it all. This shit is just for emergencies—I doubt you'll even look at it the whole time we're gone, but it's always good to be prepared for emergencies."

"What kind of emergencies?"

He shrugged. "I dunno—anything is possible. We could get separated and you may need to find a ride home. One of us could be injured and we'd need identification at the hospital. I could be attacked by a bear and hideously mangled and they'd need to ID me."

"That's not funny," I snapped.

He chuckled. "It is, a little. There *are* bears out there so there's a decent likelihood we'll see one, but

I know how to handle them."

I rolled my eyes at his braggadocio. "You know how to handle bears."

He nodded seriously. "Absolutely."

"And you snuggle them and dance with them, too, I imagine?"

"Yep. I'm a bear dancing and snuggling expert." He chuckled. "I just mean I know what to do if we encounter a bear, Izzy, that's all."

"And that would be what?"

"Make noise, and don't try to run."

"That's it?"

He nodded. "Basically. We keep our food up out of reach or in a locker at night, and we make sure we don't surprise them. If they hear us, they'll run before we even see them. Usually. They don't like people. What they say is cliché but true: they're more scared of you than you are of them."

"Have you ever encountered a bear?" I asked.

He shrugged and nodded. "Sure, several times. Only one close call, though."

"Why don't you run? And what was the close call?"

"Your brain bounces around a lot, you know that? So, I was up in the Sierra Nevadas in the early spring on a two-week hike. I was way, way up near the peak of…god, I don't remember which mountain now, just that I was up high and coming around a bend in the trail—although where I was, it wasn't really a trail so much as an old deer track I'd found. Anyway, I came around a pretty blind corner and there were these two little cubs right on the track, eating berries off a bush. I was less than twenty feet away from them, and they just stood up on their little legs and stared at me, making that funny snuffling noise bears make."

"Awww. Were they as cute as I want to imagine baby bears being?" I asked.

He laughed. "Oh man, probably at least ten times cuter in person. The problem was, their mama came out of the woods right behind me."

"Oh, shit."

He laughed even harder. "Yeah, that's a real oh-shit moment, let me tell you. A seven-foot-tall angry mama grizzly bear standing on her hind legs, snarling at you? Yeah."

"Oh my god, what'd you do?" I asked, laughing myself now.

"Pissed my pants," he said, still laughing. "No lie, I actually did pee a little. And then I started shouting. She took a swipe at me, got me with a claw right here." He lifted his T-shirt and showed me a long, thin, ropy scar running from his left nipple straight down to his hipbone. "Gave me that. I whipped out my bear spray, still yelling as loud as I could, and sprayed her with it.

She made an awful goddamn amount of noise, but she took off with her cubs behind her, growling the whole way. If she'd gotten any more of that claw on me, I'd have been split open like a sack of sausages. As it was, I got a really bad infection from the bacteria on her claw. By the time I made it back to civilization, I was sick as a dog."

"Bacteria on her claw?"

"Oh yeah, bears are omnivores, you know, so they'll eat carrion if they have to, which means their teeth and claws almost always have all kinds of nasty shit on them that'll infect you if they get ahold of you." He let his shirt fall, hiding his deliciously ripped abs. "Reason you don't run from bears is because they're faster'n fuck. Big as they are, you'd think they'd be slow, but they're not. Even the biggest, fattest, slowest bear can easily outrun a human. You run, they'll think you're prey and take off after you, and they *will* get you. You make noise; they'll get scared and run off. Even that mama grizzly that pawed at me was just protecting her cubs. I don't hold it against her. Plus, I got a cool story and a badass scar out of it."

"So you've actually survived a bear attack?" I asked, trying not to be impressed and failing.

"Nah, I wouldn't call it an attack. It was more of a warning, like 'hey, asshole, get away from my babies or I'll really fuck you up.' I'd accidentally gotten between her and them, which is why she went after me in the first place." He grinned. "But, if calling it a bear attack will win me more points, then yeah, it was a bear attack."

I rolled my eyes. "There are no points. I don't play the ratings game."

"No?"

I shook my head. "Nope. It's pass or fail with me."

He sat down on the floor and began gathering items. "Time to pack. Even distribution of weight is vital, so packing everything in here is kind of an art and a science at the same time." He began putting things into the pack, and I watched carefully, quickly picking up on the method. He glanced at me as he packed. "So. What's the criteria for pass or fail?"

I snorted. "Ha—wouldn't you like to know?"

He was quiet a moment, continuing to pack gear into my backpack. Finally, before he began packing my clothing in near the top, he glanced at me.

"Yeah, I would." There was no humor in his voice, which was unnerving, somehow.

I fought the temptation to answer the question straight—that would be stupid and dangerous, and courting drama I didn't need. So, instead, I opted for snark.

"It's pretty simple—don't be an obnoxious,

arrogant asshole." I sat on the floor beside him and took the backpack from him. "Move aside, you big lunk. I don't want your grubby paws on my unmentionables."

He laughed, but it sounded a little forced, and he slid aside to let me pack my own clothes—which was good, because the T-shirt that had my emergency sex kit wrapped up in it was right on top, and he'd have felt it and gotten curious. With my clothes packed, all that was left were a few items that Ram strapped down to the outside. And then there was only a compass and a small box I hadn't noticed him add to the pile of gear.

I picked it up. "What's this?" I asked, opening it. Inside was a Browning folding knife, the handle made of pink camo, the blade four inches of shiny metal. "I thought you said I didn't need a knife."

He shrugged. "I said you didn't need a Bowie knife." He tapped the knife on his belt, which was basically like a small sword. "You go hiking, you should have at least a little knife. They always end up being useful."

"Ah." I folded the knife and slid it into the black scabbard or whatever it was called. "So, should I put it on my belt?"

He rolled a shoulder. "Sure. Easier to get to when you need it." He nudged the compass toward me, which also came with a case that could be attached to a belt. "That too. If you have a good knife, some fishing line, and a compass, you can survive in the wild indefinitely."

I unstrapped my belt a few loops, slid the knife and compass on, and rethreaded and re-buckled it. "I see. I don't know how to use a compass, though."

He slapped his knees as he stood up. "I'll teach you." He indicated my backpack with a toe. "Try that on."

I got to my feet and hefted the bag...or tried to. "Holy fuck, that's heavy!"

He chuckled. "Yep. It won't feel as heavy once you get it on, though."

I tried again to lift it and put it on like I would a normal backpack, but it was just too heavy. I eyed him with annoyance. "Am I missing something?"

He jutted his chin at the bed. "Get it up onto the bed, back up to it, squat and buckle it on, and then stand up."

I did as he suggested, and did manage to get it on and stand up with it. "It's still heavy."

He tilted his head to one side. "Yep. But remember, you *are* carrying three-days worth of supplies on your back."

I refused to complain any more, or even let myself voice out loud the thought that was running through my head: how the hell am I going to survive carrying this thing around for three days? I'm going to die.

I glanced at Ram. "How the hell do you carry two weeks worth of supplies, if three days is this heavy?"

He stood in front of me and adjusted straps so the pack settled lower on my back, and then tightened the hip belt so the weight sat on my hips more and my shoulders less, and just like that, it felt magically lighter.

"Well, for one thing, I'm stronger than you, and I just mean that as a simple statement of fact, not as a brag or some kind of macho posturing bullshit."

I rolled my eyes. "You're a monster, Ram—of course you're stronger than me."

He smirked as he fiddled with other straps—he was close to me, so close I could smell him: a woodsy pine scent from his beard, and that indefinable deeper, muskier scent of man. "Well, you get kind of easily offended by shit like that, so I was covering my bases."

I narrowed my eyes. "You think I'm easily offended?"

He chortled. "Um, yeah, babe. You've called me an asshole at least twenty times since we got here."

"That's a ridiculous exaggeration."

"Well duh. My point is, you get offended easily. Just facts."

"Kitty!" I shouted.

"Yeah?" she shouted back from the living room.

"Am I easily offended?"

"Yeah!"

"Shut up," I groused to Ram. "That offends me."

He laughed, stepping back. "There. How's that feel?"

It was still heavy, but somehow the weight seemed easier to carry. I wiggled side to side, forward and back, hopping up and down—I was amazed to find that nothing jangled or jounced, which I'd been expecting.

"Really good," I said. "Still heavy, but manageable."

He nodded. "Good." His eyes, blue as the Caribbean and the summer sky and sapphires, locked onto mine. "So, then. You ready to head out? Trail's waiting, babe."

I let out a breath, and then nodded. "I'm ready." I laughed. "Or, as ready as I'll ever be. Let's go." I shot him a snarky look. "And stop calling me babe."

"Sure thing, darlin'."

I huffed. "Don't be annoying."

He exited my room, and I followed; we stopped at the front door and I waved at Kitty and Juneau. They both had the day off together, a rarity, and so they were spending it bingeing on a true crime docuseries on Netflix.

Kitty was the first to jump up and hustle across the room to hug me. "Be safe, okay?"

"I will." I jabbed a thumb in Ram's direction. "Or at least, I'm counting on him to do that for me."

"It's a nice easy trail," Ram said, his voice calm and reassuring. "Not quite a walk in the park, but it's not like I'm taking her up to the Garden of the Gods or something."

"What's that?" I asked.

"A park way up in the Rockies in Colorado. It can be pretty challenging."

Juneau hugged me next. "Have fun."

I laughed. "I'm probably going to die."

Ram snorted. "It's a little hike, ya'll. Relax."

Kitty laughed and patted him on the chest. "You don't know Izzy."

I stuck my tongue out at her. "You shut up."

She kissed my cheek. "Love you!" she said in a cutesy sing-song.

Ram glanced at his wristwatch—a giant digital thing that looked like it was capable of summoning Optimus Prime. "Time to go. I'm gettin' antsy." He grabbed my arm and hauled me out the door. "I'll have her back in three days, safe and sound."

I called over my shoulder as he guided me to the stairs. "If I'm not back in three days, send in the

National Guard!"

Ram just laughed, and then we began descending the stairs to the ground level. And that, my friends, was the first warning sign of the amount of trouble I'd talked myself into: just going down two flights of stairs wearing that backpack, I had sweat on my forehead and I was out of breath.

I refused to play into the "clueless city girl trying to be outdoorsy" trope, so I wiped the sweat off my forehead before Ram could see it, and forced myself to breathe slowly.

We got to his truck and I unclipped my backpack. Ram took it from me and easily swung it up one handed into the bed of his truck, climbing up onto the wheel and leaning in to strap it down. And ooooh baby, that man's ass—come to mama. Tight as a drum, hard a rock, and round as a pair of cannonballs. I had to shove my hands in my pockets to keep from reaching out and grabbing it.

With my bag secured, he hopped down and turned to face me, a happy smile on his face. "Let's get the fuck out here, yeah?"

I laughed at the eagerness radiating from every line, pore, and syllable. "You are really geeked about this, ain'tcha?"

He held open the passenger door, and I climbed up and in. "You have no idea."

It was only after he circled the hood and slid behind the wheel that I realized every single time we'd approached his truck today, he'd opened my door, waiting until I was in and buckled, and closed it behind me. It was so natural and simple that I hadn't even noticed.

I eyed him as he started the engine, put it in gear, and checked traffic before pulling out. It was kind of eye-opening, actually. Come to think of it, he opened every single door for me, always waiting until I'd gone through first.

He arched an eyebrow at me. "What?"

I shook my head. "Nothing."

He turned on the radio, and an old Western song was playing—"Ghost Riders in the Sky" by Gene Autry.

My heart clenched, seized.

Ram glanced at me and moved to change it; my hand shot out and clamped down on his wrist to stop him.

"Leave it, please," I whispered.

He frowned, slowly dropping his hand, and we listened to the song until it ended.

I was lost in thoughts and memories for a long time, as other old classic Western songs played.

"That one had some memory on it, huh?" Ram asked after a while.

I shrugged. "I suppose."

He nudged the volume a little louder as a Johnny Cash song came on. "Didn't take you for a country-western kinda girl."

I shrugged again. "I'm not. My dad is. Or he used to be, at least."

He eyed me sideways. "Used to be? He pass on?"

I shrugged a third time. "Yeah."

Ram laughed. "Okay, so you don't want to talk about it. Got it."

I sighed. "Ram…"

He turned the volume up again. "It's cool. No big deal. You don't want to talk, I ain't gonna push it."

Somehow, though, I felt words bubbling up, explanations, stories—words long suppressed, pushed down, held in, even from Kitty and Juneau.

I stared out the window, looking at the big blue sky and watching as the rugged terrain replaced the pretty town. "I used to be super close to my dad. Mom and Dad and I were all close, but Daddy and I were…it was special. Weekends were our time together. He worked long, long days during the week as the head of neurology at the hospital, but on the weekends, he was all mine. He mowed the lawn every Saturday morning, and he would always wear this hat—" I touched the brim of the hat I was wearing, "and then we would ride bikes to get ice cream.

Sometimes we'd go to the movie theater afterwards, or to the park. He took me to see movies a little girl probably shouldn't have seen, but it was my special time with him. He had a slick little Mercedes convertible he drove to work, but on the weekends, he drove me around in this ancient old beat up pickup that had belonged to his grandfather. He always left it on the same station—I don't think that radio station had changed in, oh, fifty years. It was a country and western station, and they played all those old songs, Gene Autry, Roy Rogers, Hank Williams, Roy Acuff, all those old classics, and Daddy would sing along as he drove me around. That song just...it reminded me of those weekends."

Ram was quiet for a while. "That sounds...pretty special."

I smiled at him. "It was."

I waited, expecting him to push past it, but he didn't. He seemed lost in his own thoughts or memories.

I wanted to know what he was thinking, but I didn't want to seem too eager, or overly interested, so I elbowed him. "Hey, where'd you go?"

He shifted one shoulder, a bare hint of movement, his face impassive. "I can't quite say I grew up without a parent because my dad *was* around but, for the most part, my brothers and I basically raised ourselves. Dad was a workaholic and an alcoholic. He spent all his money on booze, so he was either at work, at a bar, or passed out at home. My earliest memory of him is him sitting in a cracked plastic chair outside our trailer, a fifth of Jack in one hand, a can of Busch in the other—with a whole case of Busch on the ground nearby. I remember him sitting there drinking from one and then the other until he passed out, puke dribbling out of his mouth and down his shirt. So, your memory of driving around with your pop listening to Gene Autry? Kinda jealous."

I blinked. "Wow. I...wow. That's...I don't even know what to say."

He forced a laugh. "Sorry, I guess I just shit all over your nice memory, huh?"

"Yeah, you did," I said, laughing. "It's okay, though. The rest of that story kind of shits on itself."

"Oh? How so?"

I shook my head. "It's the kind of thing we can talk about late at night, half asleep, when I can pretend I never told you."

"That great, huh?"

"Yeah," I said with a sarcastic bark of laughter. "Really, really awesome."

We passed a good half an hour in silence, the road climbing higher into the mountains, the old classic western songs floating and wavering in the air between us, woven around the palpable tension between Ram and me. We finally pulled into a wide open dirt parking lot with a handful of cars parked here and there, and a short, fat-bodied shuttle bus idling off to one side, several mountain bikes secured to the rack on the front. An older man stood outside the folding doors, smoking a cigarette and talking on a cell phone; he was tall and lean, with a lank gray ponytail and an impressive Fu Manchu mustache, wearing dirty blue jeans and a red-and-gray-checkered flannel shirt.

Ram parked his truck in a corner of the lot, shut the engine down, and climbed out, locking the doors after I slid down from the cab. He unstrapped both of our backpacks and carried them over to the shuttle.

I frowned in confusion. "Wait, what? Why are we getting on a bus?"

Ram stepped up onto the bus and found seats for us behind a young hipster couple. The guy wore his greasy hair in a topknot, and the girl wore a tank top, stretching her arms over her head in a way that showed she wasn't wearing a bra and had probably never shaved her armpits. I sat next to Ram, trying not to feel out of place; the others on the bus included a trio of college-aged guys wearing what seemed to my inexpert eyes to be very expensive gear and chatting in a language that may have been German, a pair of women about my age talking shit about their husbands, and a single middle-aged male looking morose and lonely.

The guy with the cigarette and Fu Manchu crushed the butt with his boot heel, ended his call, and climbed in behind the wheel. "All right, ya'll. Looks like this is it for this trip. Tallyho!"

He closed the doors, put the bus in gear, and we trundled with a belch of diesel exhaust back onto the highway.

Ram leaned over to me, murmuring in a low tone. "We'll leave the truck here and take this shuttle to the trailhead—that way, when we're done, we can just hop in the truck and head home for a big ol' fancy dinner."

"Oh," I said. "I guess that makes sense."

We chatted about random things on the drive from the trail terminus to the trailhead, our low voices blending with the murmured conversations of the others around us. By the time we got to the trailhead, Ram was visibly antsy and agitated, his knees bouncing a mile a minute, his fingers restlessly plucking at his clothes and fiddling with his hat and adjusting his sunglasses. When we finally reached the trailhead parking lot and the bus grumbled to a stop, he let out an audible sigh.

"Fuckin' finally," he muttered under his breath.

"Fuckin' dying in this fuckin' deathtrap."

I laughed. "Deathtrap? This is actually a very nice bus, you know."

He was the first off the bus, and I had to hop into motion quickly to keep up even though he had both of our packs in his hands, which he carried as if they weighed nothing.

Annoying butthead.

I trotted after him as he loped with his seventy-million-foot-long legs across the wide dirt parking lot toward the edge of the forest, where there were a few wooden benches, an information sign with brochures advertising various local attractions and services, and a map of the trail. Everyone else on the bus had unhooked mountain bikes from the front of the bus and had set out already, except for the one older guy, who had shouldered a huge pack, leaned forward with hunched shoulders, and marched onto the trail with a grim resolve on his face.

I caught up to Ram as he set our bags on a bench. "I hope you don't plan on actually running the whole way," I grumbled.

He smirked at me. "Oh, I didn't mention that? We're jogging the trail."

"Not funny."

He rolled his shoulders, the muscles straining against his T-shirt, which was white, emblazoned with an "International Finals Rodeo" logo, advertising a rodeo event in Oklahoma City some ten or so years ago. "Who's kidding?"

I glared at him. "You said *hike*, not run."

He tapped the brim of his hat. "The training for smokejumping makes this look like a tea party. We'd kit out in full gear with eighty-pound packs and be expected to run uphill through mountains at a six-minute mile pace."

He had to be kidding. "Bullshit."

He arched an eyebrow at me. "You really think so?" He raised his arms and flexed like a bodybuilder, and the way his muscles bulged and rippled left my eye twitching, my thighs quivering, and my pussy dripping. "You don't get a body like this on a treadmill, sweetheart."

"Arrogant prick," I muttered.

He just laughed, clearly not taking me seriously anymore. "It's not bullshit, though. We'd go on six-, eight-, ten-, and twelve-mile runs at a pace most pro runners would be jealous of, and we'd do it in the mountains in full gear."

I shook my head. "That's nuts. I hate running in just shorts and a sports bra on a flat road."

He smirked, tightening and retying his laces. "Yeah, well, I don't risk smacking myself in the face like you do."

I whacked him across the chest with the back of my hand. "Shut up, pervert." I eyed him. "You're not really gonna make me run, are you?" I asked, unable to hide the unease in my voice.

His laugh was annoyingly chipper. "Relax, Izz. We're gonna take this at a nice slow stroll." He hefted his pack onto his back, buckled it in place and adjusted the straps, indicating my pack. "Strap up, buttercup. Time to hit the trail."

I backed up against the pack, slid my arms into the straps and stood up, buckling the hip belt, adjusting the straps. I stared at the narrow opening in the forest, nerves rifling through me.

Not for the first time, I asked myself what I'd been thinking, why I'd been so stupid as to talk myself into this.

Could I do this? I'd never been hiking in my life. I'd never once slept in a tent, or even an RV for that matter—what was it they called that? Glamping? I exercise, sure, but in a heated and air-conditioned gym, with my special sweat towels and my podcasts.

That narrow sliver of shadow-wreathed darkness between tree trunks...that was a foreign world.

Ram nudged me, smiling. "Hey, you ready?"

I inhaled deeply, held it, and then let it out, glancing up at him. I nodded once, resolutely. "Yes. Let's go."

He grinned, and in the year-and-some I'd known him, I'd never seen him this visibly happy about anything. "All right, then." He set out toward the opening in the forest, and I followed him, a few steps behind. He glanced at me over his shoulder. "Yo, Izz—this is gonna be fun. I promise."

"I wish I could believe you," I muttered, low enough he didn't hear me.

If his eyes weren't so dang pretty, if his beard wasn't so endearingly shaggy, if his grin wasn't so panty-meltingly sexy, if his body wasn't so gorgeously perfect, I'd have turned around.

But, this was Ramsey Badd, and I was a sucker for hot men.

Yes, I was only doing this because of a sexy guy. Stupid, I know. Shallow, I know.

I didn't even *like* him.

Problem: that little lie I'd been telling myself was beginning to wear thin, even in my own mind.

I entered the forest right behind Ram. It was dark and cool and quiet under the boughs of towering pines; the only sounds were the occasional chirp and warble of birds, and the sighing of the trees.

And the thunder of my own heart.

FIVE

Ramsey

Y OU'D THINK SHE WAS ABOUT TO GO IN FRONT OF A firing squad, the way she was walking gingerly behind me. Her steps were soft and short and hesitant as we entered the forest. I slowed my pace so she was beside me, and I watched her from the corner of my vision as we walked. Her head was on a swivel, looking up at the waving branches, trying to peer into the shade between the trees, looking down at the carpeting of pine needles on the hard packed dirt underfoot. She was totally rigid, gripping the shoulder straps of her backpack with white-knuckled fists, shoulders hunched, brows drawn down.

I let her walk, finding her comfort level, for about

ten minutes, getting us well away from the trailhead, but I knew she was uneasy. I stopped abruptly and turned to stand facing her, forcing her to stop.

"Isadora, you need to listen to me for a second."

She glared up at me, as if my very existence was an affront. "What?" she snapped.

I sighed, annoyed at her attitude. "This is my happy place, Izzy." I gestured around me with a wide sweep of both arms. "Out here, on the trail—this is where I'm happiest. But you, sweetheart, you're so tense you're making *me* tense, and that's seriously fucking with my mojo."

She shrugged miserably. "I just...I don't know what I'm doing."

I laughed at that, throwing my head back. "You're *walking*, Izzy. That's it! Literally that's the only thing to do, here—just walk."

"I walk to work all the time," she said, and then gestured at the forest around us. "This is different."

"Yeah," I said, letting sarcasm creep into my voice. "Out here, there are no expectations. No one is waiting at the other end for you to start working. No one is going to ask anything of you. This is the absolute nadir of relaxation. Literally, the only thing for you to do is *walk*. Breathe in the fresh mountain air, listen to the birds sing overhead, feel the wind on your face, enjoy the beauty of one of the last truly wild places left on earth, and just...*be.*"

Izzy blinked at me. "Whoa, whoa, whoa." She frowned so hard I was worried it'd give her a headache. "Did you...did you just use the word *nadir* in a sentence?"

I rolled my eyes. "Yes, Izzy. I told you, I do actually read books, and I actually do know words besides ugh and oogah-oogah."

She tilted her head backward on her neck and sighed. "Ram, that's not what I meant. I said it before—I know you're not stupid. My point is, I've never actually heard anyone use that word in a sentence before, and I was impressed."

I let out a sigh. "You're right, you're right. I'm sorry. People thinking I'm stupid is kind of a thing for me."

"Clearly," she drawled, her voice dry and droll.

I pinched the bridge of my nose. "Back to you, though. You're so damn tense it hurts just looking at you." I gently took her by the shoulders, squeezing, kneading her knotted muscles with my thumbs. "Relax. Breathe deep. Hold it, now breathe out. Let your shoulders settle. Breathe deep, and let go of everything but being right here, right now. Just let it all go."

She grinned. "You sound like a yoga instructor."

"Would you believe me if I told you I've actually

taken yoga? On a regular basis?"

She just blinked for a moment, and then burst out laughing. "I'm sorry, I just have a hard time picturing you in tree pose."

I arched an eyebrow at her as I pressed my palms together in front of my chest, slid my left foot up and braced it against my right knee with my toes pointing downward, balancing perfectly despite my backpack. "I'd show you flying turtle pose, but I'd have to take off my pack."

She shook her head. "You're full of surprises, aren't you?"

I shrugged. "Only to those who underestimate me."

"Which is pretty much everyone?"

I nodded, grinning. "Especially hot bitches who are determined to not like me."

She glared at me. "Rude!"

I laughed as I started walking again. "I was kidding."

"Well, I don't find being called a hot bitch funny."

"Who said I was talking about you?"

Izzy stopped and stomped her foot. "UGH! You're so annoying!"

"You need to learn how to take a joke, yo."

"So do you, *yo*," she shot back. "Also, I'm not *trying* not like you, I just genuinely don't."

I walked a few paces in silence, eyeing her sideways. I wanted to believe she was kidding again, but a small, quiet, but insistent part of me kept suggesting that maybe she wasn't.

A secret for you: inside every confident alpha male is that still, quiet voice that whispers doubts-- just like everyone else has; we're just better at ignoring and silencing it.

We walked in silence for quite a while, then. Izzy's head was still on a swivel, but she was more relaxed now, and it seemed like she was starting to enjoy the hike. I was content to continue in silence—I didn't need a lot of chitchat and small talk to be comfortable and, oddly, it kind of seemed like Izzy was the same way. Our silence wasn't awkward or tense, although I did still wonder how much she genuinely disliked me, and how much of that was her just trying to deny her attraction and our connection.

I glanced at my Fenix and realized we'd already made nearly two miles, which considering she was a total rookie wasn't too bad for the first hour. Granted, I was keeping the pace to what felt like a crawl, but still. I was enjoying the slower pace, come to think of it—it afforded me time to really look around, to breathe, to soak up the peacefulness.

We rounded a bend and the trees thinned out, exposing a breathtaking view of the creek, which chuckled and gurgled and rushed down the mountain. Izzy slowed to a stop, resting a hand on a tree trunk, watching the creek. She sucked in a deep breath, held it for a long time, and then let it out slowly.

Her hazel-green eyes flitted up to mine for a fleeting moment, back down to the creek, and then back to me; she was starting to get it. I smiled at her and let her take all the time she needed to just look and breathe.

After a moment, she forged onward, and now she was the one to push the pace a little, her arms swinging more freely, her breathing easy, her gaze constantly swiveling, trying to take in everything at once.

Neither of us said a word as we hiked. Every once in a while, Izzy would stop and take a moment to appreciate a view of something, and I found my-self spending as much time during those brief pauses looking at her as I did at the view.

She was stunningly beautiful, and the way she dressed really was classy—if sometimes a little on the revealing side, which I found sexy—but out here, like this, in jeans and a T-shirt and an old ball cap? This was the sexiest version of Izzy, to me. She was more...*real*, somehow. Her cheeks were flushed with exertion, her strawberry blonde hair wisping out from her swinging ponytail and sticking to her forehead and cheeks.

Her chest rose and fell deeply and steadily, swelling her breasts against the thin, faded, vintage Sonic the Hedgehog T-shirt she was wearing. Her jeans were tight and flexed with each step, and I often found myself fading back a few steps just so I could watch her walk, especially when the trail ascended a little hill here or there.

Fucking gorgeous is what she was. A woman who could rock a designer miniskirt and four-inch heels, and then turn around and kill it in secondhand jeans and clunky hiking boots? Hell yes.

I told myself to keep my head in the game—this was a hike. We were friends, if that. Assume nothing. She may not even like me—I still wasn't sure, as she was hard to read. I felt like sometimes she disguised her real feelings behind a thick layer of snark and sarcasm, and her repeated dislike of, and annoyance at, me felt like it was in that realm.

Whatever.

Whether she liked me or not, I enjoyed her presence, and not just for the nice view of her ass in those tight jeans as she hiked ahead of me, or the way her boobs bounced when she trotted down the occasional descent. The woman herself was interesting. I understood her humor; I understood her reticence to talk about herself and her past, which was why I wasn't going to push her to talk about it. Hell, I wasn't super interested in talking about my own, so why would I expect her to talk about hers?

At the top of the third hour of our hike, Izzy finally broke the silence.

"I'm hungry."

"Reach up and back with your left hand," I told her, "find the little zipper toward the bottom. I put some protein bars in there."

She shook her head. "No, I mean I'm *hungry*. I hate being the fifth wheel with Rome, Rem, Kitty, and Juneau, so I didn't eat much this morning."

I snorted, nodding. "Yeah, I feel you there. They're all so lovey-dovey it's fucking obnoxious."

"Your brothers are worse about that than Kitty or June, though," Izzy said. "They hang on the girls like they're worried they're gonna disappear or something."

"Well, that's because they are," I said. "They probably feel like Kitty and Juneau are too good for them, so they're still half expecting them to realize this and leave."

Izzy laughed. "Well, that's stupid. I'm pretty sure Kitty thinks Roman hung the actual moon specifically for her, and Juneau is the same way with Remington."

I didn't have anything to add to that, so I gestured at the trail ahead of us. "If I have our position reckoned right, we should be reaching a pretty good spot to break for lunch soon. There's a place up ahead where the trail crosses the creek. I can even see if I can catch some fish."

She eyed me. "Catch fish…and *eat* them?"

"Yes, Izzy." I laughed. "Catch fish and eat them. You ever eat fish you caught yourself?"

"I've never been fishing."

I shook my head. "Dude, what *have* you done?"

She snorted. "Um, well…? I took dance lessons for eight years—tap, ballet, and jazz. I went on vacation with my parents every summer until—well, until things…changed, and we'd go somewhere amazing every year. One year it was Spain, the next it was Italy. I've been to Iceland, Germany, Norway, Greece, Mexico, Brazil, Poland, the Czech Republic…"

"Wow, " I said, suitably impressed. "I've been to…uh, Oklahoma, California, and Alaska."

"That's it? You've never left the country?"

I shook my head. "Nope. I mean, we drove through Canada to get here, but that barely counts."

She laughed. "I took piano lessons for four years, too. And, umm…" Another laugh, a harder one. "Okay, fine! I lived a very spoiled, sheltered suburban life. I went to school and dance and piano, and I went on bike rides with Mom and Dad, and had family movie night every Friday, with popcorn Dad would make in the popper. We had a dog, a golden retriever named Charlie, and he was my best friend. I had sleepovers with my friends and we'd play truth or dare and listen to Christina Aguilera and Britney Spears and 'N Sync."

"Well, you know what they say: admitting you have a problem is the first step to recovery," I said, smirking at her.

She whacked me on the chest with the back of her hand—a gesture I was learning was actually a gesture of affection. "Shut up, butthead." She glanced at me. "So, you said you and your brothers raised yourself…what was that like? I mean, what did you guys do?"

I blew out a breath, shaking my head with a laugh. "What didn't we do?" I said. "We got into trouble, that's what. Dad worked at a factory from midnight to eight am, so he was either asleep or drinking himself to sleep by the time we woke up. Breakfast was usually a box of sugar cereal each, and cartoons—and that's a habit we still have, actually."

She arched an eyebrow at me. "You do not eat a whole box of sugar cereal every morning."

I chuckled. "No. Now we each eat half a dozen eggs and split three pounds of bacon between us, but we still watch cartoons while we eat. Nothing like the good ol' classics—*Looney Toons, Transformers, G.I. Joe, He-Man.*"

She was suppressing laughter, now. "Oh god, seriously?"

"Why is that funny?"

She glanced at me between gales of laughter. "It's just...I'm picturing you, Rome, and Rem sitting on the couch in your underwear, shoveling eggs into your mouths, hair all messy, watching *He-Man*. It's just funny. I mean, you're these big giant tough fire-fighting alpha male macho mountain men dudes, but you watch kiddie cartoons every morning."

I paused, head tilted, and then laughter comes over me. "Okay, you're not far wrong in that mental picture, honestly."

She eyed me sideways, biting her lower lip.

"What?" I asked, laughing. "You're looking at me weird."

She shook her head, turning away and walking faster—as if to hide a flush. "Nothing. It's just a...a funny image."

"Funny, huh?" I said, my voice a murmur. "You think me in my underwear is funny?"

She forged ahead even faster. "No."

I caught up easily, walking beside her as she basically trotted to get away. "You know, I don't always wear underwear, but when I do, they're tiny and black and very, very tight."

She didn't look at me. "Good to know."

"Why are you running, Izz?"

She slowed. "Because you're annoying me."

"I'm just explaining what my underwear looks like, so you can get the correct mental image. I'm helping you out."

She couldn't quite hide a smirk. "Why thank you, Ramsey. So kind and helpful."

"I live but to serve."

She shook her head, snorting a laugh. "You are such a dork."

I stopped walking entirely at that. "You know, I've been called a lot of names in my life, but I can say with one hundred percent certainty that no one has *ever* accused me of being a dork."

She halted and looked back at me. "Yeah, well, you hide it behind that facade of big, dumb, sexy macho man."

"Snap into a Slim Jim!" I quoted, in a fast, deep, gravelly voice; when she just blinked at me like I'd spoken Swahili, I laughed. "Randy Savage? Macho Man? No?" I shook my head. "What *were* you doing in the 80s?"

"Not watching wrestling, that's for damn sure," she said, breaking into a brisk walk again.

I caught up to her with a couple of quick strides. "So you *do* know who he is!"

"Just from the Slim Jim commercial."

"It's not a facade," I said. "This is me."

She then sang a few bars of a song with that phrase as the lyrics, which I'd heard a few times on the radio here and there around town. When I failed to sing along, she shook her head. *The Greatest Showman.* Duh."

I shrugged. "Nothing."

"That's a tragedy. Everyone needs to see it."

"I'll watch it with you," I said.

She glanced sideways at me. "You'd watch a musical with me?"

"Sure." I grinned. "On one condition."

She rolled her eyes. "Oh boy, here we go." She tapped her chin, glancing up and to the side, pretending to be deep in thought. "Hmmm, let me guess: your condition will involve me wearing one hundred percent fewer clothes and doing something of a one-sidedly sexual nature."

I arched an eyebrow. "I said condition, not sexual extortion—Jesus."

She sighed. "Okay, I'll hear you out. What's your condition."

"I'll watch that show dude musical or whatever it is, if you watch cartoons in your underwear with me."

She snickered, snorted, and then burst out laughing. "*That's* your condition?"

"Yup."

"Just watching cartoons with you?"

"In your underwear," I clarified.

"What constitutes underwear?" she asked.

I laughed and rolled my eyes. "Whatever you want, Izzy. T-shirt and nothing else, bra and underwear, bra and boxers…just a pair of panties." I watched her for her reaction to that last part.

Was it me, or did she blush a little, and start to bite her lip and then stop? "You wish."

"All day long, baby," I said.

"Really? All day long? You wish to see me in my underwear all day long?"

I nodded and shrugged. "Sure. You're hot as fuck, Izz. There's nothing I'd like more than to take my time getting you from fully clothed to fully naked, and enjoying every stage in between."

I sounded casual as I said this, but I didn't feel casual. My heart was thumping and hammering, my pulse pounding.

"Nothing?" she muttered, glancing at me sideways.

I let a leer slide across my lips. "Well, I can think of a few things, but they all come *after* I've stripped you naked."

She shook her head, lunging forward faster than ever. "Again I say, dream on, Bullwinkle."

I let it go, and we walked a few more minutes in silence, her a few paces ahead, and me trailing behind and just enjoying the view.

We rounded a bend which ascended a gentle hill, emerging from the forest—Izzy was farther ahead of me than I'd like, knowing all too well how suddenly you could run into unexpected ursine company. I opened my stride to catch up, but she was climbing the hill like she had a vendetta against it.

She paused at the top and glanced over her shoulder at me. "Quit staring at my ass."

I kept climbing. "I'll quote you: dream on, Bullwinkle."

She rolled her eyes and shook her head, but then smirked and wiggled her butt at me. "You want it? You better catch up!"

I laughed and broke into a sprint up the hill, causing Izzy's eyes to widen as I crossed the distance between us faster than she probably thought possible. I reached her before she had to time to react, sinking my hands into the thick meat of her juicy, wiggling backside.

"Got it," I growled.

She squeaked and darted out of my reach, looking over her shoulder at me rather than at the trail ahead. I trotted to keep up, and she laughed breathlessly, not really trying to get away.

I heard something, then. A scraping and scratching up ahead, and a whuffling groan.

"Izzy! Stop!" I called, keeping my voice calm but loud.

"No way," she called back, laughing. "I'm not letting you cop another feel!"

I hoped my voice was carrying enough to scare it away. "Isadora—*stop!*"

She heard the urgent snap of authority in my voice then and halted, skidding in the dirt. I caught up, wrapped an arm around her waist and pulled her back, shoving her forcefully behind me.

"Ram? What is it?" she asked.

"Bear," I murmured. "Up ahead."

I could still hear it ahead, snuffling, whuffling, groaning. The temptation is to step quietly so it won't hear you; instead, I grabbed Izzy's hand in mine, reaching down into the brush at the side of the trail and snagged a big stick, which I smacked against the trees as I took a couple slow steps forward, listening.

"Ram?" Her voice was low, thin, scared. "I still hear it."

"I know," I said, keeping my voice loud. "So, Izzy. What was your favorite overseas destination?"

"You're asking me this *now*?" she demanded, her voice shrill and panicked.

"I told you before, babe, you gotta make noises.

They'll hear you coming and take off." I glanced at her, keeping my hand firmly clasped in hers, dragging her forward. "So? Favorite vacation?"

We still heard it, closer now, and I realized it must have some kind of treat it was trying to get at, and wasn't paying attention to us.

"HEY!" I called. "HEY! HEY! HEY!"

I moved us to the far edge of the trail's curve so I could see as far ahead as possible—Izzy was right up behind me, pressed against my side and clinging to me for dear life.

We reached the end of the curve where the trail straightened, and there, right in the middle of the trail fifty feet away was a massive Alaskan brown bear—a grizzly. It was on its hind legs, digging in the hollow of a tree, snuffling and groaning as it withdrew its paw dripping with golden honey. Bees buzzed angrily around it, and every once in a while the bear would grumble and shake its head and swipe at the cloud of offended bees.

Izzy pressed her face against my shoulder, making a noise which I thought at first was her crying, but then I realized she was suppressing laughter.

"What's so funny?" I whispered.

She pointed at the bear. "It's Winnie the Pooh!"

I chuckled quietly. "Yeah, except in this case, Winnie the Pooh is at least eight feet tall and weighs a thousand pounds."

"What do we do?" she asked.

"We have two options—go back around the corner and wait for him to leave on his own, or try to make enough noise that he runs off."

"Which is less likely to get us mauled?"

I laughed. "Hell if I know. For all we know, we could wait back around the bend, only to find him face to face with us again."

She looked up at me. "What about your gun?"

I snorted. "Couple major issues there, sweetheart. Number one, he ain't hurtin' nothin', just getting some honey in his belly. Number two, we're in *his* home, so by rights, *we're* the trespassers. Number three, a nine millimeter would barely even tickle a monster like that even if I was inclined to shoot, which I ain't. And, yes, I own a pistol, and yes, I have a concealed carry permit, but I will never *ever* draw it unless my life is directly and immediately threatened to the point that I have no choice but to shoot to kill."

"Oh," she said. "I just meant scare him, but okay."

"Easier ways to accomplish that."

The wind shifted then, and a breeze blew up against our backs—and the bear immediately dropped to all fours, sniffing. He lumbered a few steps toward us, whuffling noisily, squinting at us nearsightedly. I felt Izzy trying to pull back as he neared us—he was twenty feet away now, and his true size was apparent. He wasn't the tallest grizzly I'd ever seen, but he was *huge*.

Izzy was making a small, scared noise in her throat, pulling backward.

My gut was churning, my pulse hammering in my ears, my heart thudding fit to burst. I straightened, took a step away from Izzy, toward the bear.

"*Ram—*" she hissed.

"HEY!" I shouted. "Hey, WINNIE THE POOH!"

The bear grunted and reared up on his hind legs again, nose wiggling as he scented the air. He let out a long, low groaning growl, waving with a paw, head tilting.

"YEAH, YOU!" I shouted. "GET! GO ON!"

He snuffled again, growled, and then dropped heavily to all fours, lumbered in a slow circle, and ambled away down the trail; he stopped about a hundred feet away, turned back to look at us over his shoulder, and then angled off the trail and into the forest.

Once he was out of sight, I started laughing. "Holy shit!" I turned to Izzy, who was frozen in place, trembling, barely breathing. "Izz, did you fucking see that? He waved at me!"

She blinked at me as I walked over to her. "He— the bear—"

I laughed again, exhilaration rushing through me

in a powerful high. "That was wicked!"

She shook her head as if to clear the fog. "You're nuts," she muttered. "Absolutely crazy!"

I laughed again, scrubbing my face with both hands. "Well, yeah. I used to jump out of an airplane into a wildfire for a living, so you're not far wrong."

"That bear was huge."

"Sure was. I've seen taller ones from a distance, but that fucker was *brawny*—an absolute unit, as the kids these days say."

She shook her head at me. "The kids say that?"

"I've heard it around."

She finally let out a soft laugh. "That was incredible. I can't believe he just walked away like that."

"Me either. He legit waved at me!"

She looked at me as if I'd sprouted a second head. "You're really amused by that, aren't you?"

I cackled. "Fuck yeah, I am! A *grizzly* bear *waved* at me."

She huffed. "Well, I'm glad you found that amusing. I think I may have peed a little."

I rested against a nearby tree trunk, eying the dead tree the bear had been digging in—the cloud of bees were still swarming with a noisy, air-shivering hum. I gestured at the bees. "That could be an issue."

She followed my gaze. "Oh…really?"

I watched them for a moment, and decided they

were mainly focusing their attention in and around the tree, so if we skirted to the farthest opposite side of the trail and moved fast, they may not even notice us.

"Let's just make a break for it," I said. "Keep to the left and move quick."

She shifted. "Is it stupid for me to be almost as afraid of the bees as I was of the bear?"

I chuckled. "Nah, there's something inherently terrifying about a swarm of bees." I gestured at the tree. "They're calming down, anyway. It'll be fine. Just hold to the edge of the trail and keep moving."

I hiked my pack up, tightened the straps a touch, and then glanced at Izzy. "Ready, babe?"

She shook her head. "Nope. Not even close." Then, with a short sharp exhalation, she tightened her straps and said, "Let's go."

And just like that, she marched forward, hugging the left side of the trail. I shook my head in amazement at her ballsy bravado, and then followed right behind her. The bees hummed and buzzed, and a few darted overhead and around us, but for the most part they stayed near the tree, wanting only to get back to the business of making honey. We made it past the tree without issue, only a few isolated bees trailing after us.

And then Izzy yelped, darting forward with a

weird shimmy to her step, twisting in place, screaming, and trying desperately to get out of her backpack. I shucked my pack in record time, snagged hers,
unbuckled it, and hauled it off of her, letting it fall to
the ground. She was yelping like a wounded puppy,
dancing and twisting in place, tugging at the fly of
her jeans.

"Izzy, Izzy, whoa!" I grabbed her by the arms and
twisted her to face me. "What's the problem!"

"BEE!" she screamed, tears in her eyes. "Bee in
my pants!"

"How the fuck?" I muttered. "Is it still in there?"

"YES!" She was dancing out of my grip and trying to undo her pants at the same time.

"Hold still, dammit," I said. "Let me help."

She whimpered, but held still long enough for
me to get her belt unbuckled, her fly undone, and
then I peeled her jeans down her legs. She twisted in
place, turning her backside to me. She was wearing
pale blue cotton underwear, and there was a small
lump inside her underwear against the skin of her
right butt cheek.

I paused, glancing up at her. "It's inside your underwear, Izz."

"I DON'T CARE! JUST GET IT OUT!"

"You know, it's a honey bee—it can only sting
you once."

"FUCK YOU, RAM! JUST GET THE FUCKER OUT!"

"All right, all right, I just didn't want you to accuse me of copping a feel."

I peeled her underwear down, and the poor little bee was stuck against her butt, the stinger's barb hooked into her skin. It was still buzzing halfheartedly, but the little thing was squished.

Squished by the squishy...

I decided not to voice that particular joke.

I pinched the tips of my fingers around the bee's body against her skin, feeling it flutter and buzz. I plucked it away and tossed it aside; I leaned close, peering at her skin where it had stung her.

She smelled of sweat and woman, making my heart flip in a weird way.

"Shit, the stinger's still in there."

She was breathing slowly out of her nose and mouth, calming herself. "I *hate* getting stung," she muttered.

I chuckled. "No shit, babe." I tugged my Bowie knife from the scabbard. "Okay, now hold still. Don't move a goddamn muscle, okay? I've gotta scrape the stinger out, and all I've got is this big bitch here."

She craned her neck to look over her shoulder, and saw me bringing the blade flat against the curve of her butt. "HOLY SHIT WHAT THE FUCK? NO!"

"Babe—hold the fuck still." I looked up at her. "Trust me."

"Get that fucking sword away from me, you barbarian!"

"It's a Bowie knife, number one. Number two, you want the stinger out or no?"

"Yes," she muttered.

"You have tweezers?"

"No."

"Then hold still and trust me." I grinned up at her. "You think I'd do anything to harm an ass as perfect as this?"

Her eyes narrowed. "Nice."

I hesitated. "So, um…this is where I cop a feel. Just, you know…forewarning you. It's necessary, though, so don't try and hit me for it."

Behold, the Promised Land. If she wasn't in pain, and I wasn't about to scrape a bee stinger out of her skin with a foot-long knife, I'd be springing major wood at having this big, round, juicy ass of hers in my face. As it was, though, I had to be something like professional about this. Or at least detach myself from my intense attraction to this woman.

The bee had stung her right butt cheek, right in the middle, and I was right handed, so in order to hold the skin taut, I had to use my left hand…which meant I had to cup the inside of her right butt cheek with my left hand. Niiiiice and intimate. Yikes. Holding the skin taut, I gently, gingerly, cautiously used the very edge of the blade to scrape downward, keeping the edge at an angle and moving perpendicular to her skin. I watched the stinger slide out of her skin. I sheathed the blade, scraping the stinger away with a fingernail and flicking it aside. The skin was reddened and swollen where she'd been stung.

She'd watched the whole process, and when I flicked the stinger away, she'd released an exhale of relief. I looked up at her, our eyes meeting.

I have absolutely no explanation for what came over me, then—no manly, masculine, macho way to rationalize what I did next.

I kissed her where she'd been stung, a gentle kiss right to the red and swollen center of her buttock.

Her breath caught.

"Ram…" she breathed.

I recovered from whatever had possessed me to do something so intimate and so personal and so tender, and I patted her bottom, and then gave both cheeks a hearty squeeze.

"There. All better."

I could tell she was working through how she wanted to react—I expected her to slap me for the butt squeeze, or give me some kind of nasty, snarky reply.

What I didn't expect was for her to twist in place. Her jeans and underwear were still down around her knees, leaving her entirely bare from waist to knee. She was as freshly shaven and waxed as I remembered her being. Tight, plump, pink little lips nestled between thick, strong thighs, with just the tiniest needle-thin gap of daylight between them. God, I wanted to…to…

Fuck it.

I curled my hands around the backs of her knees and slid them up her thighs to cup her ass; she bit down on her lower lip as I tugged her closer.

"Ramsey…" she murmured.

I kept my eyes on hers as I slowly brought my face closer and closer to her core. "Just…one…little…taste…" I whispered. "See if you're as sweet as I remember."

Her hands fluttered in the air above my head as I nuzzled my nose against her belly just above her core, brushing my mouth over her nether lips.

She huffed a breath, a whine, a whimper. "God, Ram…here? Now?"

I smirked up at her. "Ain't nobody around 'cept just us bears." I flicked my tongue against those tight plump little pussy lips. "You can tell me no."

"Now you've got me started," she muttered. "Might as well finish it."

I rumbled a laugh. "Ain't even gotten started, sweetheart," I said. "You don't want it, just say so."

She narrowed her eyes at me, mouth falling open as I lapped up her seam. "You do *not* play fair, Ramsey Badd."

"Nope." I wiggled my tongue into the little keyhole at the top of her slit, flicking the tip of my tongue against her clit. "I got a taste of your sweetness a year ago, and I've been dyin' for another ever since. But, like I said, you want to keep this platonic, all you gotta say is stop."

She knocked my hat backward off my head and buried her fingers in my hair. "Don't be a moron."

A lick, a swirl, and she whimpered again. I caressed her ass with both hands and then brought them around in front, using my thumbs to open her up, suctioning my lips around her and flicking with my tongue in a quick light rhythm until she was gasping and writhing against my face.

"Ram…fuck." Her eyelids were fluttering closed, her head tipped back, mouth open, hips thrust forward and grinding against my mouth. "How do I taste?"

"Like I want to spend every single second of my life eating you out," I murmured.

"I'd be okay with that," she said.

I could've made her come harder, faster if I'd

used my fingers, too, but I was in no hurry, and didn't want to leave her limp on the ground, as we still had half a day of hiking left before we made camp. This was just a little teaser preview of what I hoped she'd let me do to her later in my tent.

When her knees started buckling and her fingers knotted into my hair, I released the suction of my mouth and focused my efforts on the swirling of my tongue around the tight bud of her clit, faster and faster and faster until she was thrashing against me and whimpering like a trapped fox.

And then she came.

Her scream sent birds bursting from the canopy, and she flexed her hips forward in helpless thrusts. When she began to sag, I released her and stood up, catching her in my arms and holding her against me as she gasped.

"Holy….*shit*," she whispered, pushing away from my chest. "How do you *do* that?"

I knelt in front of her again, tugging her underwear up and then her jeans, letting her button and buckle and adjust. "Do what?"

She wiped at my beard with a palm when I stood up, settling my hat back on my head. "Make me come like that with just your mouth."

"It's not me—it's you," I said. "You just have a hair-trigger orgasm."

She shook her head. "No, not really. I don't have trouble reaching orgasm, but I've never been able to get there as fast or as hard as the two times you've made me come."

I felt pride swelling in my chest; her words made me feel about ten feet tall, made me want to smash my fists against my chest like King fucking Kong. Instead, I just shrugged.

"Well, let me just say that I have no fucking clue what's going on with us, or what's going to happen or not happen on this trip," Izzy said, "but I have absolutely no qualms about letting you do that as many times as you want, because sweet Lord Jesus, Ram—that was…art."

I grabbed her pack and lifted it in both hands, holding it out for her to back up into. "I might just take you up on that one, Izz." I waited for her to accept the weight, and then I settled my own pack on my shoulders. "I don't know what's going on, either, just know I have zero expectations, okay?"

She laughed as she adjusted straps and tightened buckles. "No? No expectations at all?"

I shook my head as I set off down the path, licking my lips to relish the taste of her. "Nope. Expectations are for losers. Hopes, sure. Fantasies, sure. But I like to live in a little place called reality, and the reality of you and me is that we come from two totally different worlds. You've also made it exceedingly clear I'm not exactly your favorite guy."

I was sort of fishing, at that point. I mean, she liked the way I could make her come, but liking *me*? A different story.

She caught up to me, hiking beside me in silence for a few minutes.

"Ram, I…" she said, cutting off with a frustrated sigh.

I glanced down at her. "You what, babe?"

The creek was widening and deepening, speeding up, becoming louder and closer. According to the map, I was pretty sure there was a bridge up ahead.

She didn't answer immediately. "I may have possibly overstated the case, just a little bit."

I let the silence hang yet again, for a few minutes. "Meaning?"

We rounded another curve, this one angling downhill toward the creek, and then the creek cut across the path, with a handmade wooden footbridge across it.

"Meaning, I don't *hate* you." She said this with a shy little smirk.

"You're only saying that because I just gave you an orgasm."

She shrugged and nodded. "There is that," she said, as we paused at the bridge. "But you and I both know we're each entirely capable of trading orgasms without it becoming anything personal. Actually liking the other person? That's not always a given, you know?"

"You're saying you wanna be fuckbuddies?" I asked, cutting over to the side of the bridge, where there was a small clearing.

I set my pack down and opened one of the compartments, digging out a few cans of fruit, some jerky, and a couple of protein bars.

Izzy took off her pack, set it beside mine, and sat down cross-legged on the grass, twisting to pop her back and stretch the muscles. She watched me closely as I opened the cans.

"Not necessarily," she said, belatedly answering my question.

"So you don't want to fuck."

She shrugged. "I didn't say that either. I just don't necessarily want to be fuckbuddies."

I fished a set of utensils from another compartment, stabbed a piece of fruit, and extended it to her; she leaned forward and took the bite without taking the fork from my hand.

"Then what *do* you want?" I asked.

She shrugged. "Hell if I know."

I laughed at that. "I see. Helpful."

She opened the package of jerky and slid out a

stick, taking a bite of it. "And you know what you want, do you?"

I tilted my head to one side. "To some degree."

Another few minutes of silence as we shared fruit, jerky, and protein bars, washing it down with water from our canteens. When the food was gone, Izzy lay back and let out a deep breath.

"What happened to catching fish?" she asked, watching a few wisps of clouds pass overhead.

I put away the garbage, rinsed the utensils in the creek, and secured my pack for travel, and then lay down on the grass next to her.

"No fire ring here, and it'd take time to catch, clean, and cook 'em. We'll have fish for dinner. There's a couple of nice campsites ahead, at miles four, and ten and a half. Depending on what kind of time we make, and how you're feeling, we can stop at the first one at mile four, or we can keep trucking."

She rolled her shoulders, and then massaged her quads. "I'm thinking probably the first campsite," she said with a rueful laugh. "I'm sore in places I didn't know I had."

"Ohh, just wait till you wake up tomorrow morning. Sleeping on the ground is its own kinda fun."

"Yippee," she said dryly, and then swiveled her head at me. "You said you know what you want to some degree. What's that mean?"

I tucked my hands under my head. "I know I like the way you taste, and I like the way you can't seem to help screaming. I know you've got a wicked talented mouth. I know you've got a killer fuckin' body, and I'd murder someone to get you naked." I turned to look at her, meeting those wide, expressive, hazel-green eyes. "I also know I'm impressed as fuck that you're out here, so far outside your comfort zone, and I haven't heard you genuinely complain about anything yet."

Her cheeks were pink, and she wouldn't look at me. "Ram..." she said, and then sighed. "You're impossible."

"How am I impossible?"

She shook her head. "I just...I think I know what to expect with you, and then you go and blow that out of the water, and then you go back to being an arrogant fuckboy."

I laughed. "I'd like to think that makes me more complicated than you'd originally assumed."

"You'd think right." She flexed her legs, stretched her torso. "I guess I assumed you were a prototypical country boy jock. All swagger and bravado and testosterone and muscle, and not a lot else."

"But?"

She laughed. "But you're quite a lot more than that, I'm discovering."

I decided to let it go, for now. "Ready to get moving again?"

She nodded, and I stood up, extending a hand down to help her up. When she reached her feet, she paused, standing close to me, staring up at me.

I won't say sparks flew between us, because that wouldn't be quite accurate. It was more like the first flickering flames of a runaway campfire licking at the base of a dried out tree—not much at first, but you just knew looking at it that it would grow to be something enormous and white-hot.

I was sorely tempted to kiss her.

Yank her up against me, cup the back of her head, and kiss her stupid.

She saw it, sensed it—before I could kiss her, she gave a minute shake of her head, as if to dispel a momentary burst of insanity...like letting me kiss her. And then, with a strange, soft sigh, she pushed past me, struggled into her pack without help, adjusted and buckled it, and then set off across the bridge without a backward glance.

SIX

Izzy

MY HEART WAS POUNDING IN MY CHEST AS IF I'D JUST done a dozen burpees. My hands shook. My core throbbed.

Kissing Ramsey Badd would be a monumentally stupid idea. Just because he could eat my pussy better than any man to put his face between my legs didn't mean I was ready to suck face with him. Sure, the only thing I could think about—aside from *DON'T LET RAMSEY KISS YOU!!*—was how magnificent and perfect and glorious and amazing his cock had been... assuming memory held true, that is.

The whole thing had happened really fast, mind you, so my memory was a bit hazy. All I really remember is hauling him into the empty hospital room on a horny whim, thinking I'd never see him again or, if I did, it'd be fine and dandy and no-harm-no-foul. But then I'd shoved him into that stupid little plastic-leather chair, yanked his jeans and drawers off, and had found myself face-to-face with penis perfection. I remember thinking: *Holy mother of shit! The man is hung like a goddamn rhinoceros!*

That was not much of an exaggeration, either. I'd had some nice dick in my slutty little life, but if all I ever did was suck that man's cock one time, I could die a happy woman, because it had been just that pretty.

And now…shit—I wanted it. I wanted his cock.

I didn't want complications and emotions and vulnerability and sensitivity and all that lovey-dovey, sucking face, simpering terms of endearment, ooey-gooey-rich-and-chewy romantic horseshit. I didn't want to tell him any more of my deep dark nasty secrets. I didn't want to cuddle him after we made love—I wanted him to fuck me hard and make me come until I went cross-eyed, and then fall asleep like a douchebag. I wanted him to fuck me doggy-style, legs in the air, bent over the bed, face down ass up—dirty nasty filthy sex.

What I didn't want was face-to-face intimacy, breathing each other's breath, staring into each other's eyes, whispering and shaking in the drowsy afterglow. What I didn't want was to wake up with him and never want to move.

Because people left you.

Mothers died, and fathers changed.

Men used you and abandoned you.

Fucked you and dumped you. Told you you were beautiful, fucked you in a train station, and left you dripping cum in a bathroom, alone, terrified of getting pregnant and diseased, with no money, no friends, and nowhere to go. Men called you a fat whore so you'd feel like shit, like you didn't deserve anything better than their pathetic ass—and you believed them and took the pathetic scraps they were offering, and then you'd feel even worse afterward and try to eat and drink your way to feeling okay again.

Men were walking, talking dicks: pieces of meat to be used and discarded. They weren't for liking, or wanting, or needing. You didn't get attached. You didn't see their qualities, only their flaws and faults. You sucked their bank accounts as dry as you did their dick, and felt zero remorse—not because you didn't have your own money, or because you were a sugar-baby, but because it was easier and simpler and better to use them like a coldhearted succubus than to pretend you were capable of something so human as an emotional connection.

Because you weren't.

The ability to form emotional connections with men had been seared, scarred, and taken from me a long, long time ago.

So no—I wasn't about to kiss Ramsey Badd. Because he stank of danger. He gave every indication that he was the kind of man who wouldn't even realize he was using you, and wouldn't think twice about walking away after he was done—and would leave you half-in-love and imagining a forever after a single fuck.

Nope, nope, nope. Not doing it. Not going there, not with anyone, but certainly not with him.

I stomped across the bridge, knowing full well I nearly gave away my emotional reaction to him nearly kissing me. But once across the bridge, the forest soon closed in again and swallowed the trail. I remembered all too well how suddenly we'd come across the bear, so I forced myself to slow down, letting Ram catch up—I had zero interest in running into a bear with Ramsey fifty feet away.

I kept him a few paces behind, though, because I was still feeling off-kilter and pissy, and if he tried to strike up his usual flirty banter, I'd either snap at him unfairly, or do something even dumber, like maul him.

Gah, my stupid libido was revving at the redline. Him and his stupid mouth, his stupid tongue, stupid lips. Even stupider beard, scratchy and silky at the same time as his face nuzzled between my thighs, licking me to an orgasm that had left me weak in the knees in a way I'd not felt in a very long time.

I did remember *that* part of our hospital room tryst with crystal clarity: using just his mouth, he'd made me come so hard I literally saw stars behind my closed eyelids. And listen, I'm never exactly quiet when I orgasm, but I don't typically scream like a horror movie heroine the way Ramsey made me. That's new, and unusual. And that's just his mouth. No fingers, no cock, no toys.

Argh. I'm so conflicted. I honestly feel a little desperate to fuck him, just so I can experience at least once how he can make me feel, what he can do to me with plenty of time and privacy at his disposal. But, on the other hand, I'm scared to go there with him because I do feel these tiny fragile little threads of connection to him on an emotional level, and if I were to have sex with him I'm worried those threads would grow and strengthen, and then he'd prove true to his character and abandon me like every man always has—and, in my mind, always will.

Yeah, yeah, yeah—Rome hasn't abandoned Kitty, nor has Rem abandoned Juneau. And none of their cousins—not one of the eight of them—has abandoned their respective significant others. So, I guess

I'm fully aware that the data in this case is somewhat stacked against me.

But try telling that to my heart.

It won't believe you. The numbers, the data—that means nothing to my heart.

"Izzy." Ram trotted to catch up to me. "Yo, Izzy, hold up."

I slowed my steps a bit, glancing at him. "Yeah?"

"What's the rush?"

I shrugged. "No rush."

He chuckled. "Yeah, well, you're really pushing the pace, babe. We have all the time in the world."

I focused on slowing my pace, because he was right. No point exhausting myself. I wasn't going to be able to get away from him, obviously. I needed him, because I had no clue what I was doing out here, and he did. I'd chosen to accompany him on this stupid hike, for reasons I'm not entirely clear on. Proving something to him? But why should I care? Proving something to myself? I've never cared about being outdoorsy, so why start caring now? There's no good reason to be out here with him, on a three-day hike in the Alaskan wilderness. Sure, this is a well-maintained public trail, fairly well-trafficked, not far from civilization. It's not like we were way out in the trackless wilderness of the deep bush. But still—this was more wilderness than I'd ever experienced.

Up until now, my idea of wilderness was being out of range of Wi-Fi without my no-sugar-added vanilla, almond milk, quad-shot lattes.

"You know, Izz, I'm noticing a trend, here."

I glanced at him, faking boredom. "A trend, hmm?"

"Yup." He reached back, snagged his canteen, unscrewed the cap, took a sip, replaced the cap, and secured it once more. "Whenever things get too real or personal between you and me, you start literally, physically, trying to run away from me."

"Do not."

He continued as if I hadn't denied it. "And then you blame me for being annoying which, I'll grant you, is probably partly accurate, because you're fun to annoy. But there's more to it, I think."

I wanted to deny it again, but if I denied it too hard, it'd be a case of "The lady doth protest too much, methinks," and he'd see right through that. So, instead, I took a different tactic.

"Why is it fun to annoy me?"

He grinned, rolling a shoulder. "Because your reactions are always so predictably entertaining."

I glared at him. "I am not predictable."

He just laughed. "Oh yes, you are."

I made a face of disbelief. "I am *not*. Kitty and Juneau were just telling me how *un*predictable I am."

He took his hat off, scrubbed his hand through his hair, and replaced the hat. "I'll bet you I can make you smack me."

I rolled my eyes. "Well, not anymore. You've told me the reaction you want, and now I won't do it."

He snorted. "You wish. I am absolutely certain I can get you to smack me."

"Like, a full-on across the face slap?"

"Sure. That, or just an annoyed whack to the chest or arm." He winked at me. "The trick is, I'm not gonna do it now. It's gonna be when you're not expecting it. My point is, I'm getting to know how you'll react to certain things."

I huffed and shook my head. "Yeah, right. You wish."

He bumped me with a shoulder. "You don't believe me?"

"Nope."

"Make a bet of it?"

I stuck out my hand. "I'll take that bet."

He eyed me sidelong as he shook my hand. "So…what are the stakes? I'll even let you choose."

"That's risky business, letting me pick the stakes."

We rounded a corner and reached the bottom of the steepest hill yet, and I watched how he leaned forward and took long, deep strides, pushing hard on his back leg to propel himself up the hill, and I mimicked that.

"No money," he said. "The stakes can be anything except monetary exchange, because that's boring."

I nodded. "I wasn't going to make it money anyway." I laughed as a ridiculous idea popped into my head. "Okay, I've got it."

He arched an eyebrow. "Uh-oh. You're laughing. Not a good sign."

I pointed at him. "Right! Because you have no idea what I'm about to say! Because I'm UNPREDICTABLE!"

He snorted. "I wasn't saying you're predictable as a person, or in the things you do and say—just predictable when it comes to getting you to react to something that will annoy you."

"I still call bullshit on that," I said. "Therefore, the terms of our bet are these: You claim you can do something to make me involuntarily smack you, and I say you cannot. If you succeed in getting me to involuntarily smack you, I'll walk one mile with my tits hanging out. But, if you don't succeed, you have to walk a mile with your dick hanging out."

He guffawed, halting to bend over laughing, smacking his knee. "Oh man, oh man! Seriously, Izz?" He wiped at his eyes. "You're serious? Those are your terms?"

I nodded. "Yep. You win, I walk a mile with my tits out. I win, you walk a mile with your johnson swinging."

He laughed again, shaking his head. "You realize this is a well-trafficked public trail, right? Just because we haven't encountered anyone yet doesn't mean we won't—it's basically guaranteed we'll see either other hikers or mountain bikers or both at some point."

I nodded. "I know. And the rule is no covering."

"You're crazy!" he said. "Legit nuts."

I smirked. "I'm confident I'll win."

"And so am I." He held up a finger. "Hold on, though. We have to narrow the criteria: when I say you'll smack me, I mean any kind of involuntary strike anywhere to my body."

"I'll agree to that," I said. "But I'm going to rule out any kind of jump-scares."

He stuck out his hand and we shook again. "Agreed," he said. "I wasn't going to jump-scare you anyway." He scratched his jaw. "Do you jump-scare easily?"

"Nope," I said, a little too fast. And then I jabbed a finger in his face. "And we just agreed no jump-scares."

"No, we agreed jump-scares don't count toward the bet. Not that I wouldn't jump-scare you at all."

I glared at him. "You better not, Ramsey. I'm

serious. The last person to jump-scare me got a broken nose—so do it at your own risk. But be warned: it won't be cute or funny or sexy. I'll deck the shit out of you."

"Duly noted," he said wryly.

And so we hiked in silence for a long while. The first hour, I was on high alert, anticipating something in every movement he made. Gradually, I relaxed. Which, I was fully aware, was part of his plan. Once I'd stopped startling at every movement, I focused on trying to figure what it was he thought would make me smack him. God knows he could be annoying enough that just about anything he did was capable of eliciting some kind of a reaction from me. But enough to annoy me that I'd whack him? I couldn't think of anything that would fit in that category.

Another hour passed, and by this time I was sweating profusely. We'd gone up and down several hills of varying sizes, and the weight of the pack was beginning to drag on me. I wasn't quite gasping for breath, but I was breathing hard and I knew I had rather unattractive pit stains happening. I kept adjusting my pack, hoping a different tightness or looseness of the straps would make it more comfortable. My core hurt from keeping it balanced—and by core, I mean my actual core muscles, not my...*other* core. My thighs ached. My calves ached. My shoulders were screaming. My back was in knots.

I was hungry again.

But, god…was it beautiful out here. The sky was clear blue, with only a few wisps and shreds of white cloud here and there; the sun was bright and warm. Birds flitted overhead, chirping and singing. The trees sighed in a constant breeze, the sunlight shining through them to dapple the ground with shade and light. Every once in a while, the forest would clear or we'd ascend a hill, and I'd get a glimpse of a mountain in the distance—and since we were constantly but gradually ascending, I realized the mountain top was getting closer and closer with every mile we hiked.

We reached a break in the trees where the creek cut close to the trail. I leaned against a tree and shot Ram a look. "I need a quick break."

He nodded without comment, shucking his pack and helping me off with mine.

"Thanks," I said automatically, as he set my pack on the ground near his.

Only, he didn't move away. He stayed right there next to me, not quite behind me. Just…looking at me.

I arched an eyebrow at him, laughing uncomfortably. "What? Why are you looking at me like that?"

He shrugged; I was leaning with my back against a tree, and he was leaning his shoulder against the same tree. "Just…visualizing."

I snorted and rolled my eyes. "Oh boy. Visualizing what, dare I ask?"

"You." His voice was low, a quiet rumbling murmur.

"Me, huh?" I cupped my breasts. "Imagining what I'll look like if I was to lose our little bet?" I laughed. "Keep imagining, in that case, because buddy, that's all you're gonna get."

He shook his head. "That's not what I was visualizing. I'm perfectly content to let that be a pleasant surprise." He leaned closer, and I stiffened; he was so close I could feel his breath on my ear, feel his voice as much as hear it. "And honestly, visualizing may not be the right word."

"Fantasizing?" I suggested.

"Nope." He paused for effect. "Remembering."

I caught my breath, hating how immediately I was affected by what I knew he was insinuating. I clamped down on the reaction, but it was intense and immediate and visceral—my thighs clenched, my gut tightened, my eyes widened, my nostrils flared, and I felt the dampness of desire flooding through me.

"I hope your memory is good, because that's not happening again."

He nipped at my earlobe, and I tensed even more. "No?"

"Nope. Onetime only performance."

He inched closer, and his body pressed against mine, his chest and belt buckle pressing against my arm and my hip...and something else, maybe. Something harder, thicker, longer.

"So, you've never thought about a repeat?"

"Nope. Not interested."

"You're telling me," he whispered in my ear, "that there's no part of you interested in slipping that warm, soft, strong little hand of yours in my jeans? You're not at *all* interested in wrapping your hand around my cock? Just thinking about it, I'm getting hard. You remember, don't you? Pushing me into that room, shoving me down into the chair, and dropping to your knees? I know you remember. You ripped my jeans open so fast I didn't know what was happening." His voice dropped, and I strained to hear. "You stroked me twice and then you were going to town. Or rather...going down. Your mouth was so hot, so wet, so tight."

"Shut up," I hissed. "One time. *One*."

"Yet I haven't forgotten it." He pressed his hips against my thigh, and I definitely felt him, now. Not quite all the way hard, but growing. "You remember?"

"Nope. Forgot about it completely."

He laughed. "Liar. I bet you've thought about it."

"Nope."

"I bet you considered putting those lips of yours

around my cock at least once since we've been hiking. Probably after I got done eating your sweet little pussy until you screamed."

"Have not," I breathed.

He laughed again, a quick sarcastic bark. "Lies," he whispered. "You're full of shit."

"I am not."

"Are too." He writhed against me. "You're thinking about it right now. You're thinking about my cock. You can feel it, can't you? I'm getting hard. In a few more seconds, I'll be so hard I might pop out the top of my jeans."

"Good for you," I snapped, determinedly not looking at him or his jeans or his fly or the assuredly giant ridge behind it.

"You wanna know a secret?" he whispered.

"Nope."

"These jeans are a little too big. The belt is necessary, because without it, they're easy to just yank off without even unbuttoning. One little tug is all it'd take."

"Well then, get to tugging, if that's what you're into. I'm not touching you."

"Oooh, so stubborn."

My temper flared.

Who the fuck did he think he was, calling me stubborn?

I glared at him then, giving him the evil eye. "You're a dick."

"Nah—you'd be sucking me if I was a dick."

Oh, fuck, no.

I felt my arm moving—my temper was in control by that point, and I was powerless against it. Fuck him. I felt my hand crack across his cheek with a loud *slap* that echoed in the forest.

He just grinned at me, rubbing his cheek. "Gotcha."

I made a sound that was somewhere between a scream of rage and an animal snarl—and before I could stop myself, I smacked him again. He let it happen, the bastard. He saw my hand coming, and just let me slap him again.

"Does that mean I get two miles?" he asked.

"You are *such* an asshole," I snapped.

He grinned even more broadly. "Yep. But I won."

I narrowed my eyes. "All of that...the whole..." I waved a hand vaguely, "cock-sucking stuff...all that was just to get a rise out of me?"

"Not *just*—I knew it'd work, especially if I managed to work a nice insult in there somewhere..." His grin shifted to a lascivious smirk, hooded eyes, smoldering promise and lust. "It was nothing but the raw truth."

"Which part?" I asked.

"All of it." He shrugged. "Except the part where I said you'd be sucking me if I was a dick—that was a joke, meant to get a rise out of you."

"A joke?"

"Yep."

"Because it kind of sounded to me like you were insinuating I'd suck any dick that came my way."

He moved to stand in front of me. "I know it did—that was the point. It got you pissed off enough to slap me." He laughed, rubbing the back of his neck. "I guess I didn't think this through, huh? Now you're actually pissed."

"Um, yeah."

"It was a joke. Meant to win the bet, that's all."

I glared at him, giving him the evil eye so hard it was a wonder he didn't burst into flames. "Well, congratulations, Ram, you won. And fuck you." I shoved my fist, middle finger raised, right into his face. "Was it worth it?"

I stormed away angrily, fuming inside.

A joke?

He makes a comment like that, and it's a fuck-ing joke? What the hell was his problem? Did he re-ally think I'd find that amusing? Like, oh, hahaha, you won, let me take off my top now that you've basically called me a cum-slut.

I heard him behind me, following at a safe distance.

I was still walking—or rather angrily stomping—fifteen minutes later when I realized I'd stormed off without my pack. I stopped abruptly and turned around, only to see Ram carrying my pack along with his own.

He arched an eyebrow and smirked. "Just realized you forgot something?"

I snatched it from him, swinging it onto my back and securing it. "Shut up."

"Izz, it was a joke—a bad joke. I'm sorry."

"You're just such a fucking *dick*, Ramsey! I mean, yeah, of course I'm gonna smack you if you say some shit like that! Who wouldn't?"

He moved closer. "You know, I don't think you actually find that comment as insulting as you're pretending."

I blinked at him. "What the hell does that mean?"

"It means I think there's another reason you're pissed."

"And what would that be, since you know so much about my emotions, oh infallible master of my feelings?"

He sidled closer yet, and once more he was in my personal space, staring at down at me with those big deep bright blue eyes. "I think you're pissed because I got a reaction out of you. You were on the lookout for me doing something, and I got you riled up anyway." His thumb brushed over my cheekbone, and I physically flinched away at the unexpectedly tender touch. "I think you're also pissed because I was turning you on, and you hate that I can turn you on so easily."

"Not true," I breathed.

He just kept his eyes on me. "True," he countered. "You were turned on, hating that I could turn you on, and then I came out with that boneheaded comment. I mean, it worked, and I knew it'd work. I guess I just didn't realize how well it would work."

"Congratulations," I said dryly, "you know how to piss off a woman."

He laughed. "Oh, I'm really good at that. It's basically my specialty." He smirked, and then, in a move so unexpected and sudden, he touched his lips to mine, so fast and so light I didn't know what happened and then it was over, leaving my lips tingling and my mind blank. "You're just especially easy to piss off. The problem for me is, you're sexy when you're pissed. So I'm like a cat around you—drawn to pissing you off even though I know it's a dumb idea. I just can't help it."

"I'm not sexy when I'm pissed," I huffed.

"Are too."

I narrowed my eyes. "I am *not!*"

"How do you know? You ever see yourself when you're pissed?"

"No, it's just fucking dumb! What about me being angry makes me sexy?"

"See? You're getting pissed and it's hot." He smirked, shrugging. "Everything about it is sexy. Your cheeks get all pink and rosy, and you get this wild energy like oh shit, what the hell is she going to do now? Plus, you tend to stomp around a lot when you're pissed and, baby girl, you get some *serious* bounce going on when you do that. Coming and going, you pissed is a fine sight. The trick is getting you to cool off again."

I glared. "I don't cool off easily. Once I'm pissed, I tend to harbor it for a while. So, you know, good fucking luck."

He laughed. "You drop more F-bombs than any chick I've ever met, you know that?"

"Blame my dad. He dropped F-bombs left and right. My folks rarely fought, but when they did, it was invariably about my dad cursing." I heard the words come out of my mouth, but I absolutely could not believe I'd just said that.

I'd spoken more about my father to Ramsey in the last several hours than I had to anyone at all in the last ten years.

Ram just nodded. "I see." He winked. "I happen to find it hot."

I sighed. "Is there anything about me you *don't* find hot?"

He pretended to think. "Nope, not that I've noticed."

I wanted to keep being pissed, because it was a great defense against my other emotions, but that comment sapped the anger out of me. "Well, that makes you pathetic, then," I said, falling back on snark as my first line of defense. "Because I think I've been kind of a world-class bitch to you."

He laughed. "Yeah, kind of."

"Nice." I laughed. "Let me guess—you think it's hot?"

"Nope. But the fact that you're being a bitch in an effort to pretend you don't like me and that you're not attracted me...*that's* hot."

"I'm not pretending," I snapped. "And it's not a game—I'm not playing hard to get."

"You know, I tend to spend more time outside, on my own, than around people, and I think that's made my bullshit detector super sensitive."

"It's not—"

"You said a few hours ago that you don't hate me," he interrupted.

"Sure, but that doesn't mean I like you."

"You don't want to," he said. "So of course you're not going to admit to it."

"You're impossible."

"Yep." He tapped me on the nose. "And you love it."

And with that, he pushed past me, ending any reply I might've made, because I refused to shout my comeback to his absurdly broad shoulders as they retreated.

I stomped a foot and growled in irritation—which only made him laugh. Which just pissed me off all the more.

"I take it back!" I shouted after him. "I *do* hate you!"

He turned around to look at me. "Can you do the foot stomp again? Your tits bounce when you do that."

I almost did just that out of sheer anger, but just managed to restrain myself.

I followed him, after a minute—I had to calm myself down first. It took about forty-five minutes for my temper to cool off, which meant I spent forty-five minutes mentally berating him, coming up with be-lated comebacks that I wish I'd said, plausible argu-ments for how *not* attracted to him I was, plausible reasons as to why I truly didn't like him.

But then, once all that faded and I mentally

returned to just enjoying the hike—despite my mounting exhaustion and bone-deep soreness—I started to see the humor in the whole situation.

He'd been one hundred percent right—he knew exactly which buttons to push, and how I'd react. He'd played me like a goddamn violin, and I'd responded precisely as he'd expected.

The bastard.

The smug, smug bastard.

Where the hell did he get off seeing me so clearly? How did he know my buttons so well? How could he play me like that?

I felt stupid for playing into his plan, but at the same time, it was kind of funny.

The longer I thought about it, the funnier it got.

I mean, if I hadn't been turned on and fighting it, and then pissy about being turned on and fighting it, his comment about me sucking him if he was a dick would've been funny. I wouldn't have been insulted by it in the slightest. If Kitty or June had said it, I'd have laughed and high-fived them. And probably agreed that, yes, if Ram was a dick, I'd suck him.

I couldn't help a snicker of laughter as the hilarity built inside me. Eventually, I couldn't hold it in anymore, and I had to stop to laugh.

Ram paused, glanced back, frowning, and then came to stand nearby, leaning against a tree, eyeing me. "What's so funny?"

I choked down a snort of laughter. "The whole thing."

"What whole thing?"

"The bet, and you winning it. How you won it." I breathed slowly and deeply to calm myself. "Oh man, oh man. I spent the last forty-five minutes raging inside, but now, suddenly, it's just funny. I mean, you really did play me like Joshua Bell plays a violin."

"Who?"

I shook my head. "Josh Bell? Violin prodigy? No? My mom was into classical music, and I still listen to it sometimes." I waved a hand to dismiss the subject. "Point is, you played me. Well done. You won."

He pushed away from the tree. "Yeah, well, I absolve you of the terms of the bet. I won unfairly."

"Ram." He stopped and turned, and I met his eyes. "You won fair and square."

He shook his head. "I was a dick."

"Yeah, you were. That was an asshole thing to say to me. But you *were* right in that, normally, I'd have found that funny rather than insulting. You claimed you could get me to smack you, and you did."

"Izz, I said I absolve you—"

"Very chivalrous of you," I said. "But I don't accept your absolution."

"You don't?"

"Nope."

I sucked in a deep breath and held it—looked around to make sure the trail was empty, even though I knew I was going to go through with this regardless. With Ram's eyes hard on mine, carefully watching my every move, I hooked my fingers into the neck of my T-shirt and the cups of my bra and yanked them both down to bare my breasts. Only, instead of just flashing and shaking them a little, I tucked the shirt and cups down underneath my tits. My heart thudded, adrenaline coursing through me.

Of all the inappropriate shit I've done in my life, public nudity wasn't up there for me. I've fucked a lot of guys, but I never went on spring break, and so never got the opportunity to drunkenly flash my tits at anyone.

Right now I was stone-cold sober, and had my tits out in public. Holy shit.

Ram was staring. Unabashedly, openly ogling my breasts.

I wiggled them at him. "Get a good look?"

"No, I think I need a closer one." He took a step toward me.

I held out my hand to stop him. "Whoa, hold on. This isn't an invitation to touch."

He just laughed. "Fine. Be that way."

"I will. I'm honoring my end of the bet." I

pointed at the watch on his wrist. "I expect you to be honorable and tell me when it's been one mile."

He glanced at his watch, and then nodded at me. "One mile, starting now."

I started walking.

HOLY SHIT.

I've never appreciated a sports bra as much as I did, then. Every step sent the girls bouncing, flopping, and jiggling so hard that during a jagged little downward curve I ended up having to hold them in place simply to stop the pain.

Ram kept pace with me, of course, and essentially never stopped staring.

"Is it a mile yet?" I asked, after about fifteen minutes.

He laughed. "Nope. Half."

"Shit." I couldn't help a laugh, then. "This hurts."

"Your pride, or literally?"

"Literally." I glanced pointedly at him. "If anyone's pride should be dinged, it's yours. You're the one with zero control over his eyes. It's like you've never seen tits before."

"None as perfect as yours," he said. "Besides, you yourself have said any number of times there's no guarantee of anything happening between us, so I'm just soaking it in."

I snorted. "I see." I eyed him. "Again, you used

that word—perfect."

He shrugged. "I use the words that seem to fit." He indicated my breasts, which were bouncing as we slogged up a long, shallow hill. "Those are perfect." He leaned backward to look at my butt. "That? Perfect, too."

"You're an idiot. They're just butt and boobs, Ram. Seen one, seen 'em all."

He shrugged again. "True. But seeing actual perfection is rare."

We kept walking, then. For how long? Another fifteen minutes? Half an hour? I was focused on my feet, picking my path up another hill, and so I didn't hear them until they were right on top of me: cyclists, or mountain bikers, or whatever they're called, coming up behind us.

"Passing on your left!" one of them called, as they approached from behind.

I didn't have time to cover up, which I'd have done regardless of my own rule. But they were zipping past us in a blur, two young, buff, hot college guys in expensive helmets and riding expensive bikes, with expensive backpacks and expensive sunglasses. The second rider to pass twisted to glance back at us, out of curiosity or habit, or whatever; he saw me with my pale, freckled, DD breasts casually plopped out over my shirt.

He rode off the trail, crashed into a downed tree, and flipped straight over the handlebars and into the bracken.

I covered myself with my hands. "Shit!"

Ram was laughing hysterically as he hopped over the downed tree to help the poor guy up—he seemed more shaken than hurt, and more worried about his bike than himself. He thanked Ram as he climbed over the tree and righted his bicycle, bringing it back onto the trail and checking it over.

"I'm really sorry about that," I said, still clutching myself with both hands.

The rider just eyed me. "I mean, if I'm gonna wipe out, that's a great fuckin' way to go."

His friend was stopped a few feet away, standing with his bike between his legs, twisted to watch the whole thing. "Dude, Jake, let's go. Quit ogling the hot topless chick and get your ass back on the fuckin' bike. She's out of your league, son!"

Jake, the cyclist who'd crashed, flipped his friend off with both hands. "Fuck off, Hank." He winked at me. "Can I get another look before I go?"

I glanced at Ram, who just shrugged, arms crossed over his massive chest.

"Sure," I said. "But it's gonna be fast. Ready? One…two…three." On three, I dropped my hands for a split second, and then replaced them. "There you go. Just to make up for causing you to crash. Now shoo. Go ride your bicycle, sonny."

He laughed. "Best crash ever, man." He reached out a fist to Ram. "You're a lucky motherfucker, bro." With that, he stood with one foot on a pedal, swinging on and propelling himself into movement in a single, practiced motion, clicking his other foot into the pedal as he sped away up the hill.

When they were gone again, I let my hands drop, and burst into laughter. "Oh my god. I can't believe that just happened."

Ram was grinning. "I mean, it's not that hard to believe."

"No?" I asked.

Ram shrugged. "I mean, not really. Men are pretty easily hypnotized by tits, you know. Even totally average tits will make us zone out. A big ol' pair of perfect knockers like yours? I'm pretty sure you could turn a gay guy straight with those. A straight guy? We're helpless."

I snorted, rolling my eyes even as I blushed and suppressed an embarrassingly breathy giggle of flattered glee. "You're so dumb, Ram. Seriously. They're literally just breasts."

"They're literally just the most amazing breasts I've ever seen." He grinned. "And babe, I've seen more than my fair share. Trust me on that."

"Aaaand then you ruin it with that comment."

"What? It's just the truth." He gestured at my chest. "And those are easily the most attractive pair I've ever seen. It's a compliment."

"Wrapped in chauvinistic braggadocio." I reached out, grabbed his wrist, and looked at his watch. "Has it been a mile yet?"

That was a miscalculation—grabbing his wrist like that put me within touching distance. He stared down at me, at my hand on his thick wrist. His eyebrow arched, and a smirk crossed his face.

I lifted my chin. "Don't you dare."

"Don't I dare what?" he asked.

"Do what I think you're about to do."

He leaned closer, so his forehead brushed mine, his lips ghosting teasingly over mine. "What is it you think I'm going to do?"

If I said it, I'd sound ridiculous. Pathetic. Like I had something worry about, like I was scared of him.

He pulled back, that stupid sexy mysterious irritating smirk on his face. He bent, slowly, so there was no missing his intention. Both of his big hard hands cupped my breasts and lifted them—I gasped, a sharp, aroused inhalation. My mouth opened and closed, but no sound came out. I meant to tell him to stop, to not touch me, but I couldn't.

His lips closed over my nipple, the left one,

suckling gently, and then his tongue fluttered over it and circled it, and I felt my nipples hardening to diamond points of aching arousal. He shifted to the other breast and paid the same homage to it, sucking the thick, pink aching nipple into his mouth, kissing, nuzzling, licking.

And then he backed away, straightening and grabbing the straps of his pack as if to prevent himself from going any further.

Which, at that particular moment, I may not have minded.

He sucked in a deep breath, and then reached out, tugged my bra and shirt back into place, covering me. "It's been two miles." He grinned. "My bad."

"I knew it!" I shouted. "I knew it felt like more than a mile!" I whacked his arm. "You jerk!"

He smirked, shrugged. "I lost track."

I glared at him. "Bullshit."

"Like I said—hypnotizing. I swear—I lost track."

"You have a watch that keeps track for you."

"Doesn't do any good if you don't look at it."

I stared. "I asked you if it had been a mile! You said no, it's been half a mile."

"It *was* half a mile…then. We walked a ways after that, and I got so distracted by the sight of your boobs that I forgot to keep track of the distance."

I shook my head. "Dick."

He just laughed. "Guilty as charged."

"You sound almost proud of it."

"Once again, you're getting pissy because I turned you on, and you hate that I can have that power over you."

I narrowed my eyes at him in aggravation. "You do *not* have power over me, toolbag."

"Do too."

"Do not."

He sighed. "Do I have to prove it?"

"Yeah, you do." I lifted my chin proudly, defiantly. Stupidly.

Because I knew, deep down, that he absolutely did have power over me, at least in that respect.

Plus, making him prove it could be fun. Disastrous emotionally, but fun. And I mean, if the worst thing I get out of this business with Ram is an achy, breaky heart? Well…I've survived worse. I'd be fine.

"Ohhhh man, you are gonna eat those words, sweet cheeks." He patted me on the butt as he moved past me and continued up the trail.

"I'm not the one who's eaten something today," I muttered.

He just laughed. "No, and damn right." He licked his lips. "You ready for another go around? I'm getting a little peckish."

Shit, shit, shit.

Everything kept backfiring.

I waved a hand at the trail. "Just walk, Ramsey," I snapped. "I'm ready to set up camp, and you promised me fresh fish."

He chuckled. "After all this hiking we've been doing, I'm not sure how fresh your fish is at this point, but I don't mind. I'll still eat it till you scream."

I howled a wordless shriek of annoyance, and whacked him across the chest again as I stormed past him. "YOU ARE *SO* FUCKING ANNOYING!"

His only answer was another satisfied chuckle.

SEVEN

Ramsey

GOD, IT WAS WAY TOO MUCH FUCKING FUN MESSING with her. Everything about her was sexy, funny, and arousing. Just watching her hike fully clothed gave me a goddamn semi, but those two miles she walked with her tits hanging out? My balls ached and my cock was so hard it hurt. I don't think she'd noticed, mainly because I'd done my best to direct her attention away from it.

For one thing, I hadn't been with a girl in two months—I'd been focused on helping out with the saloon, helping Rome get things tightened up so I could step away and figure my own life out. Two months without sex? In my world, that was a fucking eternity.

Or rather, an eternity without fucking.

And, truth be told, when I took care of things with the aid of lotion and Kleenex, it was always Izzy I'd imagined.

Or, more accurately, remembered.

That day in the hospital had been the best day of my life. I'd gone for a walk with her hoping to maybe get lucky, get a dirty quickie with her in the janitor's closet. Push that hot little skirt of hers up and fuck her up against a wall or something. Get a little taste of all that strawberry blonde hotness, and be done with it. If I saw her again, I'd been convinced it'd be a polite nod at each other, in a distant sort of way. I really hadn't expected Rome and Kitty to last, and I certainly hadn't expected Rem to shack up with Juneau, or for them to last either.

But they'd both made what seemed to be lasting, monogamous, long-term commitments to those girls, thus leaving them to wonder why Izzy and I had never got together. Little did they know.

But, the thing was I had no interest in settling down. No interest in romance or commitment. I was a wanderer. An outdoorsman. My life was out here, on the trail, far from people.

Especially soft, spoiled city girls.

Except Izzy was proving she wasn't soft at all. She'd hiked with me all damn day, carrying a pretty heavy pack, and hadn't complained about it once. She kept up, too—albeit our pace was slow as we weren't in a hurry.

Right now, for example, she was up ahead of me again, arms swinging, legs churning away on the trail, head on a swivel, taking in the incredible view all around us. The mountain was closer than ever, towering in snow-capped majesty over us, visible through the trees and above them. The creek chuckled noisily, birds chirped and cawed and screeched, squirrels chattered.

I caught a glimpse of something on the trail up ahead, a hint of brown fur, and I trotted to catch up with Izzy. I grabbed her arm and pulled her back, putting my finger to my lips.

Her eyes widened, those hazel-green pools betraying fear. "Another bear?" she whispered. "I thought we were supposed to be loud?"

I shook my head, finger over my lips, and crept forward. She followed, doing an admirable job at creeping as quietly as she could. We reached the end of the curve in the trail and, less than twenty feet away, standing head high in the center of the trail was massive bull elk with a spread of antlers at least six feet in diameter. It was munching on something; glancing around with bright, alert black eyes, jaw moving.

Izzy's breath caught audibly, and I watched her

hand cover her mouth in amazement. "Wow…" she whispered under her breath. "He's….*huge.*"

"Bull elk," I whispered. "Too bad it's not hunting season." I mimed raising a rifle to my shoulder and firing.

"You wouldn't shoot him, would you?"

I just smirked. "Sure would…in season. Not for sport, though—for meat, for the fur, and for the antlers."

She shook her head. "Take a picture. It'll last longer."

He heard us, then, or smelled us. His head swiveled, and he spotted us, freezing. His tail twitched. His nose wrinkled, flared.

And then, with a single leap, he was gone, nearly a thousand pounds vanishing in near silence, barely a rustle of leaves to mark his passage.

"So beautiful," Izzy murmured, still quiet even though he was gone. "I can't believe you'd shoot something that majestic."

"He was gorgeous, wasn't he?"

It was late afternoon by this point, and I could tell Izzy was reaching the end of her day, as far as hiking was concerned. Her feet were dragging, her steps were slow, and she was constantly adjusting the pack, trying to find a way to make the weight more comfortable. I reminded myself that she'd never hiked before, so even though I could have kept going for a few more hours without any issue, it was time to stop for the day for her sake.

I checked the map of the trail, compared it to the coordinates on my GPS unit, and reckoned we were only another mile or so from a camping spot. While I was figuring our position, Izzy was rolling her shoulders and stretching her back and adjusting the straps. I showed her the map, pointing at one spot.

"We're about here," I said, and then pointed at the campground. "This is our first camping spot. Not far now. You gonna make it?"

She sighed. "Well, camping here isn't an option, I don't think, so yeah, I'll make it."

"You need a longer rest?"

She shook her head. "Nah. I'd rather just push on and get there."

I smacked her gently on the ass. "Atta girl."

She frowned at me. "Stop patting me on the butt. This isn't football, and I'm not your girlfriend. It's demeaning."

"It's not demeaning, it's affectionate. Plus, I just like touching your butt."

She rolled her eyes, shook her head, and sighed. "No kidding. But I'm telling you, no patting."

I smacked harder. "How about if it's too hard to be considered a pat?"

She shoved at me. "No, you dick. No touching the butt at all."

I pouted, sticking out my lip. "No touching the butt? Not at *all*?"

She tried to stifle a laugh, but couldn't. "God, you're ridiculous."

"Does that mean I can still touch the butt?"

"No, Ram. No touching the butt."

I harrumphed. "Fine." I crossed my arms over my chest trying to look dramatic. "But that's a stupid rule and I hate it."

She cackled. "You're such a twelve-year-old." She flounced back into motion, heading down the trail. "Touching the butt is a privilege you haven't earned yet."

"How do I earn it?"

"You'll know when you do."

"I will? How?"

She just shot me a sizzling, sarcastic smirk. "Oh, you'll just know. Trust me on that."

I followed her, hungrily watching that which I was not yet allowed to touch. Despite having touched it more than once already…and having eaten her pussy till she screamed.

But, no. No touching the perfect ass.

Fine. Whatever.

I was being ridiculous and I knew it, but it made

her laugh, and hearing her laugh was worth it.

Plus, her phrasing indicated that I *would* earn that privilege, not that I merely *could*.

Yippee-ki-yay, motherfucker—I'mma touch the butt.

She eyed me. "What the hell are you grinning about?"

I shrugged, pulling an innocent face. "Nothing."

"Ram."

"What?"

"What are you grinning about?"

I gestured around us. "Being out here in this beautiful world, on a gorgeous day, with a sexy, funny woman who at the very least doesn't hate me...what else do I need to be happy?"

She had no response to that, which I took as a victory.

At long last, we reached the campsite, which was, to my happiness, empty. We might possibly get company later in the evening, but most folks used this trail as a day trip, whether biking or hiking, so I was hopeful we'd have it to ourselves. I chose the best site, tucked back under the canopy of trees and well off the trail with a nice fire ring. There was a soft bed of pine needles on the ground, which would make for great sleeping, too. I shucked my pack and immediately began setting up the tent. I gave Izzy a few minutes to rest and stretch, and then gestured her over.

"Ever set up a tent?" I asked.

She rolled her eyes. "What do you think?"

I laughed. "I know, I'm teasing." I gestured at the woods. "Can you collect some wood for our campfire? Stay close to the campsite, within shouting distance of me."

"What kind of wood?"

I stared, confused. "Um…any kind. It doesn't matter, it all burns the same."

She huffed. "No, I meant how big? Like, how big should the sticks be?"

I laughed. "Oh. Doesn't matter. Whatever you can carry in your arms. I mean, don't collect, like tiny little twigs or giant branches. Just kindling."

"I don't know what kindling is."

"You've never had a bonfire? Never watched anyone build a fire?"

She shrugged. "I mean, sure. I've been around bonfires a few times, but I've never paid attention to how it was built."

I sighed, shaking my head. "City girls, man." I set down the poles I was sorting and assembling and found a two-foot long, thumb-thick piece of deadfall. "About like this. Bigger is fine, smaller is fine. Like I said, just don't bother with tiny or huge. And don't stray too far."

She rolled her eyes. "Don't stray? What am I, a dog?"

I gazed at her levelly. "Izzy, do you remember the bear?" I gestured at the bear lockers in a line to one side of the campground. "What do you think those are for?"

"So no one steals your stuff?"

"It's a bear locker," I said. "You put your food in there so bears don't tear your shit apart looking for snacks."

"They'll do that?"

I laughed. "God, you've really never been camping, have you? Yes, bears are notorious for getting into food and garbage. They're basically huge raccoons. They'll climb into dumpsters and eat garbage, and they'll tear entire campgrounds to shreds if they catch a whiff of anything remotely edible."

"Oh."

"Just because this is a place designated as a campsite for people doesn't mean bears won't come here. They don't know it's a campground. It's in the middle of *their* forest. There's no magical bear-proof forcefield." I grabbed my bear spray out of my bag and handed it to her. "Bear spray. Just in case."

"Now I'm scared."

I laughed. "It'll be fine. You'll make enough noise tromping around looking for wood that any bears within a mile will hear you coming and run off before you even know they're there. But, sometimes, they'll surprise you, so I just want you to be, you know... alert and aware."

She hesitated. "If a bear eats me, I'm going to haunt you forever. I hope you know that."

"It wouldn't eat you, most likely," I said. "It would just rip you up a bit and run off."

"Wow. You're *really* making me feel a lot better about this, Ram, thanks."

I laughed. "You'll be fine. Sing a song."

She sighed. "Fine. But don't laugh at my singing."

I held up my hands. "Hey, I can't carry a tune in a bucket even if you carried the bucket for me, so I'm not one to judge, trust me."

She headed off into the woods behind our camp-site, and I heard her singing—I recognized a Lady Gaga tune, one of those ubiquitous songs you can't get away from that end up stuck in your head for days. She had a sweet voice, high and clear, and despite telling me not to laugh, I thought she sounded great.

I had the tent set up within a few minutes, and made sure the rain shelter was stowed where I could get to it easily in case of a sudden rain shower. I checked the fire ring, making sure there wasn't any trash or debris in it, and then grabbed my hatchet and followed the sound of Izzy's voice. I found her not far away, with an armload of kindling, singing "Once Upon A Dream" from *Sleeping Beauty.*

With her long, shimmery strawberry blonde hair gleaming in the afternoon sun, she could've been Aurora. I surprised her by joining in the song, just like in the Disney classic.

She startled, gasping. "You scared me."

"Sorry." I smiled at her. "I'm not sure why you told me not to laugh—you have a beautiful voice."

She shrugged. "Thanks, I guess."

"Wouldn't have taken you for a Disney songs sorta chick, though."

She resumed her hunt for kindling while I found a long, thick piece of deadfall and started hacking the smaller branches off it.

"My mom used to sing songs from the old classics all the time. She'd float around the house, cleaning or cooking or whatever, just singing. She had the most beautiful voice." She was quiet, almost reverent.

I'd noticed, just then and before, her use of the past tense in regard to her mother, but I didn't ask. Instead, I just nodded. "Well, your voice is just as beautiful as I imagine hers must have been."

She looked at me, surprised, probably expecting the question I hadn't asked. "You never cease to surprise me, Ram."

I set the smaller branches aside in a pile and

started chopping the branch into manageable, burnable sections. When I was done, I wiped a bead of sweat off my forehead with a forearm and glanced at her. "What do you mean?"

She shrugged. "I always expect you to ask about stuff, but you never do."

I flipped the hatchet in the air and caught it by the handle. "I don't appreciate being pressed to talk about shit I don't wanna talk about, so it'd be kinda hypocritical to push you to do it, you know?" I shoved the hatchet into my belt and gathered the wood in my arms. "I figure if you want me to know, you'll talk about it. And if you do, I'll listen, and I'll be glad as hell that you chose to trust me on it. If not, that's your business."

She followed me back to camp, and we set our loads of wood near the fire ring.

Brushing off her hands and shirt, Izzy glanced at me, as if weighing what to say next. "She died when I was thirteen." A hesitation. "My mom, I mean."

"Shit, that sucks. I'm sorry that happened."

She nodded. "It was...awful. She got into a car accident on the way to pick me up after school. She just...never showed up. Dad was at work and was unreachable, and I just...I sat alone outside the school for hours, just waiting, but she...she never showed up. Eventually I walked home, but no one was there.

Dad was head of the neurology department, so he worked crazy hours. A police officer showed up at my house an hour after I got there and asked for my dad. I told him he was at work still and wasn't really reachable, and he said there'd...there'd been an accident, and that it was important I reach him."

"Good lord."

"Yeah. So, I paged him. The rule was no using his pager number unless it was an actual life-or-death emergency because, being a neurosurgeon, his work was, literally, life or death. He called me back a few minutes later, and I gave the policeman the phone to talk to Dad. The officer wouldn't tell me what had happened, only that there'd been an accident involving my mom, and that it was best to wait for Dad. But...I knew. The way he was acting, that he wouldn't tell me...I knew."

I had no idea what to say to that. "Shit, Izzy. I..." I shrugged. "I have no idea what to say, honestly."

She shrugged. "Nothing to say. It happened a long time ago." She gestured at the pile of kindling. "Do we need more?"

I shook my head. "Nah. That's plenty. I'm gonna go chop up another branch, and I'll be right back. Just chill for a minute."

I found another good-sized branch not far from

the campsite, chopped it up, and brought it back, piling it near the fire ring. Izzy was sitting on a section of tree trunk, near the ring, that had been placed there long ago as a seat; she was eying the tent with an odd expression on her face.

"So, um…that's the tent?" she asked.

I nodded. "That's the tent."

It had been a splurge for me, being one of the nicest and most expensive two-person tents available—being a pretty big guy, I liked having a tent large enough to sprawl out in, and I didn't mind the extra weight which, as expensive as it was, was negligible. But, from the perspective of a city girl who'd never even been glamping in an RV before, I could see how the size of it would be disconcerting. It was big enough by far for one person, but for two? It would be…cozy.

"It's kind of…small."

I grinned. "Well, considering I typically hike and camp alone, it's actually big."

"When you said we'd just share a tent, I thought you meant a tent like…" She gestured vaguely with her hands, indicating a tent large enough to house six people plus possibly a horse. "Something bigger."

I shrugged. "Name of the game when hiking is to carry only what you need and no more. This is more tent than I strictly need, but I'm a pretty big fella, so I like a big tent." I gestured at it. "Climb in—we'll both fit, I promise."

She knelt in front of the opening, unzipped it, and peered in, and then turned to look at me over her shoulder. "Yeah, we'll fit...on top of each other."

I just winked.

"No," she snapped. "Nope. Not happening."

"No?" I grinned. "Sure about that?"

"Argh!" she howled. "No, Ramsey. We're not sleeping—I'm not sleeping on top of you."

"Other way around, babe. I'll sleep on you. I get real warm at night, so I'll be like a big, sexy blanket."

"Ah, such humility," she said. "Nope. That's not gonna work."

I laughed. "Well, that's the only option. And babe, if you think I'm chivalrous enough to sleep on the ground outside while you take the tent, think again. I carried the fucker in and I'm carrying the fucker out, so I'm sleeping in it."

"Nice."

I shrugged. "Izz, honey, you need to relax." I took my sleeping bag off my pack, knelt beside her at the opening, leaned in, and unrolled the sleeping bag to one side; I grabbed hers off her pack and did the same, laying them side by side, which left inches of room in between and on both sides. "See? Side by side, separate bags, plenty of room."

She eyed the interior. "Huh. I didn't think they'd fit."

I laughed again. "It's a two-person tent. Therefore, designed to fit *two people*."

"Just barely."

"Well, yeah. Did you think it was gonna have an espresso machine and a hot tub inside?"

"I wish," she said, laughing. "Fine. It'll work."

I leaned back out of the tent and zipped it closed. "So. Ready to catch our dinner?"

She blinked at me. "Am I? Or are you?"

"*We* are, babe. You're helping."

She shook her head. "Oh hell no. I'm not fishing."

"Then you don't eat." I shrugged, gesturing at her bag. "Or, at least nothing that's not in there, and I only bought enough food to supplement the fish we'd catch tonight and tomorrow."

"I don't know how to fish."

I clapped her on the shoulder. "Well, honeybuns, that's what this trip is about, right? Learning new shit. How to hike, how to sleep in a tent, how to catch, clean, cook, and eat fish, how to build a fire."

She glared at me. "Honeybuns?"

"Yup. Because those buns of yours are sweet as honey."

She shook her head, rolling her eyes with barely restrained laughter. "You are such an idiot."

I collected my fishing gear—collapsible rods, line, bait, lures, hooks, and stringer. "Well, this idiot is your only chance of eating fresh fish tonight, so I'd get a move on, honeybuns. Fish are waiting!"

She went to her pack and bent to shrug into it with an air of resignation. "Fine. Jesus."

"Uh, Izzy?"

She glanced at me. "Yes, Ramsey?"

I gestured at the pack. "You don't need that." I gestured at mine, leaning against a tree nearby. "I'm leaving mine, see?"

"Oh." She eyed the packs. "Won't someone steal them?"

"I mean, I suppose the possibility exists, but it's unlikely. Stealing someone's gear is...it's basically the worst thing you can do. The majority of the people that use these trails tend to show respect for the others on it." I shrugged. "Plus, we're close enough to both ends of the trail that we'd be fine even without it. It's not like we're in the true wilderness a week's hike from, like, Coldfoot or whatever the fuck. We're a matter of hours from the trailhead and the terminus."

She nodded. "Oh. Right." She looked around as she followed me. "So, this is, like, not really even the true bush, is it?"

I shrugged. "I mean, I wouldn't recommend

getting lost off the trail, but no, not really."

"You ever been out there?"

I shook my head. "Not like you're thinking. To get to where you need your gear to literally survive, no. It's on my list, but I haven't gotten there yet. Most of my trips since moving up here have been day or weekend trips that I can access by car. To get to where I'd really like to be, you need a plane or a boat to drop you off and pick you up."

I led her toward the creek, and then we strolled easily along it, following it upstream away from the trail and the campsite, where the fish were unlikely to have been recently disturbed. I found a beautiful little spot where the creek widened, with a big old tree near the edge throwing a nice big pool of shade across the water. It was calm but swift, stained with tannins but still clear enough to see the bottom, the water occasionally churning white around an outcropping of rock.

"This is a great spot," I said. "Let's try here."

Izzy watched with interest as I set up both fishing rods, tied on hooks and bait, and then handed her one.

"I'm guessing you don't know how to cast," I said. "Safe assumption?"

"I know how to smartcast my phone to my TV," she said, grinning, "but I'm guessing that's not what you mean."

"Uh, no."

I lifted the rod and pointed out the various parts, showing her how to cast it. It took her a good half dozen tries, in which she only got the line snarled three times, but she started to get the hang of it.

I pointed at the pool of shade over the water. "Fish like to hang out in shady spots like that. What you wanna do is cast your line into the water upstream of the shade and let it ride downstream into it, and then slowly reel the line back in."

"That's it?"

I grinned. "That's it. Fishing ain't really the most complicated thing in the world, which I guess is why we dumb guys like doing it so much. Cast, reel, cast, reel. That's it." I waved a hand. "I mean, you can *make* it complicated. Lures and bait for specific kinds of fish, special rods and reels, various line test weights, all that. But, at its essence, fishing is really just putting bait a fish'll eat on a hook, throwing it the water, and hauling it back in."

"I guess I expected it to be harder."

"The hard part is the boredom. You may cast and reel a hundred times and never get a bite, but when you do feel that line tug, feel the fish hit, it all becomes worth it. You'll see." I gestured at the river. "Try it."

I watched as she headed downstream closer to the shade of the tree, sorted out her hands on the rod and reel, worked the line release lever, and then, with an admirably smooth motion, cast the baited hook way out into the middle of the river.

"Nice!" I called. "Now let the line spool out a bit with the current until it's pretty much clear of the shade, and then reel it in nice and slow."

I figured she'd get a hit within the first few tries, so I kept an eye on her as I headed upstream a ways to a different spot, where I had to do a fancier bit of casting to get the hook where I wanted it. Cast, let it float, reel it in. I closed my eyes for a moment and just soaked in the moment. It was utterly peaceful. Just the sun on my face, breeze ruffling my clothes and cooling me off, an eagle screeching somewhere way overhead, the creek chuckling merrily. No cars, no buildings, no crowds, no bills, no saloon, no brothers—as much as I loved them. Just me and nature... and Izzy.

Which, oddly, was not as weird or uncomfortable as I'd thought it would be. I'd expected her to hold me back, drag me down, to complain and bitch about how heavy the bag was and, oh no I broke a nail, and the mosquitos are biting me. Instead, she proved to be an entertaining hiking partner, easy to talk to, fun to mess with, but quick to catch on to my weird sense of humor. Plus, hot as fuck.

I opened my eyes, reeled my line in, and glanced

at Izzy. She was standing with her feet spread apart, head tipped back, eyes closed—like I'd just been—letting her line float.

She was just flat-out beautiful. Classically, breathtakingly beautiful. Hot, sure. But...*beautiful*. She could have been a pinup model, or a black-and-white era movie star, like Betty Page or Rita Hayworth. I watched her for a minute, watched her just enjoy the sun and the peacefulness.

And then the tip of her rod bent and tugged, and she shrieked. "Ram! What's happening?"

I laughed. "You have a bite! Stay cool, babe! Just reel it in."

I reeled my line in, set the pole on the bank, and jogged over to Izzy, who was wide-eyed with excitement. The reel was singing, the line bent nearly double.

"Dude, you've got a hell of a fish on there!" I said to her with a grin. "Just keep reeling. Angle the tip upward and reel it in, let the tip sag down a second, and then yank it up again and reel it in."

She fought it, doing as I said—dragging the tip of the rod toward the sky and reeling like crazy, and then letting the tip settle downward again, only to yank it up and reel some more. "It's so...heavy!"

I caught a glimpse of the fish—a massive river salmon. "Damn, girl! You hooked a monster!"

"I feel like it's going to yank me into the river!" she said, leaning backward while reeling.

"Nah, babe, you've got it!"

"Can't you take it?"

"Sure I could, but then you wouldn't get the satisfaction of having brought that big bitch in on your own. This is your victory, not mine."

She was silent, then, as she fought the salmon. I was honestly worried either the line or the rod itself was going to break, the way it was bending, but it continued to hold.

"It's getting tired," I told Izzy. "Let the line run for a few seconds, and then reel it in hard."

She held the lever and let it float, the line sliding downstream as the tired salmon glided with the swift current, and then Izzy started reeling again, and now the fish started fighting again, but half-heartedly. Izzy slowly but surely brought the line closer and closer to the riverbank, and once it was within reach, I bent and grabbed the line, hauling the fish up out of the water.

"HOLY FUCK!" Izzy shouted, tossing the rod onto the bank and coming over to me. "That thing *is* a monster!"

It was easily two, almost three feet long and weighed several pounds.

"You hold it," I told her.

She hefted the fish in both hands, and it gave a

few exhausted wriggles, but it was too tired and out of air to fight anymore. I'd brought along a digital camera small enough to fit into my hip pocket, and I took it out, powered it on, and put Izzy and her giant fish in the frame.

Her smile was huge, exhilarated, and proud.

I put the salmon on a stringer. "You just caught dinner for both of us, babe," I told her.

She was fairly vibrating. "I can't believe I caught that!"

I laughed. "What I can't believe is that you caught *that* monster on *that* rod and line. It's a small miracle the line didn't snap, if not the pole itself. You typically need heavier duty rods and line for fish that heavy."

I collapsed the rods, secured the lines and reels, set the fish on the bank, and hauled out my knife.

"Time to clean it," I said, handing the knife to Izzy.

She just stared at me. "Um…no?"

I grinned. "Part of catching it, sweetheart. I'll walk you through it, and I'll do the tricky parts."

And, once again, Izzy absolutely surprised me— she wasn't squeamish at all. She lopped off the head like a pro, tossed it aside, and followed my directions on cleaning the fish without so much as a whimper of disgust. When the salmon had been reduced to manageable filets, and the guts tossed aside for scavengers,

I wrapped it in the tinfoil I'd brought along for the purpose, giving it to Izzy to carry.

"And there's dinner. Now we go make a fire and cook it up." We washed our hands in the cold, clear water of the river and headed back toward camp; I caught Izzy glancing at me with an odd expression as we walked. "What?"

She shrugged. "If you'd told me even a week ago that I'd be out here, wearing this, hiking with *you*, catching a giant salmon, and getting ready to cook it over a fire, I'd have laughed my ass off."

"What's funny is that you include your outfit in the unusual aspect of all this."

She shot me a side-eye. "I'm a fashion blogger, Ramsey. I don't wear jeans and T-shirts even on laundry day."

"Explain to me what a fashion blogger is," I said.

"Sort of…a tastemaker, if you know what I mean? I keep up with the latest trends, watching what celebrities and celebrity designers and stylists are doing, and I try to make it accessible for the average person. So, like, if a Kardashian or Taylor Swift or whoever is photographed wearing something cool and interesting, it's probably super expensive and out of reach for the average woman. What I do is find pieces and outfits that mimic that look in a price range a business professional or even a sale-savvy college girl can afford, and explain how to create a similar look. So I write about fashion trends, model the looks myself, and explain how to create the look at home."

Judging by the look she gave me, I think she expected me to either give her a blank look, or laugh at her; I decided to surprise her with a question I doubted she'd be expecting.

"Is that a career for you?"

She frowned at me, as sideswiped by the question as I'd expected. "Um. What?"

"Fashion blogging. It sounds cool. Is that what you're passionate about? Is that your future?"

She didn't answer for quite a long time. "I...huh. You are the last person on earth I'd have expected to ask me that."

"Why?"

A shrug. "I dunno."

"It's a question that's been on my mind about myself lately, so I guess I'm just curious."

"You've been asking yourself what your future is?"

I nodded. "Well, sure. Growing up, my brothers and I had one singular goal: get the fuck out of Oklahoma. We knew we weren't cut out for, or interested in, sports, even though we're all athletic enough we probably could've gone that route, and the military didn't interest us. So, what could three big, strong, active, troublemaking young fellas get into that would put money in our pockets and get us the fuck out of the ass end of Redneckville, Oklahoma?" I shrugged. "Wildfire fighting ended up being the answer. At first we were just thinking regular old forest service fire crew, and we got into a hotshot crew, but we didn't quite fit in. We met a couple of smokejumpers in a bar in Idaho, got to talking, and realized that was where we belonged—on a smoke-jumper crew. So we headed to Cali, joined up, and spent the next few years there, fighting wildfires with the smokejumpers."

"I heard a little bit about what you do from Kitty, but that's about it," Izzy said, as we reached our camp-site and began stacking the wood. I set about building a fire in the ring.

"So, you've got firefighter crews that work for the US Forest Service, right? But then you also have two sets of elite units that do different jobs. The hot-shots are guys you hear about a lot, especially lately with all the wildfires in California. They make up the front lines of the worst wildfires. They're true ba-dasses, those guys. Tough as hell, fit, and ballsy. But they're a tight unit, you know? Regimented, orderly, sort of quasi-military in a way. They drive as close to the fire as they can get, and then hike in the rest of the way, carrying whatever gear they need with them, and they attempt to contain the fire. Smokejumpers, on the other hand—we're a wild, rowdy bunch. Cowboys, renegades. A little crazy, adrenaline-junkie types. Gotta be, because our job is to parachute into the middle of wildfires in places so remote that even the hotshots can't get there. We jump in, and we fight the fire from the inside until the hotshots and forest service crews can get to us."

"That sounds…insanely dangerous."

I had the fire going by this time, and sat back to let it build up to a nice hot blaze. "Yup. About as dangerous as you'd think, and then some."

"Did you like it?"

I nodded. "I loved it. It was challenging, and a constant thrill. If we weren't fighting a fire, we were training, because for that job, you have to stay on top of your skills and at peak fitness, so there's no downtime."

"What brought you here to Alaska? You're not fighting fires anymore."

"Our dad had a heart attack, and he's an alcoholic. He's the only family we had left, so we had to go back down to Oklahoma to take care of him. We had enough money saved that we could take a few months off and just focus on him. But then Roman saw our cousin Xavier on TV or some shit, and got a wild hair up his ass about coming up here. He had this idea that we'd haul Dad up here, get to know all the Badd cousins we had never met, open a bar, and rake in the money while hooking up with all the hot tourists. Basically, he thought that's what our cousins were doing and he wanted to give it a go. Only, Dad wouldn't go. After we got him healthy and sober, we knew we needed to get on with our lives. Then Roman convinced Remington and me to come with him up here. Neither Rem nor I had any better ideas, so we went along with it."

"If your dad was healthy and sober, why didn't you go back to firefighting?"

I sighed. "We needed a break. We had a pretty bad experience. A fire got out of control and took an unexpected turn. A good friend of ours got killed—a friend of mine. It...um." I poked at the fire, because this was one of those things I didn't like talking about. "It was bad."

"What happened?" Izzy asked, sitting on the log next to me.

I eyed her. "You really want to know?"

She nodded. "Yeah."

I'd set a big flat rock in the ring, outside of the fire but close enough to absorb the heat, and, after seasoning the salmon, I placed the packet of fish on the rock.

"We'd split up into three teams. Rem and Rome

were together, working along the base of a ridge, and Jameson, Kevin, and I were on the opposite side of the ridge working toward the end of it, with the intent of connecting with Rem and Rome. Two other guys, Peterson and Mackie, were heading along the ridge from the north—the worst of the fire was on the top of the ridge heading north, and we were trying to stop it from spreading any further. What happened was just…a freak accident. In fires that intense, trees fall all the time. You hear it happening and know to get out of the way. It's just part of the job. But sometimes, shit happens. Jameson, Kevin and I were working together heading south along the base of the ridge, establishing a perimeter. And, …this giant Jack pine just…toppled over. No warning, nothing. There was so much other noise around us we just didn't hear it."

I was silent again, remembering. I could almost feel the heat, see the flames all around us. Hear the crackle and roar. Jameson off to my right, Kevin in the middle, me on the left.

"It was just…wham. Forty tons of mature pine crashing down without a single goddamn warning. It clipped me, sent me flying. Left Jameson on the far side of it, and Kevin right underneath it."

"Oh, my god."

"Yeah." I scrubbed my face. "Kevin was a fourth

brother to the three of us. He was with us when we first joined the US Forest Service, went through training with us, and we all got into the same hotshot crew and ended up transferring together to the Redding smokejumper crew. Kevin was…he was a great man. A good friend."

"I'm so sorry, Ram."

I shrugged. "It was…bad. I went sorta crazy, I guess. Started attacking that tree with my fucking ax like I could somehow save Kevin. And I mean, I *knew* he was gone. When forty tons of wood hits you full force, you don't survive. He was dead at first impact, but…I had to save him, had to get to him. All I could think at the time was I should've seen the tree falling, we should've taken a different route, and a million other things. Rome and Rem had to pull me off before the fire swallowed us. We'd gotten behind it trying to get to Kevin, and we almost didn't make it out in time."

She pulled her hat off and freed her hair from the ponytail, running her fingers through it. She was quiet for a few minutes.

"I wish I had some meaningful words for you," she said. "I'm sorry you and your brothers went through that. I've never really thought about what it takes to fight a forest fire, and now I have a new respect for those guys."

"Yep. I still think of Kevin every day. We all knew what we were getting into when we joined the Fire Service, but it was hard to lose a friend like that."

"So…what are you going to do now, if you're not going back to firefighting? Are you planning to continue with the saloon and work with your brothers?"

I flipped the packet of fish over with the tip of my knife. "This," I said, gesturing around our campsite.

She laughed. "I didn't know you could be a professional backpacker."

"I meant taking care of places like this. Park ranger, I'm thinking."

She set her hat on the log beside her hip, gathered her hair behind her head, and began plaiting it into a thick braid. "Seems to me you have perfect qualifications for a job like that. What's stopping you?"

"Rome still needs my help at the saloon."

"And that's not your scene, I'm guessing?"

I snorted. "Ahhh, no. Not even a little. I hate bars with a passion. I hate drinking in them, eating in them, hanging out in them. I'm a man who belongs outside. I need the sky over my head, open air around me. I feel like I'm choking when I'm in the city."

"It does feel different out here," she said. "Open. Free."

I nodded. "Exactly. So no, owning a bar, that's definitely not my scene. It's Roman's for sure—he loves that shit. He thrives on the attention, the crowds, the energy, and the atmosphere. To me, I just feel hemmed in. Might as well be put me in jail as stick me behind a bar. But …"

"But?"

"But Roman needs me. He's my triplet, so I have to be there for him. I can't just…up and leave right now. And if I were to do what I really want, I'd be out here more often than not, working in forest management. Hiking or riding these trails, maintaining them, watching the timberline, evaluating tree health, monitoring wildlife, all that. I'd basically have to leave Rome and Rem to run the place themselves, and I know Rem is pretty much done with it, too, now that he and Juneau are doing the tattoo thing, which leaves me…" I rubbed the back of my neck. "I don't have any specific answers, it's just what I've been chewing on for a while."

She was quiet, then, tracing lines in the dirt with the toe of her boot. "I like blogging. I love clothes, and fashion."

I caught a note of hesitation in her voice. "And?"

She didn't look at me. "I don't know."

I pulled the foil packet off the rock, unfolded it, and checked the fish inside—it was done. I grabbed a few cans of fruit and a bag of trail mix, divided the filets in half, and handed her a set of utensils.

"Dig in," I said.

For the next few minutes there was no conversation, just us eating. The fish was piping hot, almost too hot to eat at first, but then once it had cooled off, Izzy devoured it without pausing for breath.

I grinned at her. "So, fisherwoman. How does your first fresh-caught fish taste?"

"It's amazing!" she said, around a mouthful. "It's so good I can't stand it."

"How's it feel knowing you caught it and cleaned it yourself?"

She licked the juices off her fingers, and there was something so stupidly erotic about the way she licked her fingers clean that I had to rip my eyes off of her and focus on my food.

"It's...I don't know how to put it," she answered.

"A sense of accomplishment?"

"Yeah, sort of." She shrugged. "I dunno. I guess I just...I feel...connected to nature, somehow. Like, I have this whole new appreciation for how people had to live before civilization made everything easy."

I laughed, nodding. "Totally, I totally get what you're saying. That's part of why I love being out here. I have never fit in, anywhere or with anyone except Rome and Rem. It's not about my size or the way I look, it's just...I've always felt out of place around people." I wadded the tinfoil up and took a handful of trail mix, tossing nuts and M&Ms into my mouth before handing Izzy the bag. "Out here, it's just me. Nature was here before me; it'll be here after me. The trees, the bears, the elk, the stars, the insects, the fish, the birds...none of that cares about me. I don't have to fit in. I don't have to have a college education, or be good at math or taking tests, or talking to people. I can hunt and fish for food. I can gather berries and wild roots and herbs. I can survive in the wild with not much more than my knife, some fishing line, and my own wits. I can be just me out here, and there's no one to care. I find comfort in that."

Izzy was eying me with curiosity and interest. "I think I understand that, actually."

"So. What about you?"

She blinked. "I...I don't know."

"You said you like blogging, and that you love clothes and fashion."

"I do."

"You don't sound convincing."

"I wasn't trying to convince you of anything."

"I guess I was asking if it was your future, but it seemed like you were avoiding the question, so you got me talking about myself instead." I watched her reaction carefully.

She closed down, her eyes hardening, her expression going distant, her body language shutting down and turning inward—arms crossing, legs pressing together, turning away from me, head lowering, chin going to her chest, a frown creasing her lovely features.

She didn't answer.

"Izzy, you don't have to talk about it," I said. "I'm sorry if I'm pushing something you don't want to share. Forget I asked."

She gave a minute lift of one shoulder. "I...um. I'm gonna go for a walk down by the creek."

"Make sure you're paying attention to where you're going and what's around you. Be aware, and be present. If you need to be alone, fine, just maybe find somewhere out of sight but close by. I don't want you wandering too far."

She stood up, giving a mocking two-finger salute as she did so. "Yes sir, Mr. Ranger, sir."

"I'm just trying to keep you safe," I muttered, stung.

"Sorry, Ram. I just need to..." She shrugged. "I'll be fine."

I watched her go, braid swinging, hands shoved in her back pockets, head down. For a lively, vivacious, spirited, opinionated, independent woman, she was suddenly subdued and withdrawn. Clearly, I'd accidentally stepped in something smelly.

Evening was falling, and I was worried Izzy

would wander off, lost in her thoughts leading her to get lost in the woods, so I banked the fire, sheathed my knife, grabbed a rod and reel and bait, and followed her at a distance, making sure to stay out sight and earshot, but able to keep an eye on her.

EIGHT

Izzy

THAT MAN ASKED THE MOST ANNOYING QUESTIONS. And by annoying, I mean questions I had no answers for, because I'd spent years avoiding thinking about things like…the future. Like…careers.

Gah. I didn't want to think about this. I wanted to have my head stuck blissfully in the sand, my emotional faucet very firmly shut off, the past in the past where it belongs.

Ramsey Badd had a way of dragging things out of me that I hadn't thought about in years, and that I didn't want to think about now. Damn him.

He'd gotten me to talk about Mom, and I hadn't really talked about Mom, even with Kitty or Juneau.

Same with Dad.

Next thing you know, I'll be telling Ram about running away.

Ha. Not likely. I NEVER talk about that with anyone, ever.

I found the creek easily and meandered upstream, passing the place where I'd caught our dinner. God, that had been so fun. Thrilling, exciting, and rewarding. This whole trip wasn't at all like I thought it would be. I'd jumped headfirst into this without thinking, and really hadn't had any idea *what* I was getting into, or what it'd be like. I just know I'd expected to hate it...and Ram.

Turns out, I don't hate either one.

In fact, I was finding myself liking both the experience of hiking, and the man, a lot more than I had thought it possible to like anything or anyone.

I kept walking along the banks of the creek, staring into the water, lost in thought as I watched it ripple and churn, occasionally narrowing to a swift, white-water rush of water, other times widening to a wide, calm creek. Trees overshadowed it in places, brush thick against the banks here and there, forcing me to pick my way carefully through it, following the creek so I wouldn't get lost.

I paused and really looked around me. How far had I walked? I wasn't sure. Would I know how to get back to the campsite?

Crap, crap, crap.

I looked back at the way I'd come. I didn't recognize anything, and I could see nothing but forest. Suddenly, the chirp of birds and the chuckle of the creek seemed somewhat less peaceful. I knew all I had to do was follow the creek back downstream—if I could find the place where I'd caught the fish, I'd know I was close to the campsite.

Only…

The spot I was standing in looked almost identical to that fishing spot. And, now that I thought about it, I'd passed by a few places where a big tree leaned out over the creek to spread a pool of shadow.

Shit.

I forced myself to breathe calmly, and not panic.

I had bear spray.

I had a compass.

I had no idea how to use the compass, though—knowing which way was north wouldn't do me a damn bit of good if I didn't know where I was supposed to go.

The wind kicked up, making the tall trees around me sway and sigh, dappling the sunlight and cooling the day. It was evening, at this point—the sun would be down soon. How long had I been walking? An hour? Shit! If I had to walk another hour back, it might very well be dark by the time I got anywhere near the campsite...assuming I could find it again in the first place.

"Don't wander off too far," Ram had said. "Be aware, and be present."

Ramsey would have a shit fit if he knew what I'd done. Hopefully I could make my way back to camp before he began to worry. I'd given him a mocking salute and promptly ignored his advice, and now I was lost. Well, not lost, just...misplaced. This creek had to cross the trail at some point, because we'd crossed it on the bridge. That was miles and miles back downstream...or upstream? I wasn't sure, anymore.

Fuck.

I was starting to panic.

Lost in the woods.

Where there were bears.

I'd heard stories of cougars, too, thinking back to sitting in a dive bar with the girls, giggling as we listened to tourists exchange fish stories, and the locals swapping legends and tall tales.

Did cougars attack people?

If a bear attacked me, Ram had said, it wouldn't eat me...just rip me apart and leave me there to be eaten by other scavengers.

I pulled the bear spray out of my pocket and held the cool canister in my sweaty palm as I headed back downstream. Stay close to the creek, I told myself, and pay attention so I can spot familiar landmarks.

And stay calm.

Stay alert.

And hope Ram comes looking for me.

I was trying my damnedest to not hyperventilate as I hugged the creek's edge, watching the sunlight fade. If I was still out after sundown, would I freeze? How cold did it get out here at night? Would more scary stuff come out after dark?

Oh god, oh god.

The sighing of the trees sounded frightening now. The chirp of the birds was threatening. The chuckle of the river was mocking laughter. Squirrels scampering across branches was the crackle and stomp of a hungry grizzly bear on the hunt for silly, lost city girls with no business in the forest alone.

And then, as I rounded a bend in the river, I saw the most welcome sight in the world: Ramsey, a fishing pole in his hands, calmly casting his line out into the water, neatly plunking the baited hook underneath an overhanging section of brush. Tight jeans, boots...shirt off. The evening sun shone red-gold on his tanned skin, limning every muscle and curve and plane. He'd removed his hat and the wind was ruffling his long, loose, shaggy, messy blond hair. His arms rippled as he adjusted his rod and wound the reel.

He reeled his line in, let the baited hook swing free above the water for a moment, and then with a smooth sideways movement, cast it further downstream to another spot, letting the line spool out a few feet, and then reeling it in again.

I watched, mesmerized by the utterly raw, male perfection that was Ramsey Badd. The end of his beard fluttered gently in the breeze, and his hair flattened against his scalp. God, how could anyone be so...*much*? So powerful, so strong, yet so smart and sensitive, and so capable?

He saw me.

He winked with a knowing grin. "Hey," he called. "Have a good walk?"

He surely didn't miss the bear spray in my hand, but he didn't say anything about it. Nor was there even a hint of "I told you so" in his expression or tone of voice. He was just...here. Waiting for me, probably knowing full well I'd get lost and need him to rescue me.

I shoved the bear spray back into my pocket and moved downstream to stand near him, out of the way of his rod as he cast the line again.

"We already ate," I said, ignoring his question. "So why are you fishing again?"

He rolled a thickly muscled shoulder. "Somethin' to do. It relaxes me."

I stood far enough away from him that I wouldn't give in to the temptation to run my hands over his muscles, which looked like they'd been carved out of marble. Except, this marble was sheathed in smooth, warm skin, and rippled deliciously with every move he made. My hands itched to roam over his shoulders, to feel the slabs of muscle over his chest, the ripples across his back, the ridges of his ripped abs, to trace the bear claw scar. My hands ached to wander. To delve under the waistband of those just-tight-enough, perfectly faded blue jeans. To see if my memory of his anatomy was even remotely accurate, or if memory had added an inch, or two...or four. Because it didn't seem possible that he could be anywhere near as well-endowed as I seemed to remember.

So, I stood well away and kept my hands clenched into fists and tucked them under my arms, because I was so grateful to see him that I didn't trust myself or my libido to not overpower my better sense.

I had to acknowledge the situation somehow, though.

Meaning, the situation of having ignored his advice, and how he'd arranged to be standing here fishing, waiting for me. Neatly sparing my feelings, not making me feel like he'd had to come rescue me.

The reel on his fishing pole suddenly started whining, and the tip bent toward the river. My own heart started thumping in excitement, remembering how hard I'd had to fight to bring that salmon in. He made it look easy, letting it run, reeling it in, letting it run, dragging the tip skyward and reeling furiously, all without seeming to expend any effort. Within a few minutes, he had the fish in, lifting it free of the water, dripping and flopping and wriggling—it was plenty big, but not anywhere near as nice as mine, I noted with a smug sense of pride.

He held it by the mouth and wiggled the hook free. With a grin at me, he tossed it back into the river saying, "Good thing for you, buddy, I'm full, or you'd be our second dinner."

I sighed. "Thank you, Ram."

He collapsed the pole and secured the line. "For what?"

I arched an eyebrow at me. "The only reason you're fishing in this spot is because you knew I'd get lost and you followed me."

He winked at me. "It *is* a good spot for fishing. Two or three casts and I got a hit."

"Ram."

He tapped me on the nose. "You were upset. Wandering off upriver, lost in thought? Pretty much the most cliché way to get lost, you know?"

I faked a glare. "So I'm a cliché now?" I turned away from him and his stupid, endearing, adorable, obnoxious boops on the nose.

And because he was too close and too sexy.

He followed me a step or two. "Don't pick fights, Izz."

"Can't help it. It's in my nature. I'm an arguer."

"No, you're not." He stood beside me. "It's a defense mechanism."

I rolled my eyes at him. "Defense against what?"

"Liking me," he murmured, suddenly behind me. Too close—way too close.

"I don't like you. You're annoying."

He took me by the shoulders and turned me around...and now he was inches away, his bare chest in front of my face, his beard lit by the sunset, his eyes brightest blue and piercing straight into my secret heart, that tiny, shriveled, desiccated, atrophied little hole in my chest.

"No?" he asked. "You don't? Not at all?"

I shook my head. "Nope."

He took my hands, lifted them palms facing outward, and spread his hands against mine, palm to palm, fingers to fingers—his hand was *enormous*, so big he could bend his fingers down over mine. His hand was rough, scarred and callused, hard as concrete, yet so gentle.

"Then tell me something." His voice was like his hands—roughened by years of wildfire smoke, deep as a canyon, yet gentle and kind and strong. "Who else knows your mom died when you were thirteen? Who else knows you used to listen to Gene Autry with your dad? Who else knows you still have that hat of his?"

I blinked, swallowed. "Doesn't mean I like you."

He smirked, seeing through my thinning screen of bluster and bullshit. "Who else knows you want more out of life than fashion blogging?"

I frowned. "What are you talking about?"

"When I asked if that was your future, you didn't talk about it like I talked about becoming a park ranger. You didn't—you shut down and changed the subject." Those damned eyes of his saw me—*saw* me; saw *me*. "You want more than managing a retail store, Izz—more than blogging about the latest fashion trends. I don't know what you *do* want—maybe you don't even know—but I know that's not it."

I blinked hard, hating the burn and sting in my eyes. "Be quiet. You don't know shit about me or what I want."

"Sure I do." He wasn't fazed by my outburst in the slightest. "I don't know much about you—in a way, we're really just meeting each other for the first time on this trip. But I know enough to know you have walls a million feet high and a million feet thick. I don't need to know the details of the story to see those walls, babe. I got my own walls, my own scar tissue deep inside, and like recognizes like, you know? You want more out of life. You're just scared."

"I'm not scared of anything," I snapped. I hesitated. "Except getting lost alone in the woods...and being eaten by bears and cougars."

"You were never alone out here, sweetness," Ram rumbled. "I was with you the whole way."

"What do you mean, with me?" I asked, my voice quiet, faint.

"I mean, I stayed far enough back you wouldn't know I was there, but I was there. You needed time alone, but I figured you'd end up getting farther away than you planned." His smile was...not gloating, like mine would have been; it was soft, sweet—too much so for a man so tough, so capable, so strong and macho. "You really think I'd let you get lost? Not on my watch, honeybuns."

"Don't call me that," I snapped, but my voice lacked its usual bite.

He shook his head. "Stubborn."

"Can we go back?" I asked, suddenly tired.

I expected questions, probing, demanding. Instead, he just nodded. "Yep." He pointed off through the forest. "Trail's that way, campsite's about half a mile or so down the trail."

"How far did I wander?"

He shrugged. "Two miles or so. Quite a ways."

"Would I have been able to find the campsite on my own if you hadn't followed me?"

He tilted his head side to side. "Maybe. If I'd kept the fire going and stayed put, you probably would've smelled the fire, and if you were smart, you'd have followed your nose to the fire. Not many campsites around here, so it stands to reason if there's a camp-fire, it's ours."

He led me through the undergrowth, and sure enough, after a few minutes of traipsing in a straight line through the brush, we came upon the trail. I'd have never found it on my own, …and if I hadn't gone in a straight line, I'd have missed the trail, what with the way it wound around.

He didn't say another word the rest of the way back to camp, and neither did I.

It was such a relief to see the fire ring, and the little blue-and-gray dome tent, that I actually sighed out loud, a huff of relief. It wasn't until we reached the camp that I truly realized how scared I'd been, even though I'd never been alone, and had only been walking for five or ten minutes before I ran into Ram.

Ram squatted by the fire, rearranging logs and adding kindling and poking at the coals with a length of stick, leaning close and blowing gently. In a mo-ment, I saw flames flickering, and then in another few moments the fire was going again, blazing merrily as he added more kindling, and then another thick log.

I sat on the tree trunk facing the fire and just let myself soak in the comfort of the campsite; it was odd how quickly and easily I'd come to think of this little spot as a kind of temporary home, a place of comfort. It was just a tent and a fire, and we'd be gone by morning, but for now, it was home.

I glanced at Ram, who was tossing trail mix into his mouth, staring up at the sky, watching an eagle wheel in the drowsing quiet of sunset.

How lost would I have been without him?

I realized I was entirely dependent on him, out here. I knew nothing. Zero. I would literally get lost and die without him. Or, at least, require a search and rescue team to bring me back to my lattes and Wi-Fi.

Yet he moved with utter ease and confidence. He made it all look easy—making a fire, catching a fish, cleaning and cooking it, scaring off bears, watching giant bull elks from mere feet away, hiking out into the wildness with nothing but what he could carry on his back...he was at home out here, and he had brought me into his world.

"Do your brothers ever go hiking with you?" I asked, the question tumbling out unbidden.

He glanced at me, as surprised as I was by the question. "Ummm, no, not very often. Rem will on

occasion. He and I took a little afternoon hike up the
Deer Mountain trail a few weeks ago, but…these long
weekend camping trips? Nah. Not really their thing.
They're just as capable of wilderness survival as I am,
but they don't seek it out the way I do."

"So…you're by yourself out here most of the
time?"

He nodded. "Yep. That's how I like it, though.
I'm kind of a loner, usually." He smirked. "I think I
know what you're angling at. Yes, Izzy—you're the
only woman I've ever brought on a hiking trip like
this."

"The only one…ever?" I couldn't help staring
into those big blue eyes of his to gauge his reaction.

"The only one, ever," he said. "Hikes are…well,
they're—" He hesitated. "At the risk of sounding
melodramatic, they're sort of sacred to me. Being out
on the trail, like I said earlier today, it's my safe place.
This is my me-time, where I go to recharge so I can
stomach being stuck in that fucking dingy ass saloon
of Rome's." He sighed. "That's not fair, though. We
built a hell of a beautiful bar, and I'm proud of it, and
of him, but I just…I don't like being there."

"So when I invited myself along with you…" I
arched an eyebrow at him.

He laughed. "I honestly expected us to hate each
other, for you to demand I take you back to town

after the first few miles." He made a face. "Surprise, surprise, but…I'm having a hell of a good time with you."

I ducked my head. "It's a lot more fun than I expected it to be. I really am enjoying myself, Ram."

When had he sat on the log beside me? I don't remember him moving. The fire was blazing. The sun was mostly down, the sky red-orange and darkening to purple at the edges. There was a hint of a chill in the air, making me glad of the fire. He was close. I could smell him, sweat and man, fish, campfire; he smelled like the wilderness.

I couldn't help staring at him—he was still shirtless, magnificently so. He looked as if he just belonged, like he was part of the scenery. He *was* the wild, because there was something as wild about him as the forest around us.

I felt drawn to him in a way I'd never felt drawn to anyone.

I wanted to kiss him. Hold on to him. Lay on the pine needles with him and stare at the stars, feel his heat against me.

I blinked hard and looked away, trying to breathe away the strange, intensely powerful, deeply personal desire I felt for the man who was Ramsey Badd.

"My dad remarried when I was sixteen," I heard myself say.

Intervention. Tell a story; tell him something personal to keep the desire at bay. Maybe if he knows more about me he won't want me as much, and I won't want him to want me, and I won't want him.

Stupid, stupid, stupid me. Utterly boneheaded reasoning, but it was all I had to defend against the constant onslaught of my desire to keep him out of my heart, out of my life, and out of my body.

But he was worming his way into those three places without even trying, slowly, deliberately, and surely.

"You get on with your stepmother?" he asked.

My snort of laughter was bitterly, derisively negative. "Not exactly. My nickname for her is Evil Cunt. And her daughter is Evil Cunt Junior."

He blinked. "Wow. Okay. So no, you didn't like her."

"Honestly, even though I came up with those names when I was just a teen, those names turned out to be pretty accurate." I stared into the fire rather than looking at Ram; I let my words flow, unsure where they were coming from, or why I was telling him any of this, but I couldn't stop it and I knew better than to try. "After Mom died, Dad just…fell apart. There was nothing physically wrong with him, he was just literally brokenhearted. Sick from losing her. Physically sick. He spent most of the first month isolated in his study, coming out only for the funeral and for food. He could barely talk to me, and his friends and colleagues couldn't reach him at all. After two months, he decided to take time off, so he got a leave of absence from the hospital—a year sabbatical, he called it." I sighed, pausing. "I thought maybe we would spend time together and heal together, but he didn't seem to realize that I was hurting too. He sent me to live with my aunt, his sister. He said it would just be until he could get back on track—just for the summer. They lived way across the country and we didn't see them all that often, but he still packed me off to live with them, and two months turned into a whole year."

"Jesus."

"Yeah, it was…not great. I hardly knew them. And they already had four kids and were barely making it. I just added to their stress, but I was family so they took care of me. But it wasn't…loving. It was tense and awkward. I was grieving, but I was in a strange home with people I didn't know, in a new school with no friends, and I didn't want to make any new ones because I was still hoping Dad would bring me back home. I was fucking miserable."

"Did he ever bring you home?"

I nodded. "After a year. A little less, actually. I moved to St. Paul in March, and moved back to

Memphis the following January."

"Was your dad any better?

I laughed again, bitterly. "No. He was worse, if anything. He'd...drawn inward while I was gone. He went back to work. He'd always worked long hours, but when he went back, he went back with a vengeance. He basically lived there, leaving me alone pretty much all the time."

He huffed a laugh. "I know how that feels."

"Yeah." I took a twig and snapped it into pieces, tossing the smaller pieces into the fire one by one, watching them catch fire and burn. "He was never the same after Mom died. He'd been fun, funny, charming, talkative, easygoing. After I moved back, he was just...angry. Cold, distant, and totally shut down."

"So you went from having two loving parents to no parents at all in the space of a year."

I nodded. "Yeah. And then it got worse."

"He met your stepmother?"

I nodded again. "Yep. He met her online, I guess, and then they met in real life, and within six months they were married. I told him flat out I hated her, told him she only wanted him for his money—I saw that the first time I met her. She had him buy her all sorts of stuff every time they went out—jewelry, purses, clothes, for her and for her daughter." I sniffled, against my own will. "He never bought me a damn thing. Barely looked at me. Acted as if he couldn't stand me."

Ram frowned. "God…*why*?"

I shrugged, shaking my head. "I really don't know. I think it must have been because I look so much like Mom. I sound like her too."

"So he married the greedy gold digger."

"Yep. She was divorced from a rich old guy who'd seen through her bullshit, but by then she was used to a certain lifestyle. She saw her opportunity in Dad, so she took it. I think he just wanted someone to warm his bed, you know? He never loved her. I don't think he even liked her, but…" I shuddered. "She put out, so he married her and let her bleed him dry, because he just didn't care."

"Yuck," Ram muttered. "That's bullshit."

"What's bullshit is that she only cared about spending money on herself and her spoiled bitch of a daughter, who she'd had with her first husband—I think she literally nagged that poor bastard to death, from what I understand. She didn't do shit except shop. I took care of Dad, fed him, did his laundry, cleaned the house because no one else would."

He eyed me. "So should I start calling you Cinderella?"

I snorted bitterly. "More than you know. This went on for about two years, and then Dad just…

died. Literally, actually *on* my eighteenth birthday. He just…wasted away right in front of me and I couldn't do a thing about it. He got thinner and thinner, ate less and less, slept less and less. Talked less and less. And then one morning I found him dead in his bed."

"Jesus, Izz."

"So yeah, things got worse from there. Evil Cunt took over. Kicked me out to the little loft over the garage."

"How could she kick you out of your own house?"

"She controlled the money. I'd been buying food and whatever else with his credit cards, and she took them and cut them up and got new ones. And I was just so depressed already, and then further devastated by Dad dying that I just stopped caring, stopped fighting her." I'd run of twigs to snap, so I grabbed another and resumed breaking it into smaller sections and tossing the pieces into the fire. "I reached a point where I couldn't do it anymore, couldn't handle Tracey or Trina anymore. So I left. I'd managed to save a few thousand dollars, essentially siphoning it off while taking care of Dad—it was stealing, if you want to get technical about it, but I guess deep down I knew which way the wind was blowing and took precautions. So I had some money, and I ran away. I mean, I was eighteen, so it wasn't really running away, just leaving. I ran into some people I used to babysit for. They'd lived in the same neighborhood as us for years, and they had three kids a lot younger than me, so babysitting was a way to earn some spending cash, because Dad didn't believe in allowance. Anyway, they'd moved to a different neighborhood, and I got talking to the mother, and it came up that they were looking for a live-in nanny. So…that was how I survived for the next couple years."

He eyed me with curiosity. "You? A live-in nanny?"

I laughed. "Don't sound so surprised. I do have a nurturing side."

"I guess I just have a hard time visualizing you changing diapers and making bottles."

I laughed again. "Oh, no. The kids were older by then, kindergarten, third grade, and fifth grade. I was mainly there to keep them from burning the house down, or killing each other. I also prepared the meals and did laundry, since the mom and dad both worked full time out of the house. Live-in nanny basically means housekeeper and babysitter in one."

"Isadora Styles, domestic goddess."

I snickered. "Hey, I can make a mean lasagna, and fold baskets of laundry faster than you can blink. I'm out of practice these days, though."

He grinned at me. "I'm definitely interested in the lasagna."

"If you're really nice, I'll make it for you someday."

"I can be nice," he murmured. "Very, very nice."

I flushed hot, remembering how *nice* he had been on the trail earlier today. "Don't remind me," I muttered.

He grinned, letting out a low, lascivious chuckle. "No? I think that'd be something you'd want to remember."

"How could I forget?" I closed my eyes and breathed slowly, counting to ten. "*Any*way…I nannied for them for about a year and a half, maybe two years, and then Alan, the father, got transferred here. Well, to Alaska. Anchorage, actually. I moved with them, helping with the transition, but even though the transfer was a promotion, the change in living situation meant the house they ended up buying was too small for all of them, plus a live-in nanny. And the increase in pay meant Lucy, the wife, didn't have to work as much, so they just didn't need me anymore. It was great for them, overall, but it left me out of a job and living in Alaska by myself."

"So how'd you end up in Ketchikan?"

"Alan knew someone who lived here who needed temporary help around the house—his wife was a high-risk pregnancy and on bed rest, and they needed help with the other kids and keeping up the house. So

I moved down here, and then once she'd given birth and had recovered, I was out of a job again. By that time, I was twenty-two, almost twenty-three. No college, barely enough money to survive, no friends, no family. I mean, I have Aunt Mary and Uncle Nick in St. Paul, but I wasn't about to go banging on their door again."

"What'd you do?"

"I walked by a newly remodeled retail space right as the owner was hanging up a help wanted sign. I went in, asked if I could fill out an application, and ended up getting hired on the spot. That was Angelique, and I've worked for her ever since. I went from cashier and salesgirl to manager, to now basically running the place on my own while Angelique is semi-retired. She spends most of her time in Paris, sourcing inventory."

He looked at me, long and hard and intently. "You've been through a hell of a lot."

I shrugged. "When I was a kid and my mom and dad were alive, I never could have imagined what the future held for me. I went from love and security to one impossible situation after another, just sort of... surviving."

"Don't downplay it, Izzy. You survived on your own from a very young age. You've made good."

I rolled a shoulder. "I guess."

"Why do you doubt?"

I sighed. "I just...I've bounced from thing to thing. Place to place. Working for Angelique has been amazing, and I do love blogging, and I've got quite a big following, and even a few pretty big sponsors."

"But...?"

Gahhh, here we go. The thing I hated facing. The thing I'd never even allowed myself to think about.

"But...before Mom died, I wanted..."

He waited a moment. When I didn't finish, he nudged me with a broad, hard, warm shoulder. "You wanted what, Izzy?"

I blinked hard against the tears pooling in my eyes. It was stupid—why was this so hard to talk about?

"I wanted to be a doctor." I whispered it, so low I barely heard myself. "Even after Mom died, I wanted to be a doctor. Even more so, in some ways. Like, maybe I could save someone else's mother so they wouldn't have to go through what I was going through, you know?"

"But then life happened." His voice was close, rumbling in my ear, buzzing in my bones and in my blood. "Life got in the way of those plans."

"And now I'm thirty years old with nothing but a high school diploma and a stupid fashion blog."

"It's not stupid."

"Yes, it is."

"Do you still want to go into medicine?"

I shrugged. "I don't know. Is it even possible, at this point in my life? I'd be forty before I finished."

"Anything's possible," Ram said. "Don't you know? Forty is the new twenty."

I snorted, unable to suppress a grin and a giggle. "That's stupid and you're an idiot. Twenty is twenty, forty is forty, and old is old."

He shook his head. "Now who's an idiot? You're not old. You're barely thirty."

"And I'm supposed to just...start over? Go back to school? *Med* school at that?" I laughed. "Med school is next to impossible for twenty-somethings with boundless energy and the ability to function on three hours of sleep."

He bumped me with his shoulder again. "Okay, granted. I'm just saying, it's never too late to chase your dreams. It's never too late to start over. And if you want something bad enough, you'll make the time, and you'll get through it, if it's important to you."

"Says the man still working at his brother's bar," I said, knowing I was being unfair.

"Okay, well I'm not still working there out of fear, I'm doing it out of loyalty to my brother."

I sighed. "I'm not afraid."

He quirked an eyebrow at me. "No? Then what's holding you back?"

I groaned. "Shut up. I hate you."

He chuckled. "Because you know I'm right."

"Yeah, I'm scared, okay?" I snapped. "I'm scared of going a hundred grand in debt, I'm scared of going to med school with kids ten or twelve years younger than me, smarter than me, with more energy than me. I'm scared of leaving the job I know pays the bills."

"No one is saying you have to do anything." Ram rolled a shoulder. "I'm just saying you shouldn't let being afraid stop you."

"Easy for you to say. You parachuted into wild-fires. You don't get scared."

He scoffed. "Is that what you think?"

I nodded. "Um…yeah?"

"Wrong. I was scared every single time I jumped out of an airplane. If you're not scared to jump out an airplane with nothing keeping you from smacking into the ground but some silk and some string, you're crazy—and I mean that honestly. And if you're not scared to do that into the middle of a raging wildfire, you're even more so." He added a log to the fire, send-ing sparks winkling and floating up into the night sky. "I was scared shitless my first time jumping out of the plane. The instructor had to actually shove me out, as a matter of fact. And then I was out and in the air, free falling, and it was…the craziest rush of my life. There's absolutely nothing like it. The scariest part of it is that moment when you have to convince yourself to do something legitimately moronic: voluntarily leaping out of an airplane ten thousand feet in the air. After that, it's a rush. It's fun, exhilarating, freeing. The part where you jump into a wildfire and have to start fighting it? That's a different kind of scary. That's where you have to fall back on your training. But that's scary, too. So yeah, babe, I was scared of every plane I jumped out of, and every fire I went into."

"I guess I thought because you did a dangerous job like that, that you just didn't get scared. Like, you thrived on the danger or whatever."

"You're right and wrong at the same time—you do get scared, and that fear is what keeps you alive. It forces you to double, triple, and quadruple check your gear. It keeps you alert, keeps you training as hard as possible so you stay on the knife-edge of your skills. The part you're wrong about is that people doing scary and dangerous jobs don't get scared. You're right about thriving on the fear and the danger, though. The adrenaline rush, the danger, the fear, the challenge, I did love it and thrive on it. You're never so alive as when you're hyperaware of your own mortality."

"Were you scared to move up here to Alaska?" I asked. "It's kind of like starting over, I guess."

He nodded. "Not kind of like, it *was* starting over. We'd quit jobs we'd trained for, chased after, and loved. We left California, the home we'd chosen, and we were leaving Oklahoma, the home we were born to. We had no safety net up here, no family, no friends, no jobs. We had a business loan and an idea—Rome's dream of opening a bar."

"But you did have family up here, though."

He shrugged. "Yeah, but we walked into their bar and met them for the first time…and nearly got into a fist fight with them. Actually, Rome did get decked by Bast that night, come to think of it." He laughed. "He deserved it, though. The point is, Rome had said we had long-lost cousins up here, but that didn't really mean anything to me until we met them and slowly started developing relationships with them."

"It's good you have them," I said.

He just nodded, and we were both content to let the silence stretch out, then. Ram slid off the log to sit on the ground with his back to the log, legs stretched out. He scraped his hand through his hair, and then dragged his fingers through his beard, sighing.

Eventually, a pressing need I'd been avoiding all day became too strong to ignore.

"Um, Ram?"

He eyed me, a smirk on his face. "You're finally desperate enough that you're willing to piss in the woods?"

I nodded, flushing and refusing to look at him. "Something like that," I mumbled.

"Well, obviously I ain't a girl, but from what I understand, the best way to go about peeing in the woods without a toilet is to dig a nice deep hole. Doesn't have to be wide, or more than a foot deep or so, but digging a hole keeps your pee from splashing back up on you. The other trick I've heard girls talk about is keeping your knees wide, for some reason. Not sure on that one, but I've heard it more than a few times, so I imagine it's true. Last, get your pants way down around your ankles, if not take them off entirely."

I nodded. "Got it." Another hesitation. "Um… did you bring a shovel?"

He laughed again. "I got you."

Ram stood up in a smooth, lithe movement, went to his pack, and unstrapped a small, collapsible spade from it, and then dug out a roll of TP, grabbing a canteen on the way. He jerked his head in a gesture to follow him, and guided me out behind the tent a few feet. He unclipped a small flashlight from his belt, turned it on, and handed it to me, and then dug a hole about a foot wide and a foot deep.

He gestured at the hole, leaving the spade and the canteen against a nearby tree. "Do your business, and use as little TP as possible. When you're done, dump some water on the TP to help it break down faster. This is a fairly damp area, and not really all that sensitive, so it's fine to bury the mess. Scoop the dirt and pine needles over the hole, and you're good."

"Um, so…if you don't bury it, what do you do with it?"

He chuckled. "Well, if you're hiking in an arid area, or a place where the ecosystem is fragile or sensitive, you live by the phrase 'leave no trace.' So you pack it all out with you."

I frowned in disgust. "You pack out used toilet paper?"

He nodded. "Poop too. Human fecal matter isn't part of most ecological systems, so if you're hiking in a sensitive ecosystem, you have to take it out with you."

"Oh my god, that's so gross. How do you even do that?"

"Special bags. I've done it a couple times."

I shuddered. "Nasty. This is about as far as I'm willing to go, at this point." I shooed him away. "Dump water on the TP and then cover the hole. Got it." I laughed, shaking my hands. "What a weird conversation."

"It's all natural, baby!" he said, laughing. "Okay. I'll be at the fire. Give a shout if you need help."

I snorted. "I think I can manage to pee by myself."

"Just sayin', I'll be within earshot," he said, walking away.

It felt a little silly to be so glad for the flashlight he'd left me. Away from the fire, it was pitch-black in the forest, and I could see very little. I pushed down my jeans and underwear, oriented myself over the hole, and took care of business. And, let me tell you, it was every bit as weird as I thought it would be.

Done, I dumped water on the TP, filled in the hole, and returned to the campfire, leaving the spade and canteen with Ram's pack. I handed him the flashlight as I sat down on the log. He opened a pouch on his belt and withdrew a small bottle of hand sanitizer.

I laughed gratefully. "Oh thank god," I said. "Clean hands."

"Always prepared," he said, holding up a hand in the Boy Scout salute.

"What else do you have in all those pouches on your belt?" I asked.

He winked up at me. "Trade secret, babe. I could tell you, but then I'd have to kill you."

"Wouldn't be hard," I joked. "All you'd have to do is leave me out here alone."

He chuckled. "Nah, you'd survive. You're smart and tough."

"You really think so?" I asked, stretching and yawning.

When I came out of my stretch, I discovered that somehow, I'd ended up with my legs on either side of Ramsey's torso, so he was leaning against the log between my thighs. And for some stupid, ridiculous reason, my fingers started tracing through his hair, toying with the long, feathery, silk-soft blond locks.

"Yes, Izzy, I do think so. I wouldn't say it otherwise. I'm not in the habit of sayin' shit I don't mean." He leaned his head backward, letting it rest against my belly.

What was I doing? Caressing his hair, stroking his scalp lightly with my fingernails...such intimate affection. Why?

I wasn't sure. I just knew I couldn't stop. I knew I should—this kind of intimacy was foolish, risky, too much too soon. I haven't even had sex with him. I didn't engage in affection like this with men I *did* have sex with, much less men I barely knew.

I bolted up off the log, abruptly and awkwardly, and lurched toward the tent. "I'm...tired. Gonna go see if I can figure out how to sleep in a weird bag on the ground."

Ram didn't say anything, but there was something

knowing in his silence. I bet if I'd turned around, I'd have seen him smirking.

But I didn't turn around. I unzipped the tent, took off my hiking boots and set them in a corner of the tent; they sat there for about forty-six seconds before I realized they stank to high heaven, so I set them outside the tent. I took off my bra without taking off my shirt, and climbed into the sleeping bag.

The ground was hard, but at least Ram had made sure I bought a weird little compressible hiking pillow—I pulled it out of its little bag and it sprang rapidly outward into shape, and turned out to be pretty comfy.

I'd come in here not because I was sleepy, but to escape the intimacy of the moment with Ram, but once I lay down and put my head on the pillow, I found myself drifting off to sleep faster than I'd ever fallen asleep in my life.

NINE

Ramsey

EVEN THOUGH IZZY WAS MERE INCHES AWAY FROM ME IN the tent, she was wrapped up in her sleeping bag and facing the wall, snoring softly, the sleeping bag up to her nose, only a hint of strawberry blonde hair peeking out the top. Her bra lay in the corner of the tent, and her boots sat outside, but I saw no other clothes so I assumed she was sleeping in what she'd worn that day. I typically sleep naked, even when hiking. Weird, possibly, but I just sleep better that way and always have, with the exception of those firefighting missions; tonight, though, I decided to stay clothed, for Izzy's sake.

I fell asleep thinking of Izzy. She was so defensive,

so prickly, and so sarcastic. So quick to escape any situation that even remotely suggested intimacy, vulnerability, or romance. She'd opened up a few times about her past, and I'd been shocked—and honored—each time, but she'd immediately retreated afterward, and had taken a long time to warm up to me again.

I understood, though.

What was less clear to me was why it stung so hard every time she retreated from me, closed off, put up her walls. Why did I care? What was it I wanted from her? If one of my brothers or my cousins were to ask what I wanted from Izzy Styles, I'd have said to get her naked and fuck her a few times. I wouldn't have said that I wanted to get to know her, that I wanted to understand what made her tick, that I craved non-sexual physical affection from her—her fingers trailing through my hair, her hand on my shoulder, back, neck, face; I wouldn't have said how much I wanted her to like me for who I was. I've never given a shit about who likes me, who approves of me; as long as I've got Rem and Rome, nobody else counts for shit. They're all I've ever needed, their approval and their—mostly unspoken but obvious—love. Girls are for a good time, for fun, for sex, but that's it.

Yet deep down, beneath the part of me willing to admit such things out loud, or to even acknowledge them to myself, I wanted all that with and from Izzy.

I shouldn't.

She's as committed to one-and-done liaisons as I am. Love is as nonexistent, as taboo, as anathema to her as it always has been to me.

Romance? No thanks.

Intimacy? If you mean, naked and inside a sexy woman, then yes.

Vulnerability? Bitch, please.

Yet, every minute I spend around Izzy makes that shit sound almost appealing.

Eventually, sleep pulled me under, and as I almost always do, I slept like a dead person. I woke up before dawn to the sounds of birds singing, the creek rushing in the distance, wind sighing through the trees. Sunlight glowed at an angle through the canopy, shedding long wavering shadows on the tent wall over my head. Beside me, Izzy was in the same position she'd been when I entered the tent: on her right side, facing the tent wall, sleeping bag pulled up to her nose, hair askew and escaping the braid in wisps of strawberry blonde splayed across the pillow and tent floor. She was snoring, too, an adorable little *snurk-sniff* that made my gut do weird twists and flops.

I crept out of the tent as quietly as I could, re-zipping it behind me. I was barefoot, and the ground outside the tent was cold and wet with predawn dew. I spent a few minutes rebuilding the fire. I'd made sure the coals were nice and hot, and had banked it the night before, so it was a breeze getting it going again. Once it was crackling, I dug out my pot, a change of clothes, and a bar of soap, and headed for the river. I filled the pot with cold, clear creek water and returned to the campsite, where I hung it over the flames to heat up. The tent was quiet, so I assumed Izzy was still asleep. I headed back to the river and shucked my clothes on the bank. Standing naked in the cool gray-pink dawn, I closed my eyes and enjoyed the moment, breathing in the air and letting the peacefulness of the morning soak into my bones.

And then, with a deep breath, I plunged into the bitterly cold creek. I dunked under and came up spluttering. Gahhh, it was *so* cold! Invigorating, bracing. I splashed around a minute or two, and then snagged my bar of soap off the bank and scrubbed myself clean from head to toe, working a lather into my hair and beard last of all, dunking under once more to rinse off. When I rose, spluttering and gasping again, ready to get out of the water, Izzy was standing on the bank, looking sleepily gorgeous, and bemused.

"Isn't that water freezing?" she asked, rubbing her face with both hands.

I grinned. "Sure is! Best way to wake up, though."

She shook her head. "You're nuts."

I shrugged. "I mean, yeah. But it's good for you. Jump in!"

"I didn't bring a change of clothes."

"I'll wait."

"You'll just wait in the freezing cold creek?" she asked, her voice skeptical.

"Yep. I'm used to it by now. Mostly."

She blinked at me. "You really want me to go in there?"

"Were you planning on not bathing the entire trip?"

"I…" She hesitated. "I hadn't considered that."

"Go grab a change of clothes," I said.

She huffed, but turned and shambled back to the campsite. I slid under the water again, because it was warmer to stay fully submerged; I let the current carry me downstream a ways, and then swam back upstream to where Izzy was standing at the creek's edge, a pile of clothing on the ground near mine. She was clearly hesitating, whether about stripping in front of me or getting into the water, I wasn't sure. Both, probably.

"Should I avert my eyes?" I asked. "Or are you working up the courage to jump in fully clothed?"

She narrowed her eyes at me. "Oh, shut up."

I grinned as I swam closer. "I'm gonna go

out on a limb here and guess you've never gone skinny-dipping?"

She rolled her eyes, but her grin was embarrassed. "Not all of us are exhibitionists, Ram."

"Exhibitionist? There's literally zero people for miles in any direction, except you. Not like this is a public pool, babe."

She bit her lip. "I'm not gonna get hypothermia, am I?"

"I've been in for like five minutes, Izz. Does it seem like I'm hypothermic?" I arched an eyebrow. "Take off your clothes and get in. Don't overthink it, don't ease in, just strip naked and plunge in."

"Fine," she huffed.

I watched, not bothering to hide the fact that I was staring with arousal and interest, as she peeled her shirt off and then her jeans, standing on the bank in just a pair of cotton underwear. She sucked in a breath; her eyes locked on me, and then shimmied out of those too. Even with the iciness of the water, the sight of Isadora totally nude was enough to make me hard as a rock.

She stood on the bank of the creek, heavy breasts swaying as she reached up to work her hair out of the braid, dawn sunlight bathing her golden-pink-orange, making her already perfect skin glow as if she were an actual, literal angel from heaven above. I swear, that vision of Izzy naked on the banks of the creek will be seared into the very fabric of my soul forever.

Her hair blew loose around her shoulders, and she clutched her breasts in her arms as she touched the water with a toe. "Holy hell, it's *cold!*"

I laughed. "I told you—just plunge in. It's the only way. If you try to ease in, you'll never do it."

She drew a deep breath, held it, and then with a screech she flopped forward into the water, gloriously awkward. She came up spluttering, gasping, too shocked to make a sound. Her hair was pasted against her face and shoulders, and she seemed paralyzed.

But only for a moment.

"Oh *hell,* n-n-n-no," she chattered, lurching for the bank. "F-f-fuck th-th-this! I'm out!"

I wrapped an arm around her middle and hauled her out into the deepest part of the creek, laughing as she struggled. I pulled us both under, and then rose to the surface, not letting go of her, who was thrashing like mad.

When we crested the surface, both gasping and laughing and sputtering, she twisted in my grasp. "You're an asshole," she hissed.

I used two fingers to brush her wet hair out of her face. "Yep. But now you're getting used to it, aren't you?"

We were crouching in the river, the water around

our shoulders. I found a nearby rock, slick with moss, and sat down on it, pulling Izzy with me. It was utterly natural for her to slide toward me, to straddle me as I sat on the rock chest deep in water. She wrapped her thighs around my waist, straddling me chest to chest.

My erection throbbed between us.

"How can you have an erection in this cold-ass water?" she murmured.

I smirked, shrugging. "You. You're so fuckin' beautiful, so fuckin' sexy, all I gotta do is fuckin' look at you and I get a hard-on. You, naked on the bank of the creek? Izzy, babe—I swear to Christ that's a vision I'll never forget for as long as I fuckin' live."

She visibly melted at my words. "Ram—" she breathed, choking. "Don't."

"Don't what? Tell you the damn truth?"

"We don't work out, you and me. Stop being so amazing so I can use you for your cock and move on."

I grinned. "Seems like I'm the one using you for your pussy more than you're using me for my cock. You ain't touched it since the hospital room."

"Whatever. The point is—"

"I know what the goddamn point is," I snarled. "You want me to just be the shallow, arrogant, mouth-breathing caveman fuckboy so you don't have to admit you like me." I took the bar of soap and rubbed it between her breasts and then over them in slow circles. "Sorry, babe—I can't help but be who I am, and I ain't gonna hold back telling you what I think just because it ruins your plans of remaining uninvolved and objective. I lost any chance of staying objective about you and me the moment I agreed to let you go hiking with me. This, out here? This is *my* world. *My* place. Not to put too fine a point on it, but it's fuckin' sacred to me, okay? And I'm sharing it with you. That ain't no small thing, babe."

She didn't answer, but she also didn't stop me from using the soap to scrub her pale, freckled skin. I worked a thick lather into my hands, pressed the bar of soap into her hands, and then massaged her scalp. Taking the soap from her, I scrubbed her hair against the bar until it was thickly lathered and then worked the lather from scalp down to the ends.

"Ready?" I murmured. "Time to rinse."

"No—no, no-no-no!" she protested.

I toppled us backward, and she kicked away, rubbing her hands in her hair to rinse the soap out. I caught up to her as she found her feet, coming up behind her to rub the soap over her belly beneath her breasts, then downward and downward—she took the soap from me and used it to clean her pussy, then let me take it back. I ran the soap over her back and her buttocks, and then in between the cheeks, making her gasp in surprise as I slid soapy hands over her rear entrance and further inward.

"Ohhhhhhhhmygod, Ram..." she breathed. "I was *not* expecting that."

I chuckled, scrubbing her thighs and around back up to her belly, this time abandoning the pretense of the soap, using my empty, soap-slick hand to caress her breasts. "Gotta get you clean."

"I'm clean, I'm clean," she mumbled. She twisted to face me, taking the soap from me.

"I already washed," I said.

"You missed a spot," she whispered. We were standing near the bank, the water rushing around our hips.

"I did, huh?" I said, resting my hands on her waist. "Well...better get it for me."

She scrubbed up a lather and then tossed the soap onto the bank near our piles of clothing. Her eyes flicked to mine, desire and need obvious in every part of her expression. I couldn't help but catch my breath as her gaze slid down to my cock, which stood upright, rigid, the tip swaying at my belly button as I breathed. She wrapped one soapy hand around me, and the other.

"Ohhhh fuck," I breathed, closing my eyes briefly.

She laughed lightly. "I haven't done anything yet."

"Don't have to," I mumbled, resting my forehead

against the top of her head. "Dreamed and fantasized about pretty much exactly this for the last fuckin' year."

"You have?"

I pulled back to look into her eyes. "Damn right, babe." I lowered my voice to a whisper. "Wanna know a secret?"

She stroked me, then, nodding. "Yes, please."

"Every single motherfuckin' time I jacked off, I was thinking about you, Izz. Your mouth on my cock, the taste of your pussy, the way you screamed as you came. I tried to imagine you naked but, god's honest truth, not even my wildest fantasies could even remotely come close to how perfect you are in real life."

I heard her breath catch, felt her hand tighten around me. "God, Ram. You say shit like that, and I…"

"You what, Izzy?"

She rolled a shoulder in a lame attempt at a shrug, and then shook her head. "I just…I can't help…"

Her hands slid up and down my shaft, one atop the other, and then she stroked me hand over hand, and then paused to rub the tip with her thumb.

"Spit it out, babe. Truth, and no bullshit."

"You say things like that, and I can't help almost believing you."

"Believe it, honey. It's just the truth."

"I masturbated thinking about you too," she whispered, her voice so low I could barely hear her over the chuckling burble of the creek.

My gut was tightening, her slow gentle touch making me crazy. I watched her hands play with me, never using the exact same stroke more than a few times in a row—she was playing with me for herself, I realized. Not to make me come but for her own enjoyment of my cock.

"What did you think about when you touched yourself?" I asked.

She shrugged a shoulder. "A lot of things."

"Like what?"

Her smile was aroused and embarrassed at the same time. "I...um. There were a few different... scenarios, I guess you could call them. Us kissing, touching, messing around. And then you'd...um, you'd spin me around, bend me over something—it varied every time, a bed, a kitchen counter, a car— and you'd...you'd fuck me until I screamed. Or you'd just do what you did in the woods...touch me, lick me, make me come with nothing but your hands and mouth. Or you'd ride my face, and then I'd go down on you, but you'd always insist on fucking me instead of coming in my mouth."

I growled wordlessly. "Fucking hell, Izzy."

"What? You asked." She eyed me. "What did

you think about?"

"This. Being out in nature together, naked. Fucking on the river bank. In the tent. On the ground under the sun." I shrugged. "I'd think about you showing up somewhere random, unexpected, and sucking me off, or instead of sucking me off, we'd fuck. In the office of the bar, or in the living room at the apartment, or at yours, or in a parking garage.

She snickered. "A parking garage?"

"Just somewhere public. Masturbation fantasies don't always make sense."

"Yes, that's true, they don't."

She had me gritting my teeth, resisting the urge to flex into her touch. She was taking her time, that was for damn sure. I couldn't help a groan as she used both hands to stroke me up and down slowly.

She bit her lip, shivering. "I'm fucking freezing."

I leaned close, as if I was going to kiss her, and then, at the last second, I licked her nose. "Race you back to the tent!"

I scrambled out of the water and snatched up our dirty clothes and the soap, taking off running for the campsite. I glanced behind me, laughing, to see Izzy close behind, our clean clothes in her arms, chasing me.

She'd left the tent partly unzipped, for which I was glad. I'd already gotten mostly dry on the sprint from creek to camp, so I dropped our dirty clothes on the ground near our packs and dove through the opening into the tent. Izzy was a heartbeat behind me, but she brought our clothes into the tent.

"I won," I breathed, laughing.

She hesitated in the opening of the tent, just looking at me. "Yes, you did."

I gestured at her to come in. "I won't bite," I said. "Unless you want me to."

She stared at me, biting her lower lip. "Ram, I..."

I sighed. "Izzy, this thing between us isn't going away."

"I know."

"So either dive into it with me and see where it goes, or quit playin'."

"See where it goes?"

I nodded. "It won't be just a quick fuck, Izz— you gotta know that. This ain't the kinda thing where we're gonna be able to fuck once or twice and get it out of our system. It's more than that. So, as much as I desperately want you to climb in here with me and finish what you just started, I ain't gonna lie about the fact that I *like* you. A lot. And in a way I've never liked anyone. It is what it is, and I want you, and I ain't gonna lie or apologize or make excuses. I'm no more comfortable with this kinda thing than you are. But I got balls enough to admit I'd like to feel it out."

She backed out of the tent.

I sighed again. "Got it."

She reached in and touched my foot. "No, no. I'm just—I'm getting something from my bag."

"Oh."

"So just...just wait a second, okay?"

I laughed. "I'll wait as long as you want."

I watched through the opening as she crouched by her pack, dug in where she kept her clothes, and came out with something clutched in both hands. She kept whatever it was hidden in her hands as she crouched into the tent. I reached past her and zipped it closed as she turned to sit facing me on her sleeping bag.

"What'cha got there, babe?"

She tossed several strips of condoms on the sleeping bag at my feet. "That."

"You brought them?"

She nodded. "It was Kitty and Juneau's idea. Just in case."

"Just in case?"

She smirked. "I didn't want to bring them, I guess because I knew if I brought them, I'd end up using them with you. But I think what Kitty and Juneau knew was that we'd use them anyway, and it was better to have them."

I grinned. "I brought some too. Not that many, though."

She eyed me, her gaze roaming from my face to my shoulders, down my body to my cock, which was still hard—despite the lack of attention and the cold. I just waited; I wanted to see what she would do, what she wanted, where she would take this.

She wrapped her arms around herself, shivering. "Fucking cold."

I unzipped my sleeping bag all the way, and then hers, laid hers on top of mine, and zipped them together into one large sleeping bag. Climbing in, I grinned up at her. "Coming?"

"Not yet, but you're about to," she muttered as she slid in beside me.

I reached for her, but she shook her head. "Ah-ah. This one is all me, big guy."

I tucked my hands under my head and gave a small shrug, grinning widely. "Have your way with me, then."

She rested her cheek on my chest, gazing up at me as she let her hand roam down my abdomen, teasing and dancing over the grooves of muscle toward my cock, which began to harden to a painful ache as she neared it. She grasped it lightly in one fist and lazily stroked it from root to tip several times, her touch a warm soft glide.

"I have two questions for you," Izzy said, rubbing the very tip of me with her thumb. "For...practical purposes."

"Okay?"

"First, are you clean? Like, have you been tested recently?"

"Yes."

"Good, me too." She gnawed on her lower lip, hesitating. "And second...um. How's your refractory period?"

I smirked at this question. "Well, it tends to vary. But with you, I'd guess pretty goddamn short." I reached out and caressed her breast. "Why do you ask?"

"Because I want to do...well, everything with you. And I need to know how long it'll take you to get hard again so I know where to start."

I couldn't help laughing. "It's like being at an all-you-can-eat buffet, huh? Don't know where to start?"

"Precisely."

I twiddled her nipple until she wriggled and her breath caught. "Put it this way, babe—you make me come, I'll be ready to go by the time I've given you your first orgasm."

Her eyes widened, a grin spreading across her face. "Good answer."

"So, Izz…where are you gonna…" I trailed off as she slithered under the sleeping bag. "Oh."

She grasped me in both hands, and then I felt her wet warm mouth on me.

"Ohhhhh," I murmured. "Okay."

I hadn't been expecting it the last time she did this, and it was no less shocking in its intensity this time. I gasped as she plunged her mouth around me, hands gliding slowly up and down around my base.

"Ohhh fuck, Izz," I groaned. "So fucking good."

She didn't reply—at least not verbally. She did redouble her efforts, as if her singular focus was to see how fast she could make me come. Or how hard. Or, more likely, both—how hard could she make me come in the shortest amount of time possible.

I didn't fight it, didn't try to hold back. It was futile, for one thing, and I had no interest in playing games. At least, not this time around.

She felt me beginning to thrust against her mouth, and slowed the strokes of her hand, letting me fall out of her mouth. I lifted the sleeping bag and grinned down at her.

"Okay down there?"

She smiled, an eager, pleased little grin. "Excuse me, I'm busy, here," she sassed, grabbing the fabric and yanking it back down.

I laughed, and the laugh turned into a moan as

she cupped my balls in one hand, tilted my cock away from my body with the other, and slid me into her mouth once more. This time, she wasn't just trying to stimulate me, she was...I don't even know. Taking it to a whole 'nother level, you might say. I felt her mouth around my glans, and then past it, and then she tilted me farther away and I heard her make a soft sound in her throat as she took more and more of me.

"Izzy, you don't have to—" She gave me a soft but sharp warning nip. "Okay, okay. Shutting up."

I was rewarded for correctly interpreting her meaning with a swirl of her tongue that had my eyes rolling into the back of my head and my hips flexing, an involuntary groan escaping. God, she had so much of me, I couldn't believe it. The sensation was divine, gloriously erotic. My brain was shorting out, my lungs empty. The center of my entire existence was Izzy's mouth on my cock, the swirl of her tongue and the slow wet suction and the sucking slide as she pulled back, the gentle cradling massage of her palm around my sac, the slow sweep of her fist down my shaft; her strategy wasn't hard and fast, but rather slow and intense. And holy fuck was it working. I wanted to gasp, needed to groan, but I had no breath in my lungs for either. My spine arched, and then my hips flexed to push upward, and I heard Izzy gasp for breath, swallowing hard, and then her lips suctioned around me again and rippled downward.

"Ohh *fuck*—" I grated through gritted teeth, sucking in a breath of cool oxygen. "Izzy, fuck—*Izzy*—"

Finally, she sped up—something about the ragged way I'd gasped her name had created urgency. I couldn't stop my hips from moving, from thrusting. Izzy didn't seem to mind—in fact, she pulled at me, encouraging me.

I gave her what she wanted—more. She was sucking and gulping greedily, stroking me faster and faster, and I was groaning nonstop, nonverbal grunts, curses, and whispers of her name. Again and again, as I felt myself rising to the edge.

I was moments from reaching climax when I remembered her fantasy—her doing this, and then me stopping to take her.

I pulled away just in time, scrambling out from underneath her—she protested, squeaking in surprise and then rustling under the sleeping bag and burrowing up toward the light. I ripped a condom off the strip, clenched the packet in my teeth and ripped it open, tugging the circle of latex out and rolling it on as Izzy crawled out from under the sleeping bag, blinking and looking pissed.

"What the fuck, Ram? I wanted—"

I cut her off, grabbing her around the waist and yanking her to me. I was sitting on my shins, and I hauled her onto my thighs, pulling her up against me.

"Ram—"

I kissed her. Hard, and thorough. Tongue delving into her mouth, slashing against her lips and teeth, demanding her tongue in return. She gasped, and then groaned, her hands tangling in my hair and pulling me closer, her mouth softening and opening, her warm, silk-soft body pressing up against mine. Her breasts crushed against my chest, and she had to pause to catch her breath.

"Jesus, Ram—"

I grinned, and then tipped forward so she landed on her back on top of the sleeping bags. "Get on your hands and knees, Izz."

"I—"

"Hands and knees," I repeated.

Her grin was eager and hungry and desperate as she moved to comply, going to her hands and knees, facing away from me, looking at me over her shoulder.

And holy mother of fucks, that beautiful round ass of hers all spread out for me? I throbbed, ached— I'd been a split-second from coming when I pulled away from her.

I slid two fingers between her thighs and found her slit, hot and wet and slick. I met her fingers—she was reaching back for me, and I angled my cock toward her; she grasped me, guided me to her entrance.

Her eyes met mine over her shoulder. "Ram?"

"You know how long I've waited for this, Izz?" I whispered.

"About as long as I have," she answered.

The head of my cock was nestled just barely inside her slit, a wicked, delicious, diabolical tease. She smiled back at me, bit her lip, and then drove her ass back against me, delving me inside her wild wet warmth.

I slid inside her, and in that moment, buried deep inside Isadora Styles, her soft ass pressed against my hips, her smile bright, her eyes wanting me, her whole body trembling as I filled her, I knew…

I was the one fucked.

I knew, in that moment, I would never, ever, for as long I live ever want another woman the way I wanted, needed, craved, and desired her.

TEN

Izzy

D EAR SWEET JESUS—IF I HADN'T BEEN BREATHLESS with anticipation, I would have actually cried with joy when he slid in to fill me. I'd been aching for him, and now I was aching from him. Throbbing with fullness. Burning, stretched open to accommodate his unbelievable size.

Yes, memory held true. He really was exactly that well-endowed.

My jaw ached from him.

I tasted him—precum, salt, musk, man.

I felt him—everywhere.

He was behind me, above me, all around me. Inside me—Ramsey Badd was inside me in a more than physical way. Not just impaled deep inside my trembling pussy, but inside my heart, inside my mind. Dare I say...inside my soul?

He knelt behind me, and, as I grasped his erection and slid him inside me again, I watched his expression just...melt. The patina of strength, of hardness, of toughness—the rough-and-tumble man who'd grown up roughshod in the Oklahoma boonies without a mother and a father who counted, the Boy Scout who became a smokejumper, the survivalist, the outdoorsman...all that melted away, and all that was left was *Ramsey*, the essence of the man himself. Tender but strong, rough but sweet, no formal education beyond a high school diploma, yet so smart, well-read, and insightful.

Sexy.

Powerful.

Beautiful.

I couldn't help the smile, and didn't try—I was beyond trying to pretend this wasn't something unique, something once in a lifetime, something truly worth smiling about. I met his eyes as he slid deep inside me, and I couldn't breathe. His hips dimpled against my ass, and I felt him within me, thick and hard and soft and warm, and I ached to clench around him, to feel him drive, move, thrust, fuck, lose control.

My hair was loose and wild, my lungs burning,

a whimper building inside me. My whole being was trembling already, and we'd only just begun.

"Ram…" I gasped.

He growled, his hands clawing into my buttocks with an iron grip, dimpling the flesh so hard I knew I'd probably have marks later—my skin was so pale and fair and fragile that I bruised if you looked at me the wrong way, and he was gripping so hard I squeaked. Not from pain but from excitement. Anticipation.

"I want to be gentle, Izzy," he murmured. "But I don't know if I'm capable."

I rocked forward, arching my spine down to lift my ass up, and slammed backward into him. "Don't," I bit out. "Please…don't be."

"Don't?"

"If I wanted gentle, I wouldn't be out here in the middle of nowhere with a man like you," I said, locking eyes with him. "If I wanted gentle, I'd be on my back right now, gazing up at you adoringly."

"Izz—"

I growled wordlessly, rocking backward again, taking him deep once more. "I don't want gentle, Ramsey." I rolled my hips slowly, taking him in soft, shallow thrusts. "I want you. I want this—you and me, nothing held back."

His response was to drop his head forward, chin to his chest, a rough exhale of relief escaping his lips. His hands released my ass, and he smoothed his palms over where I assumed there were pink fingerprints that would later turn to bluish shadows.

"I bruise easily," I murmured.

"Is that a license to mark you?" he asked.

I nodded, gasping. "Yes, god yes. Bruise me, Ram."

He pulled back, thick shaft sliding out for an eternity, and then he paused, nearly falling out. His left hand gripped my hipbone, and his right hand palmed my ass cheek. I watched over my shoulder, fingers digging into the soft earth under the thin skin of the tent floor—his brows furrowed, his jaw tensed, and I could tell he was riding the knife-edge already. Testament to how close he'd gotten before pulling away from my mouth. Which I'd been pissed about, initially—I had been looking forward to feeling him lose control, to milking his cock for all the cum he had until he was gasping and whimpering and bleating.

Instead, he'd yanked away at the last possible second and ordered me to my hands and knees...

And I'd nearly orgasmed just from that. I was a dominant personality, I tended to take charge, take no shit, and take no orders from anyone, men especially.

In the worst clichéd stereotype ever, though, deep down, I've always secretly longed for a man who could give me orders I wanted to obey—without cringing at the word "obey."

"Ram—move. Please move."

He slid into me with shuddering slowness, with exquisite control. "You had me there the moment you put that sweet hot mouth of yours on me, Izz," he snarled. "Being inside you? I don't stand a fucking chance."

I rolled backward into his slow, controlled thrust. "Good. Show me."

He growled. "Serious, babe. If I don't take a minute to get control, this'll be over in thirty goddamned seconds."

I grinned at him over my shoulder, rolling my hips to slide my pussy around his cock in short, shallow movements. "Good. I want it hard and fast."

His left hand released my hipbone, and now he palmed both cheeks, spreading them apart as he pushed in. He filled me so deeply my breath caught on a sob, and I shook, shuddered, and drove helplessly back into him. He grunted as I did so, and the grunt turned into a groan.

"God*damn*, Izz," he moaned, drawling the curse with that cute, sexy Oklahoma accent that came and went with his moods.

He pulled back, slowly and gently...held it for a second, a sultry, erotic smirk creeping across his mouth...and *slammed* into me, driving a shrill scream out of me.

Another—slow withdrawal…a pause…*slam*.

His hips slapped hard into my ass, his cock drove into me, filling me, stretching me, and I screamed again, the scream morphing into a wail of ecstasy as he withdrew and fucked me without pause and, as he thrust into me, his left hand cracked across my ass. His right hand roughly clutched a handful of my ass cheek, and his left hand spanked me harder and harder as his thrusts grew more ragged. Then he switched hands, his right spanking and his left clawing into the meat of my ass. With each thrust, each spank, my cries grew louder and more shrill, more desperate.

I fell forward, face down, ass up as I'd dreamed of being with him so many times—and the reality was far better, far wilder, and far more erotic than I could ever have even fantasized.

He growled my name on a chant—"Izzy, Izzy, Izzy…" my name tumbling from his lips each time he drove into my pulsating core, each time his palm cracked across my stinging, burning ass.

I joined him, chanting his name each time he filled me, spanked me. "Ram—Ram—Ram!"

It was like a plea; as if just by saying his name I was begging him to fuck me more, fuck me harder.

I reached two fingers between my legs and pressed them to my clit, and immediately began spasming, my chant devolving into wordless cries of near-feral release, my first orgasm barreling through me without warning. And then, as I rocked backward into him, my core clenching spasmodically around his shaft, I felt him change his technique—he gripped my ass in both hands, spread the cheeks apart, and thrust in hard but slow, flicking upward at the last second, and something about this sent me to the fucking moon, that last little flick of his hips driving his cock up into my G-spot and knocking me screaming and gasping and whimpering and crying over the edge a second time within thirty seconds.

Sobs, screams, gasps, whimpers—they were all one sound, now, driven out of me in nonstop succession as he found his rhythm. He clutched me and yanked me backward by my hips, and then his hands raked over my back and clawed down my spine, as if desperately seeking a new handhold with which to pull me harder, pull me closer, pull me deeper around him.

"Hair—" I snarled.

He knew. No other words were necessary. He wrapped my long loose hair around his fist and tugged my head backward, and I cried out at the tingle in my scalp, the burn in my core as he fucked me faster and faster, using my hair as leverage to drive deeper and deeper.

I felt him reach his limit, then. I felt his thick hot cock throbbing inside me, pulsing. He slowed, then, his thrusts going ragged, hard but slow, pounding in with loud slaps of flesh on flesh, his groans raw and hoarse.

He pounded in one last time and held there, tipping forward over my back, gasping for breath. He groaned, lying bent over me, thrust deep, one hand massaging my breast. And then he straightened, gasping for breath, and thrust in again, and then I felt him release, felt the blast of heat and felt him drive in, pushing deeper, harder, thrusting like that—pushing deep and trying to fuck deeper instead of pulling out. Rush after rush, groan after groan—how long would he come? God, it was amazing, a wild rush of adrenaline at the feel of this mighty man brought to such raw, ragged, helpless moans of total vulnerability.

Finally, he slowed and stopped, panting, that one hand still clutched around my breast.

I fell forward and rolled to my back immediately, staring up at him. "Ram, that was…"

He collapsed onto the sleeping bag beside me—in another fit of insanity, I did something I'd never, ever done before, not once, not with anyone, not for any reason, not even for a split second…

I slid my arm under his head and pulled him to me—he shimmied up close to me and rested his head on my chest. I cradled his head between my breasts, caressing his hair with my fingers.

Talk about intimate vulnerability?

My heart hurt. Ached. It felt swollen to bursting with something hot and shaky and wild.

I shuddered beneath him.

"Izz..." he breathed. "Your heartbeat..."

He took my hand and pressed my index and middle to his throat—I could feel my own pulse hammering, and I felt what he meant: our pulses were synched.

I laughed. "That's crazy!"

He nuzzled his head against me, sighing. "I've never listened to anyone's heartbeat like this before."

"I can honestly say I've never let anyone do this, either," I murmured.

"It's...soothing."

I laughed, but it was ragged. "God, Ramsey. What the hell are we doing? What's happening?"

He lifted up on an elbow and stared down at me. "I don't even know."

"At least you don't know any more than I do."

He shook his head. "On the surface of it, what we just did was straight up hard and fast fucking, but..."

"But it wasn't just that," I whispered, meeting his eyes. "Was it?"

"No." He bent down, and his lips ghosted over

mine. "No, it wasn't."

I blinked at the tenderness in the swift soft kiss. "Fucking hell, Ramsey."

He flopped to his back and then sat up, moved to his knees, unzipped the tent, and reached out to fish around in an outside pocket of his pack, which was right outside the door of the tent. He came back in with the kind of small white plastic bag you get your groceries in at the supermarket, stripped off the condom and tossed it in the bag, twisted it up, and set it in a corner. This done, he lay back down beside me; we lay side by side, naked, staring sideways at each other.

"Why'd you stop me?" I asked, eventually.

He shrugged. "I didn't want to waste the moment by coming in your mouth. I wanted...this."

I narrowed my eyes. "Truth, Ram."

He sighed, looking away from me. "I almost didn't pull out. I was literally seconds from coming when I remembered what you'd said about your fantasy." He paused, glanced at me, and then away again. "And I wanted to make it come true."

"Well, you did," I said. "You really, really did." I had to swallow hard against the knot of emotion lodged in my throat. Who the hell was he to make me feel this strongly? Damn him. "No one's...ah... um. No one's ever—ever done that for me before. So...thanks."

"Done what?"

I rolled a shoulder, looking away from him at the pale blue wall of the tent. "Wanted to…I don't know."

"Izz…" he whispered, palming my cheek and turning my face so I was forced to look him in the eyes, forced to let him see the tears welling in my eyes, the stupid, embarrassing, weak, broken-girl tears I was fighting like hell to keep back.

Damn him.

Damn the tears.

Damn the emotions.

I shook my head, blinking hard. "Shit." I rolled forward, yanking at the tent opening zipper and crawling out.

Pine needles and dirt stuck to my palms and knees as I crawled out, naked and awkward and ungainly—I was still weak and shaky and trembly from the wild fury of the orgasms we'd shared. I made it to my feet and stumbled a few steps away from the tent, tilting my head back as if I could force the stupid tears to drain back into my skull where they fucking belonged.

I felt him behind me.

"Don't," I whispered.

"Don't what?"

"Look at me." I shook my head. "Make me look at you."

He didn't ask what was wrong, and he didn't ask what he'd done—I think he just knew. He stood behind me for a heartbeat, and then his arms wrapped around my middle, his front pressing to my back—chest to spine, his nose in my hair, his breath on my neck, his hips against my butt, his quads to my hamstrings, his arms wrapped double around me, right hand on left waist and vice versa.

I breathed slowly, shuddering, trembling. "I'm never like this. I hate it."

"Don't."

"It's stupid. I don't even know why I'm crying."

"It's okay, Izzy."

I shook my head. "I don't cry." I sniffled, wiped at the tears as they fell, giving a lie to my words.

I had no desire to fight his arms around me—his embrace was so comforting, so soothing that I just...I fucking *needed* his arms around me more than I needed to breathe. I could only breathe if his arms were around me, and that just pissed me off all the more, making me even more weepy.

"What is it I did that no one has ever done before, Isadora?" The question was quiet but razor sharp.

I shook my head. "Nothing."

"Izz."

"No one has ever given that much of a shit about me, Ramsey!" I snapped. "No one has ever cared enough to even ask me what my fantasy is, much less make it come true."

"Why do you sound angry?"

"Because it was supposed to be *erotic*, not...*romantic*! Jesus. You fucked me doggy style in a tent in the woods, and you somehow made it feel romantic. And erotic, yes, but...fuck. I don't get it. You were supposed to be a safe bet for a quickie in a hospital room. Instead, we went down on each other, ignored each other for over a year, and then...this. Whatever the hell *this* is."

His arms tightened around me. "I give a shit, Izzy."

"I know, damn you." I wiggled in his embrace, but he didn't let go. "You weren't supposed to."

"No, I wasn't. I tried not to. Trust me, I only gave a shit against my better judgment."

I laughed at that. "Let go. I can't breathe."

He released me, and I stumbled away, stopped, and turned to face him. His eyes, to his credit, stayed on mine.

"Can we just...pack up and go?" I asked. "I need time to process what just happened."

He nodded. "Sure thing."

"I'm not trying to—"

He smiled, shaking his head as he cut in over me. "You said all you need to say, Izzy. You need time to process it, and I get it. Shit, babe, I do too. That was motherfuckin' intense."

"If you'd let me suck your cock like I was planning, we wouldn't be in this mess, you know," I said, trying to make a joke of it.

He gave me his trademark smirk—the arrogant, annoying, sexy one. "Hey, now, babe—if that's what you want, you can have it any time you want."

"Yeah?" I arched an eyebrow at him, more at home on this turf—sassy banter. "If I start going down on you, you're not gonna stop me and try to make love to me again?"

Dammit, dammit, dammit. That phrase was *not* supposed to come out of my mouth.

And yes, he noticed. His breath caught, his eyes widened.

He recovered quickly, though. "I think you'll just have to find that one out for yourself, babe."

I smirked back, giving his long, dangling, flaccid, sticky cock a playful tap as I sashayed past him. "And maybe I will. Just not when you're expecting it."

He laughed. "Get dressed, Izz. We have a lot of miles to cover today."

We were dressed, packed, and on the trail in less than an hour—the sun was still rising, only a few inches above the horizon.

I let Ram set the pace, and he set a pretty hard

one. I was sore in places I hadn't known I had, and no, they were not from fucking...I'm rather well acquainted with that kind of soreness, thank you very much.

This was new. Different. Painful. A deep ache in my lower back, shoulders, and thighs. But it was a good soreness; I felt more alive than ever before—a trite, overused phrase, but one I had a new appreciation for.

The sky seemed bluer, the clouds whiter, the trees greener, the air cleaner, sounds crisper. Everything seemed unbearably beautiful.

We'd set out without breakfast or coffee—our, ummm, activities had distracted us, so the water had boiled over, and Ram had to take the pot down to the river to cool it off and scrub the scorch marks off it. I was ravenous, and craved coffee, but it felt good to be on the trail again, following Ram's tireless strides.

Of course, I couldn't think of anything except him.

How he'd looked in the predawn—I'd woken up alone, and then stumbled out of the tent to look for him. I found him in the creek, and he'd looked like some wild, feral god of the river, standing the middle of the current, legs braced apart, heavy cock not quite hidden by the water, muscles bulging and rippling as he stood there, water streaming down his face and chest and arms, coating him in a sheen that gleamed and glimmered in the pink-gray haze. He was huge and powerful, yet beautiful. A man of raw, brutal strength and vitality, a man who could run up a mountain in eighty pounds of gear, who could survive in the wilderness with nothing but a knife and his wits—he didn't fit in this age of men. He was meant to explore the wild places in bygone eras. If he had been born at any other time, he'd have been a knight, or a king, or an explorer.

I had stood on the bank staring at him for at least a minute before he realized I was there, and in that minute, I had felt a craving for him—for all of him, all of who he was—so strong I'd nearly wept from it. It was a bone-deep, blood-deep craving. Soul-deep.

Another cliché phrase I now truly and fully comprehended: He was inside me, in my blood and bones.

My need for him was beyond sex, beyond chemicals, beyond attraction.

Goddammit—this wasn't supposed to happen.

I was falling for Ramsey…

If I hadn't already…

Yet I knew this would happen—and I'm scared out of my fucking mind.

ELEVEN

Ramsey

THE DAY WAS UNEVENTFUL FOR THE MOST PART WHICH, I think, was a good thing. No bears, no elk, no surprises. A few eagles overhead, a beautiful day, lots of miles behind us.

We stopped when the sun was overhead, and I made a small fire just off the trail—I dug out a small pit, ringed it with rocks, and stacked some kindling in the hole and created a fire just large enough to make some coffee and heat up some beans to go with the fruit and jerky. I had some fresh eggs with me, carefully packaged to survive the trip, and I was hoping I'd get a chance tomorrow morning to show Izzy what I could do with a camp stove.

By uneventful, I also mean there was nothing by way of hanky-panky between us, either. Which was a little sad, because my cock was getting pretty ravenous for another taste of Izzy. But my heart was glad for the respite, because I was still reeling from this morning. Mentally and emotionally, I was just... reeling.

I'd chosen doggy style for three reasons—one, it had been what she specified in her fantasy; two, it was one of my favorite positions, just selfishly, because as much as I was hot for her tits, her ass was what kept me up at night with wet dreams, and the opportunity to pound into that tight, round, juicy derriere of hers was one I couldn't pass up; and third, I'd assumed, wrongly, that fucking Izzy doggy style would be somehow less personal, less intimate, that I'd be able to retain some of my emotional distance from her. Instead, we'd bonded even closer. I'd felt her goddamn soul wrapping around mine as we reached climax together. I'd felt her in my guts and blood and bone and balls. In my heart. In my brain.

She was everywhere—those eyes, that smile, her sass and sarcasm, her prickliness, her quick-to-flare and quick-to-recede hot-flash temper. Her filthy mouth, dirty sense of humor, flirty touches, her annoyance with my tendency to be cocky even when I knew she also found it attractive. Her toughness, her sense of adventure.

An hour and a half or two after lunch, we reached the zenith of a hill and saw the mountains towering above us in the distance, white-capped and breathtaking; I felt Izzy come to a halt beside me.

"Wow…" she breathed. "Just…wow."

I sat down on the path and shucked my pack, leaning back against it. "Take a minute, Izz. Just soak in the view."

She sank down to her butt and leaned back against her pack but didn't take it off. "I've lived in Alaska since I was nineteen? Twenty? And I've never seen anything like this. I mean, I knew mentally, intellectually, that there was a lot of natural beauty around me, and once in a while I'd look around Ketchikan and get a glimpse of it, but I …I was too busy trying to make a living to see it."

I sighed. "Sorry, sweetheart, but I'm calling bullshit."

She turned to frown at me. "Ummm, what?"

"You weren't too busy."

"I've worked sixty to eighty hours a week for ten years."

"You could've made time to look around."

She shrugged. "I guess. I just…" She glanced at me, at the mountain, and then sighed. "You know what? You're right. I chose not to—I had my head buried in the sand."

"Why?"

She stared in silence at the vista of the mountains for a long time. "Because I wanted more, but anything I wanted seemed out of reach."

"What did you want?" I asked. "What *do* you want?"

She sniffed, brushed at her cheek. "Goddamn you, Ram." She stood up, awkwardly lumbering to her feet, hopping to get the pack higher on her shoulders, tightening the straps. "Would you quit digging into my fucking head? Jesus."

I let her walk away a few steps, and then followed her. If the pattern held, in a few hours she'd answer the question. We hiked for the next two, almost three hours without stopping. She stayed just ahead or behind me the entire time, hiking in thoughtful, if prickly, silence. It was nearing evening, and we were still a couple miles from the next campground when she stopped to take a swig from her canteen.

"I told you what I want—nothing's really changed about that," she said, after swallowing a mouthful of water, still holding the canteen with the cap swinging by its chain. "I just don't think it's possible."

"The last time we started talking about this, you shifted the conversation back to me," I said. "Not happening this time."

"Oh yeah?" she said, smirking at me. "We'll see about that."

I laughed. "You said you wanted to be a doctor, but you're scared of the time commitment, the money, and how much work it would take to get there."

She nodded. "Exactly. That's kind of a lot of things to be afraid of."

"True," I said. "But the real question is whether or not your desire for more than what you have in life is stronger than your fear of what it'd take."

"What about you?" she asked. "What about your dreams, and how you're putting them off out of loyalty to your brothers?"

I chuckled. "Nope, nice try, babe."

She huffed. "I don't know, okay? Right now, the obstacles seem pretty fucking insurmountable."

"Because you're stuck looking at the thing as a whole," I said. "You gotta break it up into smaller individual goals."

"Meaning?" she said, and took a swig, then capped the canteen and strapped it back into place.

"Meaning, instead of looking at it as, 'shit, I have to get a bachelor's degree, and then go into med school, and then do my residency, and all I have is a high school diploma,' look at it as, step one, apply to a college. From what I've heard talking to people who do have college degrees, the lower-level basic stuff isn't really important in terms of where you go to get it. So, just go somewhere local, like the community college here in Ketchikan. Get some of that bullshit out of the way close and cheap, and on your own time. Step two, get an associate's degree. Step three, get a bachelor's. Step four, decide on a university for med school. Step five, figure out how to make that work with your life and other priorities. Step six, apply, and make the move. Step seven, get through med school. Step eight, get through residency. Right now, you're at step zero—you haven't even started, so you're trying to look at the whole process at once and you get overwhelmed. Start small, start simple. Step one, babe."

"'Baby steps to the elevator,'" she quoted.

"What About Bob?" I laughed, holding out my fist and we tapped knuckles. "God, that's such a good movie." I pointed at her. "And it's good advice. Just take small, reasonable steps toward your overall goal."

"You make it sound so simple," she said, heading off down the trail ahead of me.

"I'm just saying, start by taking a couple easy courses at the community college in Ketchikan."

"I haven't set foot in a classroom in twelve years, Ram."

"So? You're plenty smart," I said, catching up to

walk beside her. "Yeah, you may be a little older than some of the other students, but I guarantee you, you won't be the only person going back to school, and you won't be the oldest person there. And if you are, so what? Who gives a fuck? You're working toward a goal. Maybe it'll take you another twelve years to get to the end of step eight, but you'll still only be forty-two by then, and even if you set your next goal as retirement by sixty-five, that's twenty-three years of practicing medicine."

"Sounds nice from here," she said, not looking at me. "But we're having a nice walk in the forest, and you're not the one going back to school."

"Izz, honey, listen—in the end, no one can make you do anything or convince you to do anything. If you want to work at Angelique's store and keep building your fashion blog then I, for one, will be happy for you—if that's what you really want. But if you want something else, you owe it to yourself to at least try, to at least take steps toward it. I have no skin in the game in terms of what you do with your life, Izzy. Right now, we're just two people who are attracted to each other, okay? Yeah, this morning was intense, but that doesn't have to mean a damn thing. I'm not saying any of this because I have any vested interest in what you do or don't do. I just happen to person- ally think it would be a big stinky load of bullshit if you have this life-long dream of being a doctor and you don't even fucking *try* to achieve it because you're fucking *scared* because it'll be *hard*."

"You didn't have to bring this morning into it," she snapped.

"Trying not to think about it?"

"No. I mean, yes. I'm trying not to think about it."

I laughed. "And how's that going for you?"

She shot me evil side-eye. "Wonderful. I haven't thought about you *or* your giant magical cock even once today. It was a totally forgettable experience, and I've definitely gotten better dick before."

I just laughed. "Okay, babe. Keep telling yourself that."

She glared at me again. "You think yours is the biggest dick I've ever had?"

I arched an eyebrow at me. "I am *not* stepping into that one, Izz. Any answer I could possibly give, you'd take the wrong the way."

"I'm not that sensitive."

"Yes, you are."

"Try me!"

"Are we talking about biggest in terms of sheer size, or best in terms of overall experience?"

"Either."

I snorted. "Now you're just being petulant."

"You have an overinflated sense of how well-endowed you are, and how good you are at sex."

I pivoted and halted to stand in front of her; I stared her down, no humor on my face, now. "If you're trying to push me away by insulting me, I'll just say be careful of getting exactly what you wish for, babe." I lifted my chin to smirk arrogantly down my nose at her. "I'm sure you've had bigger dick, and maybe you've even had better dick, but I would gamble everything I own that you've *never* in your *life* had an experience like we shared this morning, Isadora."

She stared back, blinking rapidly. "Fuck you."

And with that, she walked away. I let her, because I recognized her outburst for what it was—defensiveness. An attempt to create distance, space between us, an attempt to sever or lessen the bond this morning had created.

If nothing else, it was an attempt to piss me off so I wouldn't want to try for a repeat.

Good luck with that.

But then again, *did* I want to repeat it? Did I want to risk deepening the connection? How would that work? Rome lived in Ketchikan, blocks from the bar. Rem lived in town too, mere blocks from the tattoo studio he, Ink, and Juneau owned together. Me? I suppose I technically lived there, but it didn't feel like home. It was where I kept my shit but, truth be told, I felt more at home out here. I'd done a little sniffing around, and discovered the national parks in the area were short-staffed, so I knew with my qualifications as a smokejumper I'd get hired in a snap of my fingers. Which would mean I'd end up spending significant portions of my life out here, on the trail, in the park—exactly what I wanted, but how would that figure into having any kind of a relationship with Izzy, whether she pursued medicine or not?

It wouldn't. Even if all she did was maintain the status quo, working at the boutique and blogging, how would we ever see each other?

I scoffed out loud—was I really thinking about a *relationship* with her? What the fuck was wrong with me? I didn't do relationships. I'd never had one, didn't want one, and wouldn't know where to begin making one work even if I did.

And that's assuming Izzy wanted one with me, and it was pretty damn obvious she didn't.

The next several miles passed in silence once again, both of us lost in our own thoughts. I was mainly preoccupied with trying to talk myself out of feeling anything beyond physical attraction for Izzy— which meant reminding myself again and again to not make any moves tonight or tomorrow morning. If we had sex again, I knew without a shadow of doubt we'd only end up connecting again. It was inevitable—I could feel it simmering down inside me.

Trouble with that was, I'd never in my entire life been so insanely physically attracted to another human being. I wanted Izzy so goddamn bad it hurt. Every time she passed me on the trail, I had to shove my hands in my pockets or tangle them in my straps to keep from grabbing that perfect backside of hers. If I let my mind wander for a single fucking second, I'd be picturing the way she'd looked this morning, stepping naked from the bank down into the water like a goddess, her pale skin glowing in the predawn pink haze, her breasts heavy and full, her hips curved like a bell, thighs strong and thick and powerful, her eyes sultry and bright and aroused and eager for me.

Fuck.

If I let my mind wander, I'd end up remembering how she'd felt around my cock, that tight wet sheath pulsing around me, soft ass slapping against my hips and thighs and belly, her cries shrill and ecstatic. The way she'd looked when I lifted the blanket to peek down at her—mischievous and horny and pleased with herself.

I was a mess when we finally reached the camp-site near sundown. I was horny, irritated both at my-self and at her, hungry, and ready to just lie down and go to sleep without even making the fire or pitch-ing the tent, if only to escape my own tumultuous thoughts for a few hours.

Instead, I set about making camp with the same care as I always did. Izzy set her pack down near mine and immediately started collecting firewood, stacking piles of kindling near the ring while I pitched the tent. I chopped a couple armloads of wood while Izzy set her sleeping bag in the tent and then sat down near the newly crackling fire to rest her feet.

After I came back and set a couple larger logs on the fire, I collected my fishing gear. "Gonna go see if I can catch dinner," I said. "Wanna try your hand again?"

She shook her head without looking at me. "No, not right now."

I hesitated—she seemed morose, which was unlike her. "Izz…"

She shooed me away. "Just let it go, Ram. Not interested in talking to you right now."

I could only wonder at her thoughts, and was wise enough in the ways of women to know better than to press it. I shrugged and set off. "Fine. But stay here, please. The creek is a bit farther away from camp at this site, so if you go off trying to find it on your own, you'll just get lost."

She waved a hand at me. "Yeah, yeah. I've learned my lesson about wandering."

"Okay. I'll see in you in a while."

No answer.

I did my best to put her out of my mind as I headed for the creek. Once I found it, I chose a good spot, baited my hook, and started fishing. It was slow for an hour or so, lots of futile casting and reeling, but then after moving upstream a few hundred yards, I started getting hits. The first one got away, wriggling off the hook and taking my bait with it, and the second hit took the bait and the hook. The third hit, a good ten minutes later, netted me a decent-sized river salmon, which I put on a stringer and left in the water. I caught two more middling-sized salmon in the next thirty or so minutes; I called it a success and collapsed my pole, cleaned the fish, and carried everything back to camp.

I found Izzy exactly where I'd left her, sitting on the ground with her back against a large rock that had been positioned near the fire at some point. She glanced at me as I entered camp, but returned to staring at the fire. I decided it was best for us both if I just gave her space, so I took the fish to the other side of the fire and set about cooking them. While they roasted in their tinfoil wrapping, I heated up more beans and opened some fruit and veggies. When the fish was done, I handed Izzy her portion; she took it without comment and ate mechanically.

I was baffled by her sudden turn for the morose

and brooding, and felt a sharp urge to figure out what was wrong and try to fix it, but judging by the wary glances she kept giving me, I decided against it.

Best to just let it be, for now.

I cleaned up dinner, making sure any refuse was safely bagged and put away, and then fished my Kindle out of my pack.

Thus passed the second evening—me reading, Izzy lost in whatever thoughts were consuming her. We didn't speak a word.

Finally, well after dark, Izzy got up, took my spade, TP, and flashlight, and headed off into the darkness beyond the camp. She returned a few minutes later, replaced my things where she'd gotten them, and climbed into the tent.

I stayed up a few more hours, reading by firelight. Eventually I started yawning, so I put away my e-reader, banked the fire, and headed off into the woods to take care of my own business before heading for the tent myself. Izzy was already wrapped up in her sleeping bag, facing the wall, snoring softly, boots outside the tent, bra, socks, and jeans in a neat pile in a corner of the tent.

I fell asleep almost instantly.

I woke sometime near dawn, as usual. This time, though, Izzy was already up. I shuffled, perplexed, over to the rock near the fire, eying Izzy.

She was fully dressed, had built up the fire, and had the water heating for coffee.

"What?" she demanded. "Don't look so surprised."

"Well...I kind of am. The fire is nice and hot, and you obviously found the creek and got back to the camp on your own without getting lost."

She shrugged. "I've been watching how you make fires, and it's not that complicated, especially when you leave the coals hot like that. I can hear the creek from here, and I made sure to find some landmarks on the way there so I could find my way back."

"What'd you use for landmarks?"

"There's a tree over there that has a big double trunk with a lot of mushrooms near the base—that was the first one. Then there was a tree that had fallen across two others to make a perfect letter-A shape, and then near the creek itself there were a couple big boulders in a unique formation, so I made sure to keep the boulder formation in line of sight while I got the water and stuff, and on the way back I found the A, and then the forked tree, and then the camp."

"I bet you could've caught some fish too, if

you'd tried," I said, grinning at her as I got out the French press.

She smiled back. "I thought about it, but I wouldn't know how to bait the hook right, and I was afraid of tangling the lines and stuff, so I decided I wasn't quite ready to try fishing on my own just yet." She shrugged, looking away from me to the ground. "I was pretty proud of myself for getting to the creek and back alone, though."

"I'm proud of you, babe," I said.

"Don't patronize me," she snapped.

I frowned, shaking my head and sighing. "I wasn't. It was a genuine compliment. I don't think you'd have even considered doing that twenty-four hours ago."

She deflated, the irritation flooding out of her abruptly. "I know, I know. I'm just touchy, I guess."

The water was coming to a boil, so I pulled it off the stone and poured the steaming water over the press, set the pot in the ashes to the side of the fire ring, and pressed down the plunger.

"Hungry?" I asked her.

She nodded, eying the fire. "Yep. What's for breakfast?"

I dug the tiny camp stove out of my pack, set it up, and then carefully withdrew my package of eggs, and then the frying pan—which for such a short trip had been a bit of an indulgence, but I'd reasoned the extra weight was okay because it was a short hike.

"Eggs? Really?" she marveled, sounding genuinely excited.

I nodded. "I can't cook for shit in a kitchen, but give me a campfire and a camp stove, and I'm a fucking wizard."

"How is it different?"

I shrugged, placing the pan on the stove. "I'm hopeless in a kitchen. Too many options, too many choices. Out here, it's simple. Eggs, meat, beans, maybe some wild herbs you can find along the trail. You eat what you pack in, catch, hunt, or find, and that's it. Simple." I cracked all dozen eggs into the fry pan and stirred them up with my belt knife—which I'd also used to clean the fish and had then rinsed, sanitized, and rinsed again, and then scorched in the flames to kill any remaining bacteria. "I like things simple. Society is complicated—out here, things are a lot more basic, you know?"

I scrambled the eggs, dumped a can of beans in with the eggs, and shaved pieces of beef jerky in as well, adding a dash of my personal seasoning mix— which was just garlic, onion, and cayenne powders. In a matter of maybe ten minutes, the food was done, and we dug in.

Izzy took a couple of hesitant bites, and then

her eyes lifted to mine, wide and amazed. "Holy shit, Ram. This is incredible."

I grinned with pride. "Told you. I'm a culinary wizard on the trail. I can do a hell of a lot with a few ingredients."

She ate with gusto, occasionally blinking and coughing—I like my food spicy, so my seasoning mix contained a shitload of cayenne. "Spicy as hell, though."

"Right? Cayenne is great for you. Keeps your metabolism burning, and works as a detoxifier, too. Plus, it just adds a kick without overwhelming the flavor of the other food."

She laughed, then. "You sound like you could be on Iron Chef or something."

I echoed her words from earlier. "Don't sound so surprised."

"Sorry, you're just full of surprises. I've not known a lot of men who can truly cook." She laughed. "I mean, beyond frying burgers on a grill."

"But, let's be honest, Izz—have you ever really taken the time to get to know a guy well enough to know whether he could cook?"

I knew it was the wrong thing to say the moment it came out of my mouth. She immediately froze, lowering her fork slowly to her plate; her spine went rigid, her shoulders rolled forward, and her eyes dropped to her plate.

"Screw you, okay? What the hell do you know?"

I groaned, tipping my head back to stare at the sky. "Izzy, I'm sorry. That was an insensitive and dickish thing to say, and I apologize."

She blinked hard, sniffed, and then laughed bitterly. "What the fuck is wrong with me? Jesus." She shook her head and resumed eating, her stiff posture relaxing. "I've said pretty much exactly the same damn thing about myself, and both Kitty and Juneau have said the same thing to me, or something similar, and I just laugh it off as one of those things that's a joke but also true. I don't know why it feels different coming from you, but it does." She eyed me. "You make me so goddamned emotional, you bastard, and I hate it—mainly because I don't understand why."

"Should I speculate?" I asked.

She shook her head. "Nope," she said, her voice shutting down any further conversation on the matter.

I laughed, taking the pan, plates, forks, and my knife, and heading for the river. "Okay then. No speculation." I glanced back at her. "Be right back. If you want to use a stick to knock down the fire and spread out the coals, and then toss dirt on it, all I'll have to do to break camp is take down the tent and we can be on our way."

She nodded, standing up. "Okay." A pause. "How

long is the hike today?"

"We should reach the terminus by lunchtime or close to, I'd guess."

She nodded, and I might have been seeing things that weren't there, but she seemed a little sad at the news. But, again, no speculation, so I left it alone and went to clean up the breakfast dishes.

Twenty minutes later, we were packed up, the fire was safely killed, and the campsite was cleaner than when we got there.

I let out a gusty sigh and glanced at Izzy. "Last leg of the trip, babe," I said. "You ready?"

She met my eyes and held them for a moment, and then nodded. "Yeah, I guess so."

"Dare I ask you to elaborate?"

She scoffed. "You should know better by now."

I laughed. "Ah, right, yes. So…I'll talk to you in an hour or two?"

She set out first, not looking back at me. "You're catching on."

"Trying."

It was the best leg of the hike, by far. We saw elk and deer grazing just off the trail several times, and eagles and hawks soaring overhead, and even a bear lumbering toward the river some distance away. It was cool enough that we didn't get hot hiking, but not so cool we needed anything but our shirtsleeves. The sun was bright, bathing everything in golden-yellow light. Birds sang, squirrels chittered, the creek chuckled in the distance. Occasionally an eagle would cry high overhead, and once we even heard an elk bugle.

An hour into the hike, we were passed by a quartet of mountain bikers, two men and two women, each of them calling a cheery hello to us as they breezed down the trail.

Izzy was quiet the whole way, but she wasn't morose, now. She was alert and vibrant, looking around as if trying to see everything all at once. She had a spring in her step, her arms swinging loosely at her sides.

She didn't look at me once, though. She stayed ahead of me or behind me the whole time. And she never answered my question.

It was ten past noon when we rounded a bend in the trail and saw the terminus ahead of us—the wide lot, my truck parked off in the corner, the bus idling near the entrance to the main road.

I headed for my truck, but Izzy stopped just before stepping from the trail to the parking lot; she turned around, staring back the way we'd come, and sighed heavily.

I had an inkling as to what she was feeling, but didn't press it. I strapped my pack into the bed of my truck, took Izzy's from her and strapped it in as well, and then got into the cab.

Izzy was a little slower to get in, and when we pulled out of the parking lot, she stared at the entrance to the trail until it was out of sight. Then, once we were on the highway heading back toward Ketchikan, she let out a long, sad sigh.

"That's how I feel every single time I end a trip," I said.

She glanced at me. "How?"

"Happy and fulfilled, yet sad." I scraped a hand through my hair. "I still feel it every time, but I'm used to it by now. You're happy and fulfilled from the hike, and you're thinking about everything you saw, everything you did. You feel a sense of pride and accomplishment, but at the same time you're sad as hell because the hike is over. You're going back home, leaving the trail behind, putting away the pack and the tent, and god knows when you'll get back out on the trail again. The sadness is...complex, though. It's not just being sad that the hike over, it's...it's more of a longing. You long to be back out on the trail, under the open sky, surrounded by the woods and the rivers and the wildlife, away from everything." I waved a hand, trying to summon the right words to explain how I've felt a million times before. "Going back to civilization feels like...well, you may feel different, but to me it always feels like it felt walking into school all through my growing up. Not quite like going to prison, but close. The moment I leave the trail, I miss it and start trying to figure out when I can get back out there."

She let out another sigh. "Honestly—I'm having trouble figuring out how I feel." She stared out the window at the trees flying by. "Sad, longing, wistful, happy, fulfilled...yeah, I guess you nailed most of it. I'm also really...shocked, I suppose, at how much I—I loved it out there." She was quiet a moment or two, keeping her gaze out the window rather than on me. "I didn't expect that. I didn't expect to enjoy it at all, really. I thought I'd hate it—I really was doing it out of...of spite? Petulance? Trying to prove something to you? I don't even know. It was stupid and reckless of me, but I surprised myself. I did love it."

Finally, she looked at me, her eyes shining with emotion.

"Ram...thank you." She smiled, hesitant, careful. "You could've made me feel stupid, like a weak, useless city girl. But you didn't."

"You're not a weak, useless city girl, Izz." I paused, wanting to say a lot more but not knowing where to start. "You're not a weak, useless anything."

She didn't answer, just kept watching the scenery passing by, lost in thought as she had been since yesterday morning. I desperately wanted to know what she was thinking. I wanted inside that mind of hers as much as I wanted to be inside her in other ways.

"Penny for your thoughts?" I asked.

She scoffed, shaking her head. "You don't have enough pennies."

"Hmmm." I tapped my chin. "How about… three reciprocation-free orgasms for your thoughts?"

She laughed, eying me and then turning back to the window. "Nice try. But, no. My thoughts are not for sale."

"It was a joke."

"I know. But I just…" She rolled a shoulder. "I don't know, Ram. I'm in a weird place right now."

I felt like I was losing her, somehow. I felt her pulling away. "Izzy—"

She held up a hand. "Please, just…"

I sighed. "Okay, okay. Message received."

She looked at me, then. "Ram, I'm not trying to be bitchy, I just—"

I interrupted her. "It's fine, for real. A lot has happened on this little trip." A sliver of truth escaped me, then. "I guess I'm just hoping this isn't leading to another year of us avoiding each other."

She thunked her head against the headrest. "Gahhh—Ram. Seriously. I don't want to talk about any of that right now. I'm sorry."

"Fine. Got it." I rolled down my window and

turned up the radio.

"Ram—"

I eyed her sideways. "You don't wanna talk about, you don't wanna talk about it. No problem. Got it."

She rubbed her face, and then stared at me for a long time before turning back to the window.

The rest of the way back to Ketchikan was silent, except for the music and the rush of the wind through my open window. I dropped Izzy off at her apartment, and got out to carry her bag up for her; but, after I'd unstrapped it she took it from me.

"Got it," she said. "Thanks."

"Okay." I hesitated. "So…I'll see you later?"

She looked up at me, eyes flickering over my features, her expression carefully neutral. "Yeah. See you." She turned away and headed up to the door of the apartment building.

"Izz?"

She stopped, hand on the knob, turning to look at me over her shoulder. "Yeah?"

"That was the best hike I've had in years…if not ever."

She grinned. "That's just 'cuz you got the best pussy you've had in years, if not ever."

I laughed. "Absolutely true. Best pussy I've ever had, hands down." I winked at her. "But that's only part of why it was the best hike."

She sighed. "Okay, fine, I'll bite—what's the rest of the reason?"

I smiled, letting some of the feelings percolating deep down show on my face. "You."

Her face crumpled as if I'd said something painfully insulting or hurtful. "God*dammit*, Ram." She shook her head once, sharply, and turned away, but not before I saw the glint of a tear on her cheek.

I didn't have a chance to even start to ask what I'd said before she slipped inside and vanished behind the closing door.

Which left me nothing to do but head home, wondering.

And missing.

And wanting.

And feeling strangely empty.

Fuck.

TWELVE

Izzy

I BARELY MADE IT UP THE STAIRS AND INTO THE APARTMENT before I burst into tears. Funnily enough, Kitty and Juneau were in the same spot they'd been in when I left three days earlier, albeit wearing different clothes.

The second I entered, I closed the door behind me, dropped my pack to the ground with a loud thunk, and slumped heavily against it, finally letting out the tears I'd been fighting since yesterday morning.

Kitty clicked a button on the remote, pausing their show, and lurched off the couch to crouch in front of me.

"Izzy? What the hell?" She wrapped her arms around me. "Honey, what's going on? Talk to me!"

Juneau was right there too, then, her arms around me as well, and I couldn't breathe for their suffocating love, but it was exactly what I needed right then. I just let myself cry, and I didn't even try to hide it.

I just cried.

I hadn't bawled like this in years, and all this time I'd been pushing my feelings away, suppressing them, or repressing them, or whatever, and now it was all coming home to roost. I cried tears over issues major and minor—over my mom and dad, over being let go by the family I'd nannied for, over being poor and broke and desperate, over being homeless, over being an orphan, over being so fucking lonely sometimes it hurt...

I'd been strong and tough through all of it. But I'd been that for so long I'd forgotten how to be anything else. I'd survived on my own for *so* long.

Even after I'd found Kitty and Juneau, I'd been alone. Deep down, I knew I'd never open up to them, never let them in. They didn't know much about my past. All they knew was that I had a stepmother named Tracey who had shown up a couple years after I'd moved up here.

After sobbing for god knows how long, complete with snot and shudders and everything, I pushed to my feet and went to the bathroom, closing the door behind me, ignoring Kitty and Juneau's confused, and somewhat hurt, queries.

I blew my nose, washed my face, and spent a moment calming myself.

And then I exited the bathroom and plopped down on the couch between Kitty and June. I sighed, taking each of their hands in mine, and squeezing.

"I take it camping with Ramsey didn't go well," Kitty said, eying me warily.

I shook my head, having to stifle another burst of tears just at the mention of his name. "No, that's not…that's not quite true."

Juneau's eyes narrowed. "So, it *did* go well?"

"It went complicated, is how it went."

"You slept together?" Kitty asked.

I hesitated. "We…" I sighed. "Yes. We did."

They both stared at me expectantly, and when no further information was forthcoming, Juneau grabbed me by the shoulders and shook me. "Talk, woman! What happened? I've never seen you cry like this before, ever. Was the sex that bad?"

I sniffled, and made a sound somewhat like a laugh, but not quite a sob. "No. The sex was… earth-shaking, soul-shattering incredible."

"Earth-shaking and soul-shattering?" Juneau asked.

Kitty stared blankly at me. "So, then…what?"

I rubbed my face with both hands again. "I don't even know."

"You are being so vague and inarticulate right now, Izzy," Juneau said. "I don't even know what to ask you."

"I do," Kitty said. "What the *fuck* happened out there, honey?"

"I loved hiking," I said. "I thought I would hate it. I went into it expecting to hate it, and when we left the trail and got into his truck this afternoon, I just...I didn't want to leave. I didn't want to come back here. I wanted to keep hiking. I wanted to keep sleeping in a tent with Ram, and sitting around a fire with him, eating the fish we'd caught literally a few minutes before."

Kitty and Juneau exchanged shocked expressions.

"Um, you're serious right now?" Juneau asked.

"Absolutely."

Kitty frowned. "So...you and Ram...?"

"He literally faced down an eight-foot-tall, thousand-pound male grizzly bear." I hiccuped again, an aftereffect from crying so hard. "He surprised me so much on that hike that...I was beginning to doubt my memory of him, you know?"

Kitty tilted her head to one side. "What do you mean, doubt your memory of him?"

"Look, I know you guys have always wondered

what happened between me and Ramsey when we were all at the hospital about a year ago visiting their dad, and I met Ram and Rem for the first time."

Juneau's eyes widened. "Are you actually going to tell us what happened?"

I nodded, dropping my eyes to my lap. "I guess I haven't always been very…forthcoming…with personal details about myself, huh?"

Kitty's bark of laughter was outright derisive. "Yeah…no, not exactly."

"I'm sorry," I said. "I just…trust is hard for me, I guess."

"We can discuss that later," Juneau said.

"Just tell us what happened, and how it relates to your hiking trip," Juneau said.

I laughed. "Okay, okay." I reached down and unlaced my hiking boots, kicked them off, and stripped my socks off, wiggling my toes in relief. "I was going to just go the cafeteria and get some food and then leave. But Ram followed me out, and we started chatting as we walked, and chatting turned to flirting, and I was like, this dude is hot as fuck, right? And honestly, I was thinking you and Rome weren't going to last much longer, Kit, no offense. I just didn't see you guys lasting, much less Rem and Juneau becoming a thing. I figured in a couple weeks, a month, whatever, things would blow over and life would go back to normal and I'd never see Rem, Rome, or Ram again. So I figured, what the hell. I acted on total impulse. I didn't have a plan, I just wanted to have a little fun with a super hot dude, and that was it. Something quick, something easy, something hot but probably totally forgettable, right?"

Kitty huffed a laugh. "Not quite what happened, huh?"

I shook my head. "Not exactly, no."

"Don't leave us in suspense, here," Juneau said. "What'd you do?"

I laughed. "What the hell do you think I did? I shoved him into the nearest chair, took his dick out, and sucked him off so good he couldn't stand up when I was done."

Juneau snickered. "Oh. Right. Obviously."

I slid my arms inside my T-shirt, unhooked my bra and shrugged out of it, whipped it off, and tossed it across the room, then spent a blissful moment massaging my newly freed breasts, and then continued my story. "The dude was hung like...like no one I'd ever seen. Fucking enormous, not just long *and* thick both, but also just...*beautiful*. Like, the man's penis was a work of art.."

Kitty and Juneau exchanged looks.

"What?" I asked, laughing. "What are those looks about?"

Kitty snorted, snickered. "Honey, Ram is a triplet. Obviously there might some minute differences, but for all intents and purposes, the three of them are pretty much identical. Which means Ram's penis is an exact duplicate of both Rome's and Rem's. So... yeah. Their cocks are perfect. We get it."

I bit my lip and stifled a squeal. "Right? Fucking perfect."

"Then what happened?" Juneau asked.

"When he could finally stand up, he tossed me down into the chair, shoved my skirt up around my hips like he owned me *and* my skirt *and* my pussy, and proceeded to give me the actual best cunnilingus of my entire fucking life. I came so hard I saw stars. I screamed so loud someone called security because they thought someone was in distress. But no, it was just Ram giving me a world-class orgasm I've literally been unable to stop thinking about ever since. Then we went our separate ways after that and pretended nothing had happened."

"Except I'm stupid in love with Rome, and I happen to know for a fact that he's getting ready to propose to me," Kitty said.

"How do you know that for a fact?" Juneau asked.

"Because he took me ring shopping last week," she said. "And I picked out a ring I absolutely loved, and the store sample was my size exactly, and when I went back to try it on again, the clerk said he'd come in and bought it the very next day. And he's been acting weird lately, which means he's planning something." She waved her hands as if to dismiss this bit of information. "But we're not talking about me, we're talking about Izzy and Ram."

"The reason this story is relevant is because in the intervening year, I thought about that day nonstop." I shrugged and shook my head again. "I was doubting whether it had been real, you know? Like, had I made it up? Had I dreamed it? There was no way his cock could have been really *that* perfect, right? And there was no way his cunnilingus game was *that* good, right? A year or so later, it just didn't seem possible that it was as amazing as I remembered it."

"Understandable," Kitty said. "You said you did end up sleeping with him, though, so…was he as amazing as you remembered?"

I nodded, biting my lip. "Yeah. And then some." I sighed as I replayed in my mind the moment on the trail, and the morning in the tent.

"Wow," Kitty said, eyes wide. "You slept with him right there in the woods, on the trail?"

I laughed, shaking my head. "No. He ate me out, and then we kept hiking. He didn't even let me return the favor."

"I'm surprised you didn't insist," Juneau said,

"knowing how you feel about BJs."

"Honestly, I was so shell-shocked by the intensity of the orgasm he'd just given me, I wasn't thinking clearly." I rolled a shoulder. "Plus, I was dealing with being surprised by the fact that I was enjoying hiking with him, and enjoying his company. I mean, he's annoying and arrogant and all that, but he can be sweet and funny, and even the arrogance is kinda hot, when it's not utterly infuriating."

"Trust me, I *know*," Kitty and Juneau said in unison, and then glanced at each other, cackling.

"So then when did you sleep with him?" Juneau asked.

I laughed. "You're really antsy for the details, ain'tcha, June-bug?"

She shrugged with a cutesy, demure grin. "Yeah, I kinda am. So what?"

"So nothing. Just loving how much Remington has opened you up to the wonders of sluttery."

Juneau rolled her eyes. "It's not sluttery if it's with the one man you're in love with, ding-dong."

"Oh," I said. "Good point."

She waved a hand. "Enough chitchat. On with the lurid details."

"I was honestly still intending to not actually sleep with him, as in no actual sex. I thought maybe I'd blow him, and we'd trade innocent sexy times that didn't involve any actual intimacy."

Kitty scoffed. "Because *that* is *totally* going to work."

Juneau eyed me, frowning thoughtfully. "But... *why not?*"

Kitty elbowed her. "Because she *likes* him. Duh. And she doesn't want to like him, and she knows having actual sex with him will lead to liking him even more, if not just flat out falling in love with him and, for whatever reason, she just can't handle *that* particular possibility."

I glared at Kitty. "I am *not* in love with Ramsey Badd."

"Anyway, I fell asleep in the tent, and when I woke up the next morning, he was gone. So I went looking for him. I found him down at the river. And he was... god, he was naked. Beautifully, gloriously naked. The man's body is just...just...pure art. He was hip-deep in the water, and his cock wasn't quite covered, and he convinced me to get in the river with him, and—"

"Wait," Juneau interrupted. "The river? You went skinny-dipping in the river? Wasn't it cold?"

I laughed. "Fuck yes it was! Breathtakingly cold. But he was in the water, so I got in. And we...we horsed around. Just played in the water together, and scrubbed each other with a bar of soap ...it was like a sex scene from a historical romance novel. This big, rough, long-haired, bearded, ripped sex-god of a man, naked in a river? It was absolutely fucking primal. *He* was primal, and you know I don't use fancy words like that lightly. We washed each other, and then I ended up getting my first full, erm…hands-on, shall we say, look at his cock since that day at the hospital. And it was every bit as perfectly, gloriously mouthwatering as I remembered."

"So then you fucked in the river?" Juneau asked.

I laughed. "Nope, wrong again. We didn't fuck in the river. Or on the bank." I couldn't help another dreamy grin and sigh. "We raced naked back to the tent, and we fucked in the tent."

"And?" Kitty demanded.

"And what?"

Kitty glared at me. "And what was it like? We are your best friends, and we demand all the dirty, filthy, salacious details."

I hesitated a very, very long time. "I…it was…" I sighed. "I don't know how to describe it."

Juneau snorted. "Yes, you do." She wiggled her eyebrows at me. "You just want to keep the details to yourself."

I considered this. "I guess maybe you're right." I groaned, putting my face in my hands. "Which is weird. I've never felt any hesitation about sharing details before. I don't understand it."

Kitty wrapped an arm around my shoulders. "Izzy, babe. Sweetheart. My dear, sweet, clueless friend—"

I stood up and paced away, shouting. "I AM NOT IN LOVE WITH RAMSEY, GODDAMMIT."

"Why don't you want to be?" Juneau asked. "Once you get over the initial scariness of it, being in love is amazing. Having someone in your life every single day, all day, all night, all the time, who loves you, accepts you, as you are, who is committed to you, who wants you even when you feel ugly and stupid and crazy and hormonal? It's absolutely the best thing ever."

"Our lives don't match up!" I cried. "He's going to join the park rangers and live in the fucking woods, and I—I…" I was about to sob again, and took a moment to gather myself before starting over. "I want to go back to school."

My friends exchanged yet another shocked stare. "You…what?" Kitty asked.

"It's something Ram and I talked about during the hike. I've always wanted…" I swallowed hard. "I've always wanted to be a doctor."

Juneau shot to her feet, laughing abruptly. "Really?"

"Why the hell is this the first we've ever heard of this?" Kitty asked.

I groaned again. "Because it's stupid. I'm thirty. I barely graduated high school. I have zero work experience outside Angelique's shop."

"You want to be a *doctor*?" Juneau said, as if trying to figure out what the words meant. "Why?"

"My dad was a doctor."

"Why do I feel like you went on that hike with Ram and the Izzy we've known for years came back as someone else entirely?" Kitty asked.

"I—" I shrugged. "He has this way of...of...of getting me to talk about myself in a way no one else ever has. He made me think about myself, my past, and the things I've been trying to escape for twelve, fifteen years, things I've been trying to hide from, and to forget about."

Juneau sat back down beside me. "You're going to have to elaborate, Izz."

So, I told them the story I'd told Ram over the course of two days. I opened up to Juneau and Kitty in a single long, unbroken tale. Growing up in an idyllic home with a mom and a dad who loved each other deeply, and me especially, being a spoiled rotten only child, weekends with Daddy, dance class and shopping after school with Mom...and then Mom dying in that accident, and that endless afternoon waiting for my mother to show up...

"I...I guess I've always felt like Mom...abandoned

me," I whispered. "She never showed up that day. Up until that point, Mom was my constant. Dad was always at work during the week, and a lot of weekends, being one of the best surgeons in the state. But Mom was…she was my true north. Always there. And then, one day, she wasn't."

"She didn't abandon you," Kitty said, hugging me close. "Not on purpose."

"I know!" I wailed. "I know! Intellectually, I *know* she didn't, like, *leave* on purpose. She was killed in an accident…" I sucked in a sharp breath and held it till my lungs hurt. "She didn't die immediately. She was taken to the hospital—the same one my dad was at. But he wasn't her surgeon. Someone else was. And he couldn't save her. They worked on her for hours, I guess, but they couldn't save her. She died on the operating table."

Juneau sniffled, burying her face in my shoulder. "Oh, honey. And you feel like if you could be a doctor, you could save others."

I nodded. "Yeah. Except I never got that chance. I was so busy taking care of Daddy and the house that I missed a lot of school. If I made it to school half the week, I was lucky. When he was home, Daddy needed me constantly. When he wasn't home, I was the only one capable of or willing to keep the house up. Then he remarried and my life got even worse. She and her daughter were worse than lazy and useless. All they cared about was Dad's assets. I don't even have a single fucking thing of my mother's to remember her by, because Tracey bagged up every last item of my mothers and carted it all to fucking Goodwill while I was at school." I sobbed, wiping my eyes. "I was so mad, you don't even know. It took both Daddy and Trina to hold me back from physically beating the shit out of Tracey for doing that. I never spoke to her again until that day she showed up here trying to swindle me out of my inheritance."

"So that's what that visit of hers was about?" Juneau said, piecing the events together.

I nodded. "Yeah. She'd convinced Dad to write a new will, leaving everything to her to administer. His lawyer, the executor of his estate, fought for two years to get it tossed it out, but because I wasn't there to be part of the court hearing, Tracey won—she just needed me to sign off, relinquishing my claim on Daddy's estate."

"Holy shit," Kitty breathed. "What a bitch!"

"You didn't sign, did you?" Juneau asked.

"Yeah, I did."

Juneau boggled at me. "But...*why*?"

I shrugged. "I didn't care anymore. At that point it was just money, you know?"

Kitty shook her head. "No, Izzy, we don't know."

I scrubbed my face. "After Mom died, Daddy gave up. I reminded him of Mom, so he avoided me, except when he needed me to do things for him. He worked eighteen to twenty hours a day, seven days a week for three years straight, until he finally just died. I think technically it was a heart attack, but it was in his sleep. He went to bed one night and died of a broken heart. Tracey had just been someone to keep his dick wet and his bed warm until he was ready to die."

Kitty reared away from me in disgust. "Isadora Styles, that's a *horrible* thing to say!"

"It's the fucking truth!" I shouted, standing up and stomping across the room to whirl around on them both. "He's the one who really fucking abandoned me! Mom died and he gave up! He shut down; quit caring about me, about himself, about our life, about everything. Once Mom died, I was alone. Then he sent me away to Minnesota to live with an aunt I'd never even met, because he didn't fucking want me anymore! When he did finally let me come back home to Memphis, he was just…gone. His body physically existed, but his mind and heart were in that grave with Mom, and I was alone."

"Oh my god, Izzy, I'm so sorry," Juneau said with tears in her eyes, "—*we're* so sorry. I wish we could do or say something to make it better, but please, just know we're here for you, we love you, and we support you."

"So this is why you won't let yourself be loved by anyone," Kitty whispered. "Because your mom died, and then your dad abandoned you, so now you don't trust anyone else not to do the same thing."

Juneau shuddered, a sigh escaping her lips. "Even us, you've never really trusted us."

"It wasn't you," I whispered. "I love you guys more than I can say, and I don't know what I'd have done without you. I just...I don't know *how* to trust anymore."

Kitty slid off the couch to kneel in front of me. "Izzy. Listen to me, please. If you love me, if I've ever said anything that you're capable of truly hearing, let it be this."

I saw her through a wavering haze of tears. "I'll try."

"You've spent the last fifteen years of your life alone, isolated, cut off from everyone, even us."

"I know," I whispered.

"One person, in all those years—*one*—has been able to see through your mile-high, mile-thick walls to the woman you really are inside. *One* person has gotten through those walls, and in a single weekend, he broke you open like a coconut." She took my face in her hands. "Ramsey opened the floodgates, Izz. He saw your pain and the bullshit you hid behind, he called you on it, and got you to open up to him in a way no other human being ever has. You felt safe enough with him to trust him with your past—we've been your best friends for almost *ten* fucking goddamn *years* and we didn't know *any* of this. But you told *him* about it?" She sobbed, sniffed, and then sighed. "I admit I'm more than a little hurt by that, to be honest, but if Ramsey Badd can accomplish all this in two and a half days? I'm all for it. But it's all *him*, Izzy. It's him. Don't you see that?"

For the second time that day, and the third time in as many days, I was ugly crying.

"I know," I whisper-sobbed. "I know."

"So admit you love him, you idiot!" Juneau shouted, louder than I've ever heard her shout in her life. "Get off your big fat ass and go tell him you love him!"

"My ass is *not* fat," I said, hiccuping.

Juneau rolled her eyes. "Oh, get over yourself," she snapped. "It's an expression and you know it. If anyone in this room has an actual fat ass, it's me, but you don't see me whining about it, do you?"

"Your ass isn't any fatter than mine or hers," Kitty said, "so you can shut up about that too, June."

I let out a bark of amused yet annoyed laughter. "Can we stop talking about our big fat asses for five seconds and get back to my fucked-up life?"

Kitty shook me like a rag doll. "You just have to woman up and accept that you're in love with Ramsey, and see where that leads you."

I blinked away tears. "I'm so scared, though. What if he—"

"He won't," Juneau cut in. "Rome didn't. Rem didn't. Ram won't either."

"Give that man half a chance, and he'll love you so hard you'll be looking for ways to get away from him for five seconds so you can even pee alone," Juneau said, laughing. "Trust me on that."

"So what do I do?" I asked. "Just...show up and be like, hey Ram, I'm in love with you, please love me back and don't abandon me?"

Kitty and Juneau both nodded seriously, as if I hadn't obviously meant that sarcastically.

"Yes," they both said in unison.

I blinked. "Wait...really?"

Kitty shrugged. "Those men don't play bullshit games. Give him the raw unvarnished truth—just tell him how you feel, what you're afraid of, and give him a chance."

"Just like that? After one weekend?"

"One weekend?" Juneau laughed. "Woman, you fell in love with that man that day in the hospital. You've been in love with him for over a year--you've just been running away from it."

I frowned. "I was in love with his penis, and his oral sex skills. I knew literally nothing else about him."

"Izzy, at least be honest with yourself," Kitty said. "It was never about his cock, or his oral sex skills, or his looks, and you know it. You *connected* with him on a whole different level than with anyone else, and that's why you ran from him the way you did. But you spent the intervening year building it up in your mind, doubting it, fantasizing about him…and then when you actually did have sex with him—"

"It was even better than my fantasies," I whispered. "I told him my fantasy, or one of them, at least, and he made it come true, and my fantasy was silly and pathetic and stupid compared to what the reality with him was like."

"Because at the root of it all, it's not about the sex," Kitty said.

"The sex is just icing on the cake," Juneau added. "Really hot icing on a really hot cake."

I sighed. "Fine. Fine, fine, fine. You're both right, and I know it. I've always known it."

"You're in love with him," Kitty said. "Let me hear you admit it out loud."

I shook my head. "No. He's going to be the first person to hear me say those words."

Kitty clapped her hands and squealed in joy. "Yes!

That's exactly what I was hoping you'd say."

"Now go get him!" Juneau said, shoving off the couch.

"I need to shower and change first," I said. "The only bath I've had in the last three days was in the river, and it was followed by sex."

"Nope," Juneau said, and she and Kitty hauled to my feet. "Now. Just like you are."

They shoved me to the door, opened it, and pushed me out.

I protested, "Wait! I at least need a pair of shoes!"

Kitty tossed a pair of flip-flops at me. "There. Now go."

I still hesitated. "I'm fucking terrified."

"Good," Juneau said. "That means its all the more real. Buck up, buttercup. You can do this. You *have* to."

I took a fortifying breath. "Fine. But I'm going to do it my way."

They both nodded, and Kitty leaned forward to kiss me on the forehead. "Fine," she said, "do it your way, whatever that is. As long as it results in you telling Ramsey Badd that you love him, want him, and need him, and that you're not accepting no for an answer."

And so I marched down the stairs, forty-eight hours without a shower, wearing Kitty's too-small flip-flops, braless, to tell a man I was in love with him.

THIRTEEN

Ramsey

T HE BOYS WERE BOTH GONE—REMINGTON WAS DOING a tattoo, and Rome was off taking a food service management course, and my cousins were running the saloon. This left me to putz around the apartment by myself. I cleaned and put away my gear, contemplated taking a shower but didn't have the energy for it, contemplated making food but didn't feel like expending the effort…

I found myself at the refurbished iMac my brothers and I shared, updating my resumé and emailing it to the HR department of the National Park Service, attaching the letter of recommendation my brothers and I had all received from our superiors in both the hotshot and smokejumper crews. And then, with nothing better to do, I changed into workout clothes and jogged over to Baxter's gym.

His gym was huge, clean, well-lit—and the center of the warehouse space was dominated by a boxing ring. There were massive power racks along three of the outside walls, and racks of high-end bumper plates at regular intervals; the fourth side was reserved for a trio of hanging heavy bags and a pair of speed bags, and the doorway to Baxter's little office. I walked in and was assaulted by a palpable wall of sound—grinding, chugging, shrieking heavy metal pounding from expensive speakers suspended from the ceiling at all four corners of the warehouse. Bax himself was in the ring, barefoot, shirtless, a mouthguard protecting his teeth and professional gloves on his hands—he was sparring with a lean, hard, quick-fisted young Hispanic guy. Bax was obviously going slow and letting the younger boxer take his shots, only occasionally taking a jab here and there. I watched them spar for a few minutes, and noted the way Baxter danced and ducked and weaved, getting his trainee to reveal his strengths and weaknesses. Finally, when the younger guy started to visibly flag, Bax held up a glove to stop the fight. He used his teeth to untie his right glove, wedged it under his left arm and tugged his hand free so he could remove his mouthguard. The other fighter did the same, sweating profusely and out of breath, whereas Bax was barely winded and only had a light sheen of sweat on his forehead.

"Okay, Luis, I've got some homework for you, buddy," Bax said. "Number one, conditioning, man. You're smoked and we only went fifteen minutes, and I was going easy on you. You've got the foot-work down pat, no question, and your hands are quicker'n greased lightning, but you gotta be able to last longer. Number two, strength—you need to build up a bit more power behind your punches. I ain't gonna even put you in the ring yet. You could win fights, probably, but I think if you spent a few more months training, you'd go into the circuit and you'd seriously wreck some motherfuckers. So I want you to focus on those two things—endurance, and power. You're plenty strong, but you need more power, and you gotta be able to sustain that power for several rounds."

Luis was nodding. "I gotchu, Bax, I gotchu. Power and endurance. Got it."

Bax clapped Luis on the shoulder with his still-gloved left hand. "Hit the road, kid. You're good for today."

Luis swung out of the ring between two of the ropes, hopped down, and headed for the showers, which were next to the office. Bax hopped down too, unlacing his other glove and heading over to me.

"What up, cuz?" he said, holding out a fist.

I shrugged, tapping knuckles with him. "I need to blow off some steam."

Bax jerked his chin at the ring. "That kinda steam?" He jerked a thumb at the closest power rack, next. "Or that kind?"

I indicated the power rack. "That kind."

Bax nodded, but I could tell he was scrutinizing me. "Tell me one thing, first."

"Okay?"

"Are we trying to shred you out of thinking about a certain someone?"

I sighed in frustration. "Honestly, yes."

Bax nodded again. "A'ight. I'll work you out till you're half dead, but I'm gonna warn you right now, it won't work for long."

He was as good as his word—for the next eighty minutes Baxter put me through the most brutally punishing workout of my life. For those eighty minutes, I benched, squatted, deadlifted, pushed and pulled a loaded sled, did dozens of burpees and hundreds of pushups and pull-ups. By the time Bax called it quits, I was barely able to stay on my feet, and couldn't lift my arms more than waist high.

He was as good as his word in another respect as

well—the minute I stopped exerting myself, I started thinking about Izzy again.

Bax saw it, too. "Told you."

I groaned, leaning against the boxing ring. "It sucks, dude. I don't know what to do."

"Want to talk about it?"

I shrugged. "Not much to say. We went hiking together, camped out together...finally slept with her, and it was...well, better than I'd even imagined it could be. But after that, after we slept together, she just...withdrew."

"Sex or love?" Bax asked.

"Huh?"

"Was it sex...or was it love?"

I growled. "Fuck if I know."

"Can't help you if you don't tell me the fuckin' truth, cuz."

"Neither, and both."

Bax chuckled. "That means it was love. Or the beginnings of it. If you have sex with a chick and it's just fucking, and you both know it, that's easy-peasy. But if you have sex with a girl and you both know it's something else, too? That's when shit gets complicated, and complicated means at least one of you, and probably both of you, have feelings you're not willing to deal with. Which means it's most likely the beginnings of love—*at least* the beginnings, if not flat out the real deal."

I laughed. "Okay, Dr. Phil."

Bax eyed me weirdly. "You know, last time I talked to Izzy, she said basically the same thing--she called me Dr. Phil. What the fuck is with that?"

"You're like some love expert or something."

"Nah," he said, waving a hand. "I am an expert on bullshitting myself into thinking I'm not in love when I am, though. Eve had to bludgeon me upside the head with the fact that we were perfect for each other before I could accept it, and now I guess I'm just more easily able to see that in others, and articulate it."

"But if she won't see it, if she won't even give us the chance to talk about that possibility, what the fuck am I supposed to do?"

He shrugged. "Jack off a lot and hope she comes around eventually."

I cackled. "Wow. I don't think Dr. Phil would say that."

He slapped my shoulder. "Dude, I wish there was something else I could tell you, but if she's still in denial about her feelings or whatever, there's just not much you can do. Neither you nor anyone else can force her to accept the reality of being in love with you. If she doesn't want it, can't handle it, won't consider it, you're just...fucked. You can keep trying, but eventually you're going to either get through to her, or...not." He eyed me. "You in love with her?"

I stared at the floor and lifted one shoulder about half an inch. "I could be."

Bax was silent for a moment. "That's a pussy answer."

I stared hard at him. "Fuck you."

He just laughed. "You know I'm right. You wanna lace up and step into my office"—here, he gestured at the ring—"be my guest."

I growled again. "Fuck, man. How can I say I'm in love with her if I've only spent the one weekend with her? We fooled around a bit and slept together one time, and then she barely spoke to me the rest of the trip. Said she needed time to 'process' things."

Bax shoved me toward the door. "Go home, bro. My advice? Give her time. If there was a connection and she's got the balls to own it, she'll come around."

I sighed. "Yeah, I guess you're right."

"You wanna talk, spar, or work out, I'm here more often than not. The door's always open for you, Ram."

"Thanks, Bax."

He grinned, clapped me on the shoulder. "That's what family's for, dude. Now go shower. You stink."

I gave him the finger over my shoulder as I headed for home. Lost in thought, I trudged home, sore everywhere, my legs jelly, my arms and chest and shoulders burning, my abs shredded. I barely saw the sidewalk at my feet as I walked, so lost in thought was I.

If she never came around, what would I do? Get over her, eventually. But I knew for a fact that even if I managed to get hard for another woman, she wouldn't make me feel the way Izzy had. And I didn't want another woman—I wanted *her*.

God, this sucked.

Would she come around? She didn't seem willing to even talk about what had happened between us, so what did that say about my chances? Not much of anything good, I decided.

I reached the apartment, trudging absently through the kitchen to the hallway, stripping on the way to the shower. I smelled something odd—a note of...perfume? Something like that. I chalked it up to Kitty or Juneau having been here recently, and shrugged it off, twisting on the shower. While I waited for the water to heat up, I brushed my teeth.

I got into the shower, hissing at the scalding hot water. I washed my hair and beard, and was rinsing, my eyes squeezed shut, when I thought I heard something. A door opening somewhere? I waited, listening, but I had shampoo in my eyes so I didn't open them to look.

Another rinse, and then wiping my face I opened my eyes.

Izzy was in the shower with me, naked, her hair loose around her shoulders, damp and sticking to her pale skin.

I blinked. "Ummm. Hi. You're—here."

She didn't smile. "Yeah. I'm here."

I still had suds in my beard, and had a palmful of conditioner. "I…um. I wasn't expecting you."

She laughed, a quiet huff. "I know."

A long, tense silence blossomed between us. I couldn't take my eyes off of her, and didn't bother trying. She was so beautiful, so perfect.

My heart ached, just looking at her.

"Izzy, I…" I had no idea where to start, and trailed off.

She stepped forward, took my wrist in her hand and twisted my palm face down over hers, smearing the conditioner off of my hand onto hers. She rubbed it between both hands, and then reached up and began massaging it into my hair, working it from scalp to ends with her fingertips. I groaned at the feeling of her strong, nimble fingers massaging my scalp, and let my eyes close.

I felt her splash water onto my beard, rinsing

out the last of the suds, and then felt her fingers comb through my beard, smoothing it, playing with it.

I opened my eyes and looked down at her, wanting to say something—to ask what this was, if it was more of what we'd had in the tent: sex that meant *something*.

Her eyes were wide and full of expressive emotion, a myriad of meaning, a hazel-green tumult of intensity.

"Izz—" I started.

Two of her fingers touched my lips. "Shush, Ramsey," she muttered. "Close your eyes again."

"But I want to talk about—"

"I know," she cut in. "I know. We will."

"We will?"

She touched my lips again. "Yes. Later. Promise." She brought her fingers up to my eyelids, and ever so gently touched them. "Close your eyes, Ram. Trust me."

She twisted me so my back was to the far wall of the shower, opposite the showerhead, the water beating down on her back. Reaching up, she tilted the head so the water sprayed more directly downward, and then stared up at me, waiting.

"Come on, Ram," she said. "I'm here. Just... trust me, okay?"

I heaved a deep breath, and then nodded. "Okay."

I closed my eyes.

Leaned against the wall, and let my hands hang loose at my sides.

I felt her hands roaming my body, skating over my shoulders, tracing my chest, my abs. I groaned as her hands wrapped around my cock, and then I gasped aloud when I felt her slide me into her mouth. I had to look—had to open my eyes. She met my gaze, her eyes full of lust and heat and…more. Something else.

I didn't dare speculate what, though.

For another minute, almost two, Izzy caressed my balls with one hand, stroked my cock just below where her mouth slid and out in a slow, sucking rhythm. And then faster, and faster, and the faster she went, the harder her tits bounced against my thighs, and the harder my balls ached, the harder my cock throbbed inside her warm wet mouth.

"Izzy—" I groaned. "Fuck, fuck, fuck…that feels *so* fucking amazing."

"Don't stop me, this time," she said, her lips whispering against the tip of my cock.

"Izz…"

"Please. Promise me you won't."

I shook my head. "I can't promise you that."

She huffed in annoyance, and then her expression shifted, to one of defiance, or determination. Massaging my balls with both hands, then, she buried me deep in her mouth, in her throat, swallowing around me, and started bobbing, cradling my sac in her hands, caressing them ever more tightly, until she finally placed her middle and ring fingers along the underside of my sac and pressed hard, taking my cock deeper and deeper, bobbing hard and fast—faster than I'd have thought was possible.

God, oh god, oh god—it was too much, too much to hold out against. I knew what she was doing—she was saying goodbye. One last hurrah before she vanished from my life for good.

"Izzy, *fuck...*" I growled, snarling my fingers into the thick wet mass of her golden-copper hair. "I don't want to say goodbye like this, goddammit."

She paused, then, and pulled away so my aching cock plopped free of her mouth, swaying in front of her lips as she glanced in shock up at me. "Say goodbye? What are you talking about, Ram?"

I kept my expression carefully neutral. "That's what this is, I assume. You, saying goodbye. Trying to be nice or something, get one last bit of fun out of me, the safe way, before you leave for good."

Her brows furrowed as she stared up at me. "That's what you think this is?"

I nodded. "Well…yeah."

"Why?"

"I mean…it just seems like that, I guess. Why else would you show up in my shower and want to suck me off me instead of just having sex with me?"

She stood up slowly, her expression shifting from puzzlement to…I honestly wasn't sure what. All I knew was she was caught in the grip of some strange, strong emotion I didn't understand, couldn't read—she was acting weird, and that worried me.

She turned off the water, shoved aside the curtain and snagged the clean towel I'd hung there. With soft, slow, gentle movement, Izzy toweled me off and then herself. Tossing the towel to the floor, she stepped out of the shower and led me by the hand out of the bathroom and into my bedroom.

She closed my door, and locked it.

"I guess I went about this all wrong, didn't I?" she said. "I thought you'd want that instead."

"Want what?"

"My mouth."

"Instead of what?"

"Instead of…me," she said, gesturing at her body with a sweep of her hand.

"Honestly, Izzy, I have zero fucking clue what's going on with you right now, or what you want, or what you're doing. I just know I'm freaked out."

She stared at me in silence for a moment, blinking slowly, owlishly, thinking hard. Choosing her words, her next action.

"This is hard for me, Ram. What I'm doing—what I want. I don't know how to do it, how to say it. I was trying to show you instead of having to say it, but I guess that didn't work."

"Izzy, let me make one thing clear to you. There is a huge difference to me between you blowing me, us fucking, and whatever the hell that was we did in the tent yesterday morning, which, by the way, was a helluva lot more than just fucking. To me, you blowing me is…extra. It's fun. I enjoy it. Obviously I do—it feels amazing, and if I could have you do that forever without having to come, without having it end, that would be heaven." I brushed my palm against her cheek. "But having sex with you? We only did it once, and it was…better than heaven. It was more than just fucking, Izzy, and we both know it. If you're saying goodbye, if this thing between us, whatever it is, is over—if you're leaving for med school, or just aren't interested or willing to explore what's going on with us, then by all means, finish what you started in the shower. If this is goodbye, Izzy, then get on your knees and put those lips around my cock, and take my cum down your throat. That'll be goodbye enough for me."

She stared up at me. "Ramsey…"

I waited. "Isadora?"

She sucked in a deep breath, reaching up with visibly shaking hands to rake them through her damp hair. "Lay down on the bed." She put her warm hands on my chest and pushed me backward toward the bed. "Please?"

I did as she asked, scooting onto the bed and lying in the center, my head on the pile of pillows, watching her. I expected her, truthfully, to kneel over my hips and do as I'd said—to say goodbye.

Instead, she crawled onto the bed from the foot end, prowling on all fours over my body, her breasts draping against me. She paused with her breasts over my cock, using the tips of them to caress me—and holy fuck were they soft, and warm, making me throb painfully. Instead of staying there, she kept going. Continued prowling up my torso like a hungry lioness stalking her prey. Her eyes were bright, fiery, fierce, determined. That nameless emotion I kept seeing flashing through in brief but powerful glimpses was fully evident now, and I saw the shape of what it was, but didn't dare think it.

I wanted to hope, wanted to believe, but didn't dare.

So, I let it play out.

I kept my hands tucked under my head, my

expression neutral.

She crawled up until her knees were on either side of my hips, her hands beside my face. Her soft, heavy, warm breasts slid to drape hot against my chest. "This isn't goodbye, Ramsey."

"No?"

She shook her head. "No." She lifted one hand, showing me how it was trembling. "I'm fucking terrified right now, Ram."

"Just tell me what's going on, then, if it's not goodbye."

She huffed a frightened laugh. "Can't you guess by now?"

"I don't want to guess, Izzy." I needed to touch her—had to. While she was still here. I didn't quite believe her, and wouldn't until it was crystal clear, spoken out loud between us. "I want to *know*."

I caressed her, then—ran my hands over the hot silk of her skin from shoulders to waist, over her arms, reaching down to clutch her ass before sliding my palms up her back, burying them in her hair. Back down to grip her hips, and then gave in to the need that ruled beneath all—

I palmed her face in both hands, and brought her mouth down to mine. I kissed her, slowly, deeply. I demanded her breath, demanded her tongue. I kissed her as if it was goodbye—I kissed her as a plea to not let it be goodbye.

Shaking all over, I ended the kiss.

She parted from my lips with a sob, touching her forehead to mine. Bracing her weight with one hand, she caressed my cheek with the other, tracing my lips with a thumb.

"Ram…" she breathed. "God, the way you kiss me…"

"What about it, Izzy?"

"Do it again. Kiss me like that again." She tangled her fingers in my beard. "Kiss me like that again…and this time, Ram? Don't stop."

I nearly sobbed at that myself, but didn't. My breath did catch, though, and my throat burned. My chest filled, swelled, expanded, cracked. Shaking all over, I wrapped my arms around her, enveloping her entirely, and kissed her with everything I was.

I devoured her mouth, let all my need and desperation and fear and wonder explode. She gasped, and returned the kiss with all of that, and more.

Her lips trembled against mine, her breathing came in gasps and snatches—we had to pause to breathe, and then our mouths clashed together again, lips and tongues and teeth crashing and tangling.

She whimpered and pulled away reluctantly, as if too overcome to be able to kiss me any longer but my kiss was life, breath, and meaning. "Ram…Jesus, Ram," she breathed.

"Tell me, Izzy," I whispered against her lips. "Tell me. Show me."

"Ram."

"Tell. Me." I held her against me, pinned her body hard against mine. "Say it—*say…it.*"

She lifted her hips, reaching between us to wrap her fist around my painfully hard erection. Stroked me once, twice. Lifted further, so she was on her hands and knees again. I let her rise, but I watched her. Held on to her hips with both hands.

She clutched me tightly and just held on to me for a long, tense moment. And then she fell forward against me, smashing her breasts to my chest and her mouth against mine, sobbing.

"Ram—" she wept.

And with a single slow writhe of her hips, I was inside her slick wet center. I cried out, a pathetically soft, weak, shaking moan of sheer ecstasy—we were bare, nothing between us. I knew it, she knew it. Our eyes met, and the meaning of it passed between us, the fact that I was buried bare deep inside her, our hips pressed together, her belly trembling against mine as she fought to breathe, her breasts flattened against my chest, her forehead now bumping against mine.

We didn't move. We just stayed like that, Izzy on top of me, fully impaled on me, shaking all over, whimpering softly, shuddering as if restraining sobs. I ached. I was so full with the need to release that it was a sharp spearing pain, but I held on. A single thrust, and I'd explode inside her, and we both knew it.

I shook with the exertion of holding back. "Izzy—" I snarled her name, and then bit her lip. "Say it."

She shook her head, lifting up on her hands, head hanging, sobbing. "I can't. I'm so scared it's not real, that you're not—that you won't—"

I held utterly still, moving only my hands, then. I cupped her face in my hands and lifted her chin so she had to look at me—except she had her eyes squeezed shut tight.

"Open your eyes, Isadora."

She obeyed, slowly. "Ram. I...I want to, I'm trying to; I'm just..." She shook her head without taking her eyes from mine.

So very softly, gingerly, carefully, I touched my lips to hers. Kept my hands cupped around her cheeks so she couldn't look away.

"I fucking *love* you, Izz," I said, snapping it. More softly, then. "I love you."

She sobbed again, and brought her face to mine,

tears streaming down her cheeks—I tasted her tears as she locked her lips to mine.

"Say it again," she pleaded in a barely audible whisper.

"I love you, Izzy."

She laughed softly, her lips curving against mine. Then, pulling her face away an inch or so, enough that she could look into my eyes, she writhed her hips away from mine, gliding my cock between those sweet, tender, tight lips of hers. Paused at just the right moment, when the very tip of me was left nestled just inside her.

She knew—she *knew* somehow how close I was. She felt it, felt me.

Another laugh, louder, more joyful and less disbelieving. She fell forward against me, burying her face in the side of my neck, her hands on my cheeks, fingers tangling in my beard. She fluttered lightly, teasingly, drawing a pained moan from me.

"Izz, fuck..." I snarled. "You need to hear it again?"

She laughed, nodded. "Yeah, I do. One more time."

I slid my hands down her back, grinning at her as I cupped her ass, holding her in place. "I love you, Isadora Styles." I held the crease of her hips, thumbs against the twin points of her hipbones. "I love you,

Izz. I love you."

She sobbed another laugh, and slapped her hips down against mine, driving me into her. I cried out, a feral snarl as my climax ripped through me like a lightning bolt. "Ram—Ram…I love you, god, I fucking love you, Ram!" She snaked her arms around my neck as I lifted my head to smash my mouth against hers, even as she began to chant those three words in time with our clashing, manic thrusts.

"I love you—I *love* you—I *love* you," she breathed, over and over, her hips rolling fluidly against mine, taking me into her again and again as my orgasm shredded through me.

I came so hard I saw stars, a nova-hot explosion blasting me into gasping, snarling pieces. I thrust helplessly up against her, but now the pace and movements were all hers, I was too rigid with the crushing, grinding intensity of the climax. She bit my neck and then nipped my lips, and then we were kissing, and Izzy's hips rolled and her ass slapped against me and I drove into her. She was so wet, so slick, so tight—I felt myself coming inside her, felt her pulsating around me, and I'd never in my life felt anything so wild, so intense as Izzy spasming around me, heard nothing so sweet as her screaming that she loved me as she came.

Her lips fumbled against mine, and she was still

chanting *I love you, I love you, I love you* every time our bodies met, every time I crushed into her hot clenching wet center, and I felt her coming, felt my release pouring out of me, and I couldn't speak, couldn't breathe, could only just barely manage to pray her name—*Izzy, Izzy, Izzy*—as I lost all control.

I rolled over, arms around her, clenching her against my body with all my strength, so hard she squeaked and gasped, but her own grip on me only tightened to match the ferocity of mine, and we were grinding together, gasping mouth to mouth, salt on my lips and on hers—my tears or hers? I didn't know, didn't care, didn't care if I was crying because like this, with her, it was right, it was perfect, it was love.

At last—at long, long last, Izzy rolled us again so she was on top once more, and she lifted up to sit upright on top of me. I cupped her breast, tweaked her nipple, and she giggled, writhing away but not stopping me.

Her eyes fixed on mine. "It's not goodbye, Ram," she breathed. "It's...hello. It's I love you."

"Izzy—"

"It's please, please, *please*—" and here her voice broke. "Please...promise me you'll love me and never stop. Promise me, Ram. Promise me you won't abandon me."

Her hands raked compulsively down my chest. I was still inside her, and I'd just come—but how long had we lain together in panting, delicate silence, gasping, wrapped up in each other, clenching together, refusing to relinquish the moment?

"I could promise you that," I said, and paused just for effect. "But..."

She froze. "But what, Ram?"

"It wouldn't be enough."

Izzy flopped forward against me, laughing. "You bastard. You had me for a second."

"I've got you forever," I said.

"Swear?"

"No." I shook my head. "Because promises can be broken. This? You and me? It's so much more than that. It can't ever be broken."

She sat on me, stared down at me, and let me play with her breasts, and she raked her fingernails down my chest and over my abs. "God, Ramsey. You really do have a way with words, you know that?"

"It's just the truth, Izz."

She leaned forward, bracing a palm on my chest, and reached back behind herself, finding my tender, tingling balls, and began massaging them in her palm. I was inside her, still, and she clutched the base of me and my sac together in her hand, slowly caressing and stroking. Her eyes stayed on mine, love now open in her expression.

"I need you again," she murmured.

"Keep doing that," I said.

She grinned hungrily. "Oh, I am. I feel you growing inside me."

As I hardened, she let the sliding strokes of her hand cease and began a subtle roll of her hips, and then I was thickening inside her tight slick core and my physical heart was slamming fit to burst, and my metaphorical heart was exploding with love, and I couldn't breathe for how it felt to be like this with her, to know this was real with this woman, so imperfectly perfect for me.

How long, then? I stopped keeping track of the seconds, the minutes, the hours. I cupped her breasts and she rode me, rising and falling with unhurried lazy love. And then, when I touched her clit, she cried out and began to ride me faster as I touched her, and she was grinding on me so hard her breasts were shaking and jouncing and our bodies collided with resounding claps and she screamed and cried and I roared—

And we came in the exact same moment, our voices and bodies merged. Her fingers interlaced with mine, pressing down so all of her weight was on my hands as she helplessly writhed on me, whimpering and wailing, and I supported her with shaking arms while driving up into her clenching core.

We never got tired of saying those three little words. We said them a million times that day, just to hear them, just to say them, knowing that whatever lay ahead, our love for one another would always be enough.

EPILOGUE

Izzy

I T WAS THANKSGIVING. SIX IN THE EVENING.

We were on a boat somewhere in the Pacific Ocean, sailing along the channels between Ketchikan and Vancouver. When I say *boat*, though, that's somewhat misleading. This thing is…well, it's almost as big as the cruise ships that ply these waters.

It belonged to Xavier Badd and his wife, Harlow Grace; she still goes by the surname Grace professionally, but she did legally change her name to Badd when they married, and she's been slowly transitioning professionally to Xavier's last name. A credit here and there, listing it as Harlow Badd in press releases and things like that. She invited all of us onto

their ridiculously massive superyacht for a Badd Clan
Thanksgiving.

And by all of us, I do mean ALL:

Sebastian and Dru, Zane and Mara, Brock and
Claire, Bax and Evangeline, Canaan and Aerie, Corin
and Tate, Lucian and Joss, obviously Xavier and
Low, Roman and Kitty, Remington and Juneau, and
Ramsey and me. Plus Zane and Mara's two kids, and
Tate and Cor's set of twins plus their three-month-
old girl. Dru was four months pregnant, Eva was six
months pregnant, and Brock and Claire were in the
process of adopting a baby.

So, the boat was full.

Badd's Bar and Grille now featured three locations across Ketchikan—the original bar on the
wharf, Badd Kitty Saloon, plus a third recently opened
location evenly co-owned by Bast, Zane, and Rome,
called The Badd Night Bar, which was built around a
theater-in-the-round concept, where Canaan, Corin,
Aerie, and Tate all performed together three nights
a week as a quartet, complete with dueling electric
guitars performances by the boys, Tate and Aerie on
cello and piano, and Canaan and Aerie doing songs
from their triple platinum, Grammy-winning Canary
albums, as well as up-and-coming local acts scouted
by the boys' homegrown label.

I was three years into my pursuit of a medical

degree—I'd discovered an aptitude for schoolwork that had surprised me, so after a couple toes-in-the-water semesters, I'd thrown myself in headlong, taking fourteen to sixteen credit hours per semester, plus summers, so I was already nearing my initial degree.

Ram was climbing the ranks in the National Park Service, having started as a ranger in the Tongass National Forest, but he was well on his way to taking charge of the entire region.

Rem, Juneau, and Ink's tattoo parlor had become such a success they'd had to expand and hire new talent, and had wait lists a year long each—Remington had been featured in a couple magazines for his work on a handful of A-list celebrities. While Juneau hadn't reached that caliber of public exposure, her work was, in a way, more meaningful—she traveled the world, teaching others how to apply modern technology to ancient tattooing methods; she'd traveled to Indonesia, Hawaii, Siberia, Greenland, and all over Canada—wherever indigenous peoples had histories of ritual, cultural skin-marking. Her work had been featured in both academic and pop culture magazines, and in a three-part documentary.

Xavier's work in robotics was transforming public opinion of what robotics was and could become, and his academic work was in that field, specifically as it related to Asimov's Laws of Robotics and artificial intelligence. Harlow was still one of the most popular leading ladies in film, and her popularity was only growing with each film she did.

Brock's air taxi service had expanded into a small airline, and he was in talks to sell a minority stake to Virgin Airlines. Claire…well, I wasn't sure what Claire did, exactly, only that it involved computers and a lot of private video conferences. She called it White Hat hacking, and had tried to explain it to me, but I'd gotten bored by her explanation after thirty seconds.

Dru was one of Ketchikan's premier realtors; Mara had opened a corporate consulting firm and was rapidly expanding.

Joss and Luce owned a chain of coffee shops-slash-bakeries across the city, each one with its own unique feel and theme.

Evangeline's artwork had been recently chosen for display at top-tier galleries in Manhattan, Paris, Tokyo, and Sydney, with eye-watering price tags and international buzz surrounding her work.

Zane, Bast, and Rome had garnered the least amount of attention of the entire clan, but they liked it that way—they ran their bars, slung drinks, and made plans for new locations.

We were all sitting around in the cavernous but somehow cozy living room of the yacht—which Xavier called "the saloon." There was a fire flickering inside a glass case in the center of the room, crackling merrily and giving out heat. A giant eighty-inch TV on one wall was playing a classic Disney movie, which the older kids were watching while playing with a bucket of Xavier's famous line of toy robots—called Magneti-Bots: they were a game and a puzzle and a toy all in one, and had sold millions within the first year. The adults were sitting in little clusters at tables and on couches, playing cards and chatting. Cane and Cor had brought a bunch of instruments, obviously, and Corin was teaching his youngest son how to play the guitar—the boy was barely one and half, so he spent more time keeping the kid's mouth off the strings than anything, but they both seemed to enjoy it. Canaan was actually playing, serenading his wife with a song that sounded happy and cute and fun, but was actually rather salaciously worded if one were to pay attention.

I marveled at all this, at all these people gathered together. This family had built itself, through love and determination and hard work, through loyalty, fearlessness, sacrifice, and humor. We all fit—we all belonged.

Bast was sitting on a couch, his arm around his wife, who was rubbing her belly and wincing now and then as the baby did intrauterine gymnastics; I watched as Bast locked eyes with Zane who was sitting across from him—the pair looked around at the gathered clan, nodded, grinned...and bumped fists, laughing at some inside joke.

But I think I got it.

In a matter of five or six years, they'd gone from a failing little bar being half-heartedly kept alive by Bast alone. The brothers had been scattered across the globe, the triplets jumping into wildfires, all of us women living our own isolated, separate, lonely lives.

And now, a handful of years later, we were together, a real family, all of us successful beyond our wildest dreams—and, most importantly, we had each found love, and the meaning it gave our lives, the unity it provided through this extended family, was immeasurable.

I, a single child, an orphan, now had ten brothers and ten sisters and, well, a lot of nieces and nephews, with more to come.

I nuzzled back into Ram's arm, kissed his bearded jaw, and settled in to watch the kids play, the adults mingle, and the stars twinkle to life out over the rippling ocean.

Was it possible to get any happier than this?

Probably.

But right now, this was more than enough.

The End

Jasinda Wilder

Visit me at my website: **www.jasindawilder.com**
Email me: **jasindawilder@gmail.com**

If you enjoyed this book, you can help others enjoy it as well by recommending it to friends and family, or by mentioning it in reading and discussion groups and online forums. You can also review it on the site from which you purchased it. But, whether you recommend it to anyone else or not, thank you *so much* for taking the time to read my book! Your support means the world to me!

My other titles:

The Preacher's Son:
Unbound
Unleashed
Unbroken

Biker Billionaire:
Wild Ride

Big Girls Do It:
Better (#1), Wetter (#2), Wilder (#3), On Top (#4)
Married (#5)
On Christmas (#5.5)
Pregnant (#6)
Boxed Set

Rock Stars Do It:
Harder
Dirty
Forever
Boxed Set

From the world of *Big Girls* and *Rock Stars*:
Big Love Abroad

Delilah's Diary:
A Sexy Journey
La Vita Sexy
A Sexy Surrender

The Falling Series:
Falling Into You
Falling Into Us
Falling Under
Falling Away
Falling for Colton

The Ever Trilogy:
Forever & Always
After Forever
Saving Forever

The world of *Alpha*:
Alpha
Beta
Omega
Harris: Alpha One Security Book 1
Thresh: Alpha One Security Book 2
Duke: Alpha One Security Book 3
Puck: Alpha One Security Book 4

The world of Stripped:
Stripped
Trashed

The world of *Wounded*:
Wounded
Captured

The Houri Legends:
Jack and Djinn
Djinn and Tonic

The Madame X Series:

Madame X

Exposed

Exiled

The One Series

The Long Way Home

Where the Heart Is

There's No Place Like Home

Badd Brothers:

Badd Motherf*cker

Badd Ass

Badd to the Bone

Good Girl Gone Badd

Badd Luck

Badd Mojo

Big Badd Wolf

Badd Boy

Badd Kitty

Badd Business

Dad Bod Contracting

Hammered

Drilled

Nailed

**The Black Room
(With Jade London):**
Door One
Door Two
Door Three
Door Four
Door Five
Door Six
Door Seven
Door Eight
Deleted Door

Standalone titles:
Yours

Non-Fiction titles:
You Can Do It
You Can Do It: Strength
You Can Do It: Fasting

Jack Wilder Titles:
The Missionary

To be informed of new releases and special offers,
sign up for
Jasinda's email newsletter.